UNDISCLOSED DESIRES

Book 1

CARLY MARIE

Editing Services: Susie Selva

Cover By: Soxational Cover Art

For Carrie, who fell in love with Caleb
when Desires was only a brainstorm and has
forever staked a claim on him.

TABLE OF CONTENTS

CHAPTER 1

Travis

The last place I wanted to be that morning was a physical therapist's office. I needed to get to a jobsite, but after having surgery on my ankle following a nasty fall, I had to be there to get rid of a persistent limp and hopefully the dull ache that was beginning to plague me on a daily basis. I'd done the basic PT through a different office, but their schedules never seemed to line up well with my work, so I decided to try a place with earlier appointments for the more intensive therapy I now needed. I just hoped the physical therapist would be able to help me along quickly so I could waste as little time as possible.

My phone was vibrating like crazy with text after text from a jobsite foreman relating to an issue with an order we were trying to track down. It had started with a few missing cabinets for the kitchen and had snowballed to missing pieces and parts for the entire house. The supply company was trying to figure out what had happened to the shipment, and in the meantime, our completion date was shot to hell.

The constant texts and added stress were making it

impossible for me to focus on filling out the necessary paperwork for the therapist, and I could already tell this was going to be the Monday from hell. Was it possible to go back to bed and start the day over? Maybe with two or three more cups of coffee before leaving the house.

Ben: *Hey, boss, sorry to bother you. I've been making some calls. Finally got the owner of Canter's on the phone. Seems at least part of the order was shipped to another jobsite… not ours.*

Me: *Fuck! What about the rest?*

Ben: *No clue. But the stuff that was shipped to the wrong place can be recovered tomorrow. He's got a new person in the ordering department, he figures there was a mixup with that.*

I sighed and ran my hands through my short hair that seemed to be getting grayer at an alarming rate recently. It was now more salt than pepper and it was making me feel every day of my forty-one years. It was probably a good thing I was in physical therapy for a bum ankle and not complications due to a heart attack with the amount of shit I'd been dealing with lately.

Me: *Keep on him—*

"Mr. Barton!" a high-pitched voice called from the doorway of the waiting room, interrupting my text before I could send it. I shoved my phone into my pocket and plastered on a fake smile, hoping it looked genuine. My nerves were already shot and if I had to listen to this mousey-voiced woman for an hour, I might end up on blood pressure meds by the end of the morning.

As I joined her, limping along and wanting to curse my sore ankle, she smiled up at me. "I'm Lisa. I'll be taking you

2

back to see Caleb. He's going to be your therapist."

First good news of the day—my physical therapist was not the woman who barely looked like she was out of high school. As we entered the therapy space, there were only a few patients working at different machines so, thankfully, the place wasn't absurdly loud.

Lisa walked me to a chair at the side of the room. "Caleb is running just a minute or two behind. He'll be with you shortly. If you haven't had a chance to finish the paperwork, feel free to do so now." She shot a pointed look at my mostly blank packet as she walked away.

From the small room beside me, two voices could be heard disagreeing... arguing maybe. It took me a moment to hone in on the conversation but once I did I couldn't help but smile to myself. The deeper of the two voices sounded exasperated. "They aren't toys!"

The other voice scoffed before responding. "Cal, your desk is covered in dragon toys! I'm pretty sure this one came from a Happy Meal."

"Leave Puff alone! He didn't do anything to you. And leave my desk alone."

The second guy was gasping for air as he laughed. "Cal, dude, they're named! You've named the toys on your desk."

Voice one sounded irritated when he responded. "It's Puff from Pete's Dragon you imbecile."

My phone buzzed again and I zoned the two out. I needed to figure out what the fuck was going on with my supply shipment and how I was going to get things where they needed to be to avoid further delays. We were into

3

spring and I couldn't afford to fall behind on even one job because work was stacking up faster than I cared to admit. I'd never been so thankful to have someone like Ben working for me. I pulled my phone out and finished my text to Ben.

Me: *Keep on him. We need to figure out where everything is. I'll be at the office as soon as this damn appointment is over.*

Ben: *If you keep limping around the office bitching about your ankle, the guys are going to force you to take leave. I recommend focusing on your PT.*

I cursed but picked up the incomplete paperwork and began to fill it out. I didn't get far before the conversation from the office beside me caught my attention again.

"Shut up, Dex. I'm late for my appointment because of you. *Get out of my office, now!*" the voice huffed.

A tall ginger-haired guy in his mid-twenties was pushed out of the office just ahead of a muscular man an inch or so shorter than the redhead. The office door slammed shut and the muscular guy crossed his arms and stared at his co-worker. There didn't appear to be any malice in his eyes, so I figured they were friends, though I thought the redhead might be pushing his luck given the stern expression on the muscular guy's face.

The redhead held up his hands in surrender and walked away shaking his head. "We're going to talk about your little obsession later, Caleb."

The muscular guy appeared embarrassed by his friend's words and turned pink while he shook his head in frustration. "Ugh! You're impossible. I'm going to lunch with Lisa!" For some reason I suspected the threat was empty.

The redhead shook his head again as he walked across the physical therapy floor and into another small office before shutting the door behind him.

The muscular guy turned his head toward me with a faint pink blush still staining his cheeks. "You must be Mr. Barton." He held out his hand and flashed me a bright smile that was clearly trying to push his discomfort away. "Sorry to keep you waiting. I'm Caleb Masterson. It seems you're stuck with me for a while!"

I bristled at being called *Mr. Barton*. That always reminded me of my dad and made me feel old. "Please, call me Travis."

Caleb smiled. "Nice to meet you, Travis. You can call me Caleb. I hear you've recently had surgery on your ankle?" he probed, quickly glancing down at my work boots. He was likely judging my choice of footwear. I hadn't thought much about it when I'd left the house that morning. It had been over two months since my surgery, and I was annoyed that the recovery hadn't been quicker, despite the surgeon telling me it was going to take time. I wouldn't own a top-rated, custom home building and remodeling company if I weren't stubborn and impatient. My ankle, however, didn't seem to realize I had deadlines and projects that needed my attention.

"Yeah. I need to get this thing back in shape. I really don't have time for a weekly appointment."

"Twice weekly," Caleb corrected, fighting a grin.

I balked. "Twice a week?" *When had I agreed to physical therapy twice a week?*

Caleb nodded while looking at the small laptop in his hand. "Yes, it was confirmed when the appointment was scheduled."

Ben. I'd left it to him to find me a new physical therapy place when the last one wasn't working out. It was a good thing the guy was a hard worker and knew his shit because I wouldn't normally take too kindly to this type of surprise. I had to concede that Ben also knew me too well after working for me for over two years. If he'd told me I was going to be coming here twice a week for the foreseeable future, there would have been no way I'd have come to the first appointment. But now I was here and stuck.

I sighed. There was nothing else I could do. "Alright, we might as well get a move on. What's first?"

Caleb shook his head. "You're clearly used to being the boss, but here, I'm in charge. So you can just sit yourself down on the table and take your highly-inappropriate-for-physical-therapy boots off so I can see where we're starting."

Big hazel eyes glanced over the clipboard that I'd set beside me. I watched as he looked at the incomplete paperwork on it and shook his head.

"Well, since you didn't get this all filled out, tell me how you managed to land yourself here when you'd, clearly, much rather be working."

I gave him the condensed version of events, avoiding an explanation of *how* I'd broken my ankle, while he focused on my ankle and the scars on either side from the surgery I'd had. "This is my busy season, and I need to get this ankle back into shape quickly. The last physical therapist I was at couldn't work with my early morning schedule."

"Well, the only way you're going to get it there is to put in the appropriate time in therapy and do the exercises I give you. Oh, and don't do more than you're ready for. I can already see you're likely one who will push through the pain and end up injuring yourself more." He sighed and shook his head. Apparently, I wasn't the first stubborn patient he'd had to deal with. "So, what did you do to yourself, Travis?"

I couldn't help the exasperated huff I blew out at my own stupidity. "I was coming down a ladder, missed the last rung, and landed on my ankle. Not one of my finer moments."

Caleb fought a grin at my expense. I couldn't deny he was adorable as he tried to remain professional, but the twinkle in his eyes gave away a playful personality just below the surface. Even if I wanted to be frustrated with him, the little dimple that appeared in his left cheek was enough to wear me down slightly. "Sounds like a freak accident. It's going to help if you wear tennis shoes here, though." He was rotating my ankle and shifting his attention from my ankle to my face, likely watching for any signs of discomfort.

He squeezed and turned and rotated it more than my doctor had at the last appointment. He seemed to be making mental notes of every tight spot, slight pop, and anything he perceived as discomfort from me. After a few minutes, he went to my right ankle and repeated the process. It felt like it took ten minutes before he'd compared every movement.

Caleb finally opened his laptop and began typing rapidly. The tip of his tongue stuck out slightly as he worked, making him look younger. When he was done with his notes, he asked me all the questions I hadn't answered on the paperwork and by the time we were done with all that, our time was almost up.

He shut the laptop and smiled at me. "Well, unfortunately, we didn't get much done today. The good news is, we've got all the boring stuff out of the way, so we can get right down to fixing you up on Friday."

The last thing I wanted to do was spend another hour each week in physical therapy, yet I had a feeling Ben was right—boss or not, the guys were at the end of their rope with me. I was going to find myself persona non grata at my own company if I didn't start taking physical therapy more seriously.

"Yes, see you Friday," I agreed reluctantly.

Caleb smiled and nodded like he'd won a battle. "Have a good week, Travis. See you Friday."

CHAPTER 2

Caleb

After Dexter's ribbing about my dragon collection that morning, I *did* go to lunch with Lisa. He'd been shocked that I'd actually made plans with the new patient care coordinator. She was too bubbly and chipper for me to want to spend much time with her in or out of the office, but I'd happily tagged along with her to the sandwich shop. I almost enjoyed myself. It would have been more enjoyable if she'd stopped talking for more than fifteen seconds at a time. I wasn't even sure how she'd eaten at all. But, at least I didn't have to be civil to Dexter for the rest of the day.

Thankfully, the big construction worker who had been my first appointment of the day hadn't seemed to notice my frustration with my colleague and best friend. He had probably been too wrapped up in whatever had him scowling at his phone when I'd stepped out of my office. However, Dexter's teasing about my dragon collection had thrown me for such a loop, I'd had a hard time looking my patient in the eyes for the first half of our appointment. Or

9

maybe it was because I'd found the growly construction worker's deep brown eyes and salt-and-pepper hair incredibly attractive...

I'd been so frustrated with Dexter, I managed to make it all the way back to my house without speaking to him. Unfortunately, I forgot that, aside from being my best friend, he also rented the townhome attached to mine. My quiet brooding lasted precisely long enough to kick my shoes off and go to the fridge and open it up. I was still debating between a chocolate milk and a beer when there was a tentative knock on the backdoor. The only person who used the back door was Dexter. I sighed and hung my head for a moment, staring longingly at the chocolate milk sitting on the fridge shelf. I was reaching for it when Dexter knocked again.

"Fuck," I cursed, as I shut the fridge and walked the ten feet to the door, unlocked it, and flung it open. "What?"

"Sorry, Cal."

"For what, exactly?" I growled. I may have been shorter than him, but he was wiry while I was muscular. I didn't know why I was acting like I was actually thinking about not forgiving him. Or that I hadn't already. It was a given I'd forgive him; I always did. No matter how much Dexter drove me insane, he'd been my best friend since fourth grade. His filter was, and always had been, broken. Dexter opening his mouth when he shouldn't was just part of his personality. The fact that he knew so much about me and still hadn't spilled more than my love of dragons to the office surprised me every day. *What were the odds that we'd pursue the same career and get a job in the same damn office after college?*

Having my best friend a few feet away from me all day was a huge relief many times, but sometimes, like today, I wanted to kill him. It had been one of the more aggravating days I'd experienced with him in a while. It was bad enough he'd made me miss my start time with my first appointment of the day. An appointment that turned out to be with a sexy as fuck silver fox in a light blue dress shirt tucked into snug-fitting jeans with a gorgeous brown leather belt that matched his brown leather boots—the boots he shouldn't have been wearing to physical therapy. I would have been stumbling over my words without him possibly overhearing there were dragons on my desk. *Fucking Dexter and his big mouth.* And just like that I was annoyed with him again.

"Why are you so angry?"

And not even an apology.

I sighed. The guy just didn't get it. "Dex, you know stuff about me that no one else knows. *No one else.* Do you get that? You can't go announcing to the office, in front of clients, that I've got dragon toys."

Dexter's brows pulled together. "But you *do* have dragon toys, Caleb. You have them in your office where anyone can see them."

I pounded my head on the counter. Sometimes, talking to my best friend was a lot like talking to a brick wall. "Yes, Dex. I *know* I have toys—*at home!* At work, they are just a collection. They are things I collect. Like Lisa collects those

11

stupid dancing flowers! No one at work needs to know any different. Including patients!"

"You're still upset about that conversation from this morning?"

I threw my hands in the air. "You really don't get it do you? My personal life needs to be kept out of the office. If you had any sense of boundaries, you wouldn't even know as much about me as you do."

Dexter grinned at me. "I didn't say anything that would give you away. You know what you need? A sexy older guy. Speaking of which, oh my god, Caleb, your first patient was hot. I mean, I don't go for silver foxes, but he's totally your type. Wonder if we can find out if he's a Daddy? You need a Daddy."

I sighed. One day, *one day*, Dexter's brain to mouth filter would catch up with the rest of him. When that day came, he would be horrified by the amount of stuff he'd blurted out over the years. Unfortunately for me, today was not that day. Today, I was going to be answering another slew of uncomfortable, borderline inappropriate questions for the next twenty minutes while he figured out why I was stumbling for words.

"Dex, my private life is *private*. I don't want to bring it to work. I especially don't want patients knowing about it."

Dexter looked contemplative for a few seconds. "But he was everything you're looking for!"

"I don't even know if he's gay!" Despite not knowing anything about him, the man had filled my thoughts throughout the day. Dexter may have had a horrible case of verbal diarrhea, but he was definitely right about the sexy man ticking all my boxes. "Besides, even if he *is* gay, what I want is way outside the box. The Daddy I'm looking for is not just going to show up at work one day!"

"It's not that weird, Cal." Bless him, Dexter really did believe that identifying as a little was not strange in the least. "You want a strong older man to love you and care for you. That isn't weird at all."

As Dexter spoke, he walked toward the cupboard next to the fridge and reached up to the top shelf. "I don't understand why you haven't looked harder." He pulled out the blue cup with green and purple dragons on it.

"Simplifying it like that makes it seem totally normal, but it's not. It isn't like I'm telling some guy I want to call him Daddy while he dominates me in the bedroom, then gives me aftercare for a bit. I want someone to put a diaper on me and let me play with my toys while he watches over me. I want someone to make decisions for me and put me first. What I want isn't a simple role-play thing. I want more. I'm high-maintenance, even by high-maintenance standards."

Dexter had been working the entire time I talked and was putting the purple top on the sippy cup he had filled with the chocolate milk I'd been eyeing earlier. "It's not high-maintenance, Cal. You just know what you want and need. There's a guy out there for you. And he's not going to think you're a chore or a bother. He's going to want the exact same things you do… well, he's going to want to be what you want. Come on, let's go watch TV." He held up the cup and shook it lightly.

13

Weirdest conversation ever. Okay, *second* weirdest conversation ever. The first had been when I'd actually had to talk to my best friend about my desires. I'd hidden my little side well, until Dexter and I had decided to room together in college. He had no concept of boundaries, so when I'd left my laptop open to run to the bathroom, I'd come back to find him pouring over my bookmarks. I'd thought I was going to kill him, or die of embarrassment, either had been a likely option at the time. He'd been so earnest and open about the entire thing that it had been hard to stay mad at him for long. I'd tried to ignore the situation, but Dexter wouldn't leave it alone.

Eventually, Dexter's curiosity got to the point that I had to talk to him about it. He'd started pestering me with lifestyle questions at the most inopportune moments.

On the way to the dining hall. "Hey, what does ABDL mean?"

On the way to class. "Cal, do *you* like diapers?"

On the way back from class. "Do you like to play with toys too?"

In the lecture hall. "*How* little do you like to be?"

If I didn't have a talk with him about it, I was going to end up a puddle of embarrassed goo on the sidewalk or the lecture hall floor. The last thing I wanted was to become the talk of the college campus. I finally had to swallow my anxiety, fear, and nerves, and have a long conversation with Dexter about my little side.

Explaining to Dexter that being little was just as much a part of me as my hazel eyes or being gay hadn't been easy.

I'd been fascinated with regressing for as long as I could remember.

Finally figuring out that it was something others enjoyed had been a relief. Making friends online who shared similar desires had helped me accept myself, but hadn't made telling another person any easier. If anything, it made me realize that my desires were so far outside the box that I wasn't going to find a guy who understood my feelings just by chance. I wasn't comfortable with fetish clubs and had no interest in a long distance relationship, so I settled on keeping my fantasies to myself.

My needs were a huge part of why most of my relationships had been short-lived. I could only hide little Caleb for so long before I became frustrated and it drove a wedge between me and my boyfriend. The longest relationship I'd had in the past seven years had lasted all of seven months and it had only gone on that long because he was older and more take-charge. It had been nice not to have to plan dates or think about what we were going to do from day to day. The day he freaked out when he saw my teddy bear on the bed instead of on my dresser, I knew there was no chance he'd be okay seeing little Caleb, and our relationship had rapidly deteriorated from there.

Over the years, I'd talked with littles who were perfectly fine never wearing diapers or only wanted to be little sometimes when life got to be too much. I knew that wasn't enough for me. I didn't need to have a Daddy to know I needed it more than occasionally. I loved wearing diapers whenever time allowed. I thrived on letting the adult world slip away, even if I didn't have a Daddy with me. I'd collected a large selection of *little* things over the years—cups, plates, clothes, diapers. Even if it was just having my sippy cup while watching TV, it helped ground me and make me more relaxed. I just couldn't see finding a man who was okay with how integral my little side was to me. I also couldn't see myself getting comfortable enough with a guy that I'd trust him enough to tell him about little Caleb, much less *see* him, only to have him find it weird or repulsive.

I sighed and followed Dexter to the living room. We'd never been, nor would we ever be, anything more than friends, but after he'd found out about me, he'd begun to recognize I was struggling. Trying to be Caleb to my various boyfriends while also dealing with my desire to be cared for and let go of everything had been exhausting. At some point along the way, Dexter had stepped into the surrogate big brother role. We'd never talked about it and I'd never even thought about it before. Then one night, he appeared beside my bed with his laptop and the sippy cup I hid under my pillow. We'd spent the next few hours curled up together on my tiny dorm bed watching cartoons on Netflix while I drank my juice.

As time went by he'd managed to coax me into seeing *most* of my little side. Even as open as I was with Dexter, he'd never seen me diapered. That would be reserved for my Daddy—if I ever found him. Dexter could read my moods better than anyone else in my life, and to him, making me a sippy cup and watching cartoons with me as I played with blocks some evenings was as normal as going out to the bar other nights.

As I sank down onto the couch, I took the sippy cup from Dexter and ran my fingers over the dragons on the cup. I allowed myself a moment to imagine a Daddy in Dexter's spot. Sometimes, it was fun to pretend that one day I'd have a Daddy who would diaper me and let me curl up next to him on the couch while we watched TV and I had a bottle before bed.

CHAPTER 3

Travis

It hadn't been until I got home Monday evening and had time to actually think about something other than work, that I began thinking about my physical therapist. My mind had been so wrapped up with the supply mixup that I hadn't been able to think much about the appointment. Caleb had been so flustered when he'd first come out of his office and his eyes had widened comically when he'd gotten his first look at me. At the time, I hadn't thought much about it, but as I replayed it, I realized he might have been checking me out.

He was far too young for me. I was sure he wasn't even thirty yet, and I was on the wrong side of forty. He had big hazel eyes and when he'd shooed his friend away, his cheeks had been stained a bright shade of red.

Was I remembering something about dragon toys on his desk? I couldn't help the smile that spread across my face when the conversation came back to me. Caleb had been quite defensive about his collection, specifically the one he called Puff. Though, that had been a number of minutes before he'd appeared in front of me. I'd clearly missed some of their conversation while I'd been engrossed in trying to find the missing supplies and doing a half-assed job of finishing up the registration paperwork. I wondered what I'd missed that had the cute therapist blushing when he'd greeted me.

I was kicking myself for being so frazzled that morning. Had my agitation led to Caleb being so nervous for the first few minutes of the appointment? He'd apparently gotten over it quickly, and I'd liked that my size and gruffness hadn't seemed to intimidate him after he'd pulled himself together. He'd been able to properly chastise me for my footwear choices, and he hadn't backed down when I'd balked about the twice weekly appointments. Ben had given me a smart-assed grin when I complained about it. There was a time that my gruffness had made people bend to my will. I must be going soft in my old age. I groaned at myself. I was forty-one and it sounded like I was already planning my death.

By Tuesday morning, my focus was fully back on work while I hobbled around the office bitching about not being able to walk normally. Ben rolled his eyes at me and threatened to quit if I didn't go to the next appointment. I made a more concerted effort to not bitch and moan about my ankle for the rest of the week.

As I was getting ready to go to bed on Thursday night my phone buzzed with an incoming text.

Ben: *Just so you know, I have my resignation letter typed up. If you are in the office before 9:30 tomorrow, it will be in your inbox before you sit down at your desk.*

When I'd hired Ben, he'd been fresh out of college and hardly said two words. It had been hard to get him to talk even when I'd asked him direct questions. He was so driven and had an attention to detail that even I admired, and he was quickly working his way up in the company. At some point over the last two years, Ben had come out of his shell. He'd opened up and told me about his boyfriend, Asher, and their struggles to keep a roof over their heads the first few years they'd been together. With the other guys, he was able to give as much shit as he got. Being so young, he certainly took a lot of good-natured ribbing from the guys.

Unfortunately, I wasn't convinced he was completely lying about the resignation letter.

Me: *It's on my calendar. I'll go. Whether I want to or not.*

I didn't need to tell him that I'd been thinking about the therapist on and off all week and was actually kind of looking forward to going to the appointment. At least having a cute therapist would be worth it.

Not being completely opposed to returning unfortunately didn't translate into me making it to therapy on time. It drove me nuts to be late anywhere, but when I pulled into the parking lot it was already 8:33 a.m. and I was three minutes late. Jobsite issues didn't care if I had to be somewhere at eight thirty. When work called, I answered. That was how I'd won the awards I'd won. It was also how I'd become the go-to custom home company in the county.

I put work above everything else in my life. Boyfriends, friends, even family had been put on the backburner for my career, and I didn't see that changing any time in the near future.

I rushed into the office as quickly as I could and signed in. I hadn't even made it to a seat when Caleb's head popped out from behind the door. "Travis, you're up," he announced brightly. Thankfully he didn't bring up my tardiness, but I still felt bad for keeping him waiting.

"Sorry about being late," I apologized as we headed back to the therapy area.

He shrugged. "We'll call it even. I started late on Monday. Let's both try to be better about being punctual going forward." The hesitant smile he gave me was enough to make me grin.

As we arrived in his little area, I caught him glancing down at my feet. When he spotted the tennis shoes, he nodded in approval. "Much better choice of footwear."

"I guess I should have asked this on Monday, but my boots are okay for jobsites, right?" The clunky steel-toed boots had saved my feet more times than I could count. I ripped my guys a new one when they showed up on a site without a pair of boots. They'd never let me live it down if I started showing up in tennis shoes.

Caleb, for his part, didn't dismiss my concern. "It's probably better for you to wear them in your line of work. And hopefully, they will give you some more support in your ankle than tennis shoes."

After he logged onto his laptop, Caleb looked over at me. "Take a walk across the room for me."

It seemed pointless to walk back to the door after we'd just walked from there to here, and I couldn't help but tease a bit. "What, are you showing me the door already?"

A lopsided grin played across Caleb's face. "I watched you a bit on Monday, but you weren't in the right shoes so it was hard to gauge how you were actually doing. I want to see where you're at so I know what to focus on. Now, walk," he pointed toward the door.

I chuckled at his stern expression but started to walk toward the door as Caleb glanced back down at his laptop. When I arrived at the door, I turned and looked back over the forty or so feet to where Caleb was standing. His eyes were wide, and his jaw was slightly slack. I couldn't help but wonder if he'd been checking out my ass while I walked.

He pulled himself together and was tapping furiously at the keyboard by the time I got back to him. I had to push a bit though. "Like what you see?"

He stammered as color bloomed on his cheeks. "I-uh-what?"

He was so easy to tease, I couldn't help myself. "Did I pass the walking test?"

Caleb's mouth made an adorable "O" shape, and he nodded. "Oh. Oh yeah. Um, I got what I needed. Yes."

"Great." He couldn't have been any cuter, and I caught myself checking him out a few times while he wasn't looking. Broad shoulders and powerful legs were clear even through his work clothes. I even noted the lack of a ring on his finger, but that didn't mean much. Even if he was single and gay, he was so much younger than I was there was very little I could offer him aside from cold dinners, broken dates, and frustration. He'd drop me faster than a hot potato.

"You're doing really well. If you keep this up, you should be back to dominating your crew at full strength before you know it." I saw his eyes widen and his cheeks turn pink when the words left his mouth. "Er, managing would have probably been a better choice of words there."

I bit back the urge to tell him just how dominant I was and to ask if he wanted to find out before I finally smiled and thanked him. I was heading toward the door when his friend appeared.

The redhead bounced around excitedly. "Beans and Brew for lunch?"

Caleb glanced at his computer. "Yeah. I'm free at noon."

"Great." And the friend bounced back across the floor to his work area.

I couldn't help it if Beans and Brew suddenly sounded like a great place to grab a sandwich and a coffee at lunch. It was close to my office, and I hadn't eaten breakfast anyway. It definitely didn't have anything to do with wanting to learn a little more about Caleb, even if it was from a few tables away while I worked on my newest estimate.

CHAPTER 4

Caleb

I yawned as we waited in line at Beans and Brew. "This is a double-shot type of day."

Dexter sighed and looked from the specials menu on the chalkboard by the cash register to my face, worry lines creasing his forehead. "Didn't sleep well again last night?"

"Like shit." I shrugged like it was no big deal. "That steak salad sounds good."

Dexter shook his head. "We're at a pub, why in the hell are you going to get a salad? That bison burger sounds amazing though. They have the best fries here!"

I gawked at my best friend. I'd grown up with him, lived with him, and ate lunch with him almost every day, yet I couldn't figure out where he put the food he consumed. "How are you not the size of a house?"

Dexter waggled his eyebrows playfully. "There are plenty of ways to work off calories."

I shuddered. "Gross. I don't need to know what you do in bed."

He pushed me gently. "Are your sweet little ears too innocent?"

I growled. He was not about to bring this up in public.

"Did you turn your night light on last night?"

Apparently he was.

"Dexter…" I warned. Then I sighed. "Yes, I turned it on. Happy, jackass?"

Dexter's face scrunched up like he'd just bitten into a lemon. "Actually no, not really. I would rather be able to say, 'Told ya so!' than have you unable to sleep even though you did what I told you to do."

The words didn't make a hell of a lot of sense as they flowed out of his mouth, but I understood what he was saying, and I appreciated his sincerity. However, I needed to get over the irrational fear of something hiding under my bed. Seriously, one fucking ghost story as a child and I'd been afraid of the dark ever since, especially on windy nights like last night had been.

"You need a Daddy. Some sexy silver fox who could hold you tight while you fell asleep. Like your first appointment this morning."

"Travis?"

Dexter shrugged. "I don't know his name. But the silver-haired guy with huge muscles who always sccms to have a scowl on his face… unless he's looking at you when he doesn't think anyone's looking."

"He does not look at me. If he does, it's just because I'm his physical therapist."

"Right, because I look at my massage therapist like he's a piece of meat and I'm a starving animal everytime I go to get a massage."

I pushed Dexter's arm. "He doesn't. But you *do*. You've told me your massage guy is good looking… and incredibly straight."

He brushed me off. "Minor technicality. Your guy is hot."

"He's not my guy, Dex. He's a patient. How much more inappropriate could you possibly be?"

Dexter sighed and put his head against mine. "He won't always be your patient. Why won't you even entertain the idea that he's exactly your type?"

"Dex, I'm not denying that. But he's a successful business owner who hardly has time to take an hour out of his schedule for PT twice a week. I know nothing about him. The only thing I know is that he doesn't have a wedding ring on his finger and he's growly and scowly. The lack of a wedding ring doesn't mean he's gay. It doesn't even mean he's not married! I have nothing to offer him."

The way Dexter deflated, I knew a lecture was coming. "Caleb Masterson, you are smart and sweet and there's a Daddy out there just waiting for you to crawl into his lap. But you're never going to find him if you don't actually put yourself out there a *little* bit. You've got a sexy-as-sin silver fox eyeing you up like you're a tall drink of water on a hot day and you can't even see it."

"Dexter O'Connail, even if he *does* look at me like that, that doesn't mean he's looking for a relationship. Guys don't want someone as high-maintenance as me. Especially when they're already established in life. They want someone like them."

"Cal," he sighed sadly. "It kills me that you don't see how amazing you are. There's absolutely nothing wrong with you. It's the guys you've found. Mainly because you've never even tried to find the *right* guy for you."

I leaned over and spoke quietly into Dexter's ear. "If a guy can't take finding out I have a teddy bear, how the hell can I expect someone to accept the *rest* of me?"

We were getting close to the front of the line by that point and I hoped like hell this conversation would be over, but it was Dexter I was talking to. I'd probably be getting a lecture through my entire lunch.

"What if you just went for an older guy and enjoyed having a sexy silver fox for once? At least give yourself the chance to have *something* you want. Your first appointment guy—Travis—I bet he'd rock your world… and your bed if you gave him a chance."

Thinking about Travis in my bed made my cock start to fill. "I'm going to murder you in your sleep," I hissed at my best friend. "I have a key and I know my way around your place!"

We moved up to the front of the line and Dexter ordered some horrendously greasy burger slathered in various sauces and condiments, a huge order of steak fries, and a soda with enough sugar in it to give an elephant diabetes.

"How are you so damn skinny?" I grumbled. I gained five pounds just listening to his order. I began rattling off my order—the grilled steak salad with a side of fruit and a large coffee with two shots of espresso. I was pulling out my card to pay for my meal when a deep voice spoke up behind us, causing both of us to jump slightly.

"That much caffeine isn't good for you."

I didn't have to turn around to know who that deep voice belonged to. *Dexter was a dead man... I just didn't know what exactly he'd done, but there had to have been something he did to bring this upon me.*

Dexter's face showed enough shock as he turned around to see Travis standing there that I knew instantly it wasn't actually his doing.

What was Travis doing here?

Dexter leaned over to the person taking my order. "Um, something's just come up. Can I get my order to go?" He pulled out his phone like someone was texting him.

"Dexter!"

"Oh, yeah. Um, Lisa had a scheduling mix-up. I'm uh, going to go help her out." He was lying through his teeth, and I was going to kill him.

"Your screen isn't even on, asshole!"

"Um, yeah, well, I need to get back. Sorry!" He leaned over and gave me a gentle kiss on the cheek. "You'll thank me for this," he whispered into my ear.

"I know where you sleep," I called as he walked away to wait for his order.

"Can you just add that order to mine?" Travis asked the cashier. "And please remove the extra shots of espresso from his drink."

I balked at the man standing beside me and wanted to ask him who he thought he was. The cashier apparently had the same thought because she looked at me with questions written all over her face. As much as I wanted to be pissed that he was making a decision about what I was drinking, the part of me that craved having someone take decisions away from me, even about something as stupid as how much caffeine I could have in a day, was already conceding and nodding approval.

The cashier seemed as confused as I felt but edited my order and added Travis's before giving him the total. As the shock of his appearance, and him changing my coffee order wore off, I realized I had no clue how long he'd been behind us, and my nerves went into overdrive.

As we moved to walk past the to-go order line, Dexter pretended to be engrossed in his phone so I couldn't even catch his eye. He was a dead man. There was no way around it. I was going to kill him the next time I saw him.

Travis led me to a table away from most of the lunch crowd. I slid into the seat across from him and debated about how or where to begin. Thankfully, he took the lead so I didn't have to think too hard.

"Do you always drink that much caffeine?" Was that concern I heard in his voice? At least I was able to answer that question without crawling in a hole and dying of embarrassment.

I shook my head. "No, I just didn't sleep well last night."

He looked at me for a long time. I couldn't decide if he was trying to figure out if he believed me, or if he was wondering how much of a nutcase I was because of what he'd overheard. Was he trying to figure out how to tell me he didn't want me as his physical therapist after overhearing the conversation Dexter and I had had? I hadn't thought we'd been too loud, but he'd been standing right behind us.

The silence finally got to be too much for me. "What are you doing here?" I blurted out.

CHAPTER 5

Travis

I guess I should have expected the question. That didn't mean I was ready to answer. *What the fuck was I doing here?* I couldn't remember the last time I'd taken a lunch break at a restaurant. I didn't usually eat lunch unless one of the guys was ordering something or if I was going out to lunch with a client. Caleb definitely wasn't a client. I also hadn't intended to buy him lunch.

My original plan had been to get there at the beginning of the lunch rush and find a secluded booth where I could maybe spot the cutie and see if I could learn more about him. Like, maybe if he and the redhead were a couple. I'd been ready to write off even inconspicuously ogling him if I found out he was with someone. I hadn't intended to walk in the door just as his friend was ordering his lunch.

They hadn't noticed me, so I almost kicked myself in the ass when I'd told Caleb his drink had too much caffeine in it. The way his friend almost jumped out of his skin and his eyes got huge at my appearance made me think they were a couple. But then he'd made some sorry excuse for having to take his order to go and had ignored Caleb's wide-eyes and freaked out expression. Through the hushed conversation between the two, I could see easily that his friend was a force to be reckoned with. His personality seemed to be as fiery as his hair.

I wondered for a brief second if I'd been mistaken about their relationship when the guy leaned over and gave Caleb a light kiss on the cheek before turning and heading to the pick-up line. Caleb had stood there for a few seconds too dazed to speak and that was when I'd asked to buy his lunch. My brain had apparently taken its own lunch break because the reasonable thing for me to have done would have been to back off and let the guy eat in peace, but there had been something alluring about him since I'd begun thinking about him Monday evening.

I realized I hadn't answered his question when Caleb cleared his throat. *Shit*, to tell the truth or lie? The truth sounded like I was a creepy stalker. *You are a creepy stalker* my brain reminded me as I opened my mouth. "My office is just around the corner." Not *exactly* the truth but close enough that I was going to count it.

Caleb narrowed his eyes. "Why haven't I seen you here before, then? We come here pretty often."

Busted.

Before I could come up with an excuse, Caleb's eyes narrowed and he looked at me suspiciously then seemed to make a decision and softened slightly. "Thank you for buying my lunch. It was unnecessary."

"You're welcome. I know I didn't need to, but I wanted to."

Caleb ran his hands through the carefully styled hair at the top of his head causing a few pieces to fall out and across his forehead. It wasn't hard to picture how adorable it would be all sleep-mussed when he woke up in the morning.

"Had you been here long?" he asked carefully.

Our food was brought to the table, so I waited until the guy left before I responded to Caleb's question. When we were alone again, I shook my head. "I walked in as your friend was ordering."

Caleb seemed to sag in relief at the admission and I wondered what they'd been talking about before I arrived. It wasn't any of my business, but it didn't change the fact that I wished it was, and that thought took me by surprise. I had to remind myself that I had very little to offer Caleb. He was young and successful. My long hours at work and my controlling personality would drive a young guy like him insane in no time.

He took a small sip of his coffee, when he decided it was cool enough he took a longer sip and sighed in delight as it went down. "Oh my god, I needed this so bad."

"Why aren't you sleeping well?" I asked without thought.

Caleb flushed and set his cup down, tracing the lip with his finger. "Sleep and I just aren't great friends," he admitted to the table.

I wondered what he wasn't telling me. Of course, there were countless reasons he might not sleep well, and again, I had to remind myself it wasn't my place to pry into those reasons. Instead, I settled on something that could possibly give me a better glimpse into Caleb. "Are you and the guy who left…" I trailed off, not exactly sure how to finish the question. If he was straight, which I didn't think was likely, I didn't want to offend him. I didn't want to touch on a sore spot if there was something there, but I wanted to know more about the wide-eyed man across the table from me.

Caleb barked out a surprised laugh. "Together? Me and Dex? Oh, hell no." He chuckled again. "Dex is my best friend. He's been the most constant person in my life since I was in fourth grade. I don't think I could get rid of him if I tried."

The way Caleb said he'd been his constant told me there was something in his past that would probably piss me off if I found out about it. How could a best friend be the most constant thing in his life for so long? Where were his parents? I didn't know if I wanted to know.

A genuine smile spread across his face for the first time as he laughed. "Dex and I would kill each other within two days if we tried to date. He's too excitable."

Well there was one more question answered. But excitable seemed to sum up what I'd seen of his friend. "How did you two end up being best friends and both working at the same place?"

Caleb grinned again. He looked so carefree when he let some of his walls down, and it made him more intriguing to me. "I ask myself that question about three times a day."

I chuckled. I had a feeling that answer was more honest than he'd want to admit. "What drew you to physical therapy?"

"My mom was a physical therapist. I grew up with it, and I found it fascinating." He went quiet for a moment, like he was remembering something. I picked up on the *was* and wondered if she'd retired or if something had happened to her. We didn't know each other well enough for me to press him on something so personal. He'd open up if he wanted to tell me more. It quickly became obvious the topic was off-limits when he turned the question back on me. "You own a construction company, right?"

"Yes. I own a custom home building and remodeling company. I started it after college, against my dad's advice. He told me I was too young and I needed more experience, but I'd been working in construction since I was in high school and couldn't stand the idea of working for someone else. My friend is a genius with money and while I was in grad school, he helped me start investing what I was making through my job. Within a few years, I had enough money to start my own business. For a while it was me and one other guy. It took a long time, but for the last handful of years, I've had more work than I know what to do with. It makes me pretty terrible company outside of work."

"I don't know about that. You've been pretty nice company so far." Caleb snapped his mouth shut and looked surprised at his own words.

"I appreciate that, really. But anyone who knows me

would tell you I work too much. I can't even remember the last time I took a vacation."

Caleb looked a bit sad for me for a moment before he asked another question. "Are you originally from around here?"

"Born and raised. My dad owns a bar called Steve's Tavern. I think he was upset I had no interest in taking over the bar. He always imagined it being a legacy."

"No siblings?" Caleb asked, reading between the lines.

I shook my head. "Only child."

"Me too. I always wanted a sibling. I got Dexter instead." His face softened a bit when he thought about his friend. It was clear Dexter wasn't going anywhere, and for a number of reasons, I felt like Caleb needed someone who wouldn't leave him.

By the time my phone started buzzing repeatedly in my pocket, we'd covered a variety of subjects and conversation was flowing easily. We hadn't talked about the bits and pieces of the conversation I'd overheard on Monday that had made me so intrigued in the first place, but Caleb seemed to be set on staying with surface level topics and not letting me dig too deep. It really didn't matter, we'd had a nice lunch, but there couldn't be more to it than that. Even if I allowed myself to think about going out with him again, I could only see it going badly when I inevitably hurt him by putting my work first. From what he'd let slip, he didn't need that type of pain in his life.

"Shit," Caleb cursed when he looked at his phone. "My

next appointment is in ten minutes. I hadn't realized time had slipped away so fast."

"Honestly, someone's trying to get ahold of me right now. I've been ignoring them for a few minutes. I guess I can only escape the office for so long before someone notices."

Caleb smiled. "Thanks for lunch. It was nice. I'll see you on Monday morning."

"I'll be there."

CHAPTER 6

Caleb

Monday morning was far colder than it should have been for early spring. I was still cursing the weather and trying to warm up when Travis hobbled back to my station. I couldn't help the smile that spread across my lips when I saw him. He'd been featured in more than one fantasy since Friday afternoon, but I needed to put that out of my head quickly or I'd be sporting a very inconvenient and uncomfortable problem.

Travis had mentioned he wasn't good company, but I hadn't found that to be the case at all. I had a feeling that was his way of saying he wasn't meant for a relationship and for whatever reason that made me sad for him. I thought he'd make a great boyfriend but maybe that was because he'd told me not to drink too much caffeine before buying me lunch. *And if a man telling me I needed to watch my caffeine intake suddenly made him potential boyfriend material, maybe I needed to reevaluate where my life was headed.*

"Morning." I shivered as I rubbed my hands together.

"Good morning. Are you okay?" His brows drew together and concern creased his face as he watched me wringing my hands.

I chuckled and nodded. "Sorry, I'm fine. I'm a freeze baby. It's not even that cold, but my goosebumps have goosebumps."

"You look like you're about to be sick."

"Gee, thanks. You look good today too." *Shit, I shouldn't have said that. The cold was affecting my brain.*

Travis smirked. "Glad you think so."

Don't flirt with the patient, Caleb.

I set up a few uneven mats and some disks that were similar to rocks for him to walk across. The goal was to get his ankle more stable. This would go a long way to seeing how close we were. I didn't like the way he winced as he tried to balance.

"Have you been doing your exercises?" All signs pointed to no, even before he gave me a guilty grin.

"I've tried, but I haven't been great at them."

I sighed and ran my hands through my hair. "Three days, Travis. Three days and I can already tell you're not following through with your end of the deal. If you only work on this stuff here, you're never going to get back into shape." I'd never talk with another client like this, but after he'd taken over my lunch break on Friday, I didn't feel too bad about giving him hard truths like I would a friend.

"You're right, and I'll work on doing my exercises more often."

"Good, because if we have to keep working on what you already should have, we're going to be doing really boring work for a long, long time. Even I don't enjoy doing this stuff."

He chuckled. "Consider me properly scolded."

It felt good to correct the big, burly, sexy as fuck, silver fox, construction company owner and have him actually listen to me. Okay, after using that many adjectives to describe him, I might need to admit I'd been thinking about him too much.

Thankfully, Travis seemed more focused on his therapy after that and we were able to get quite a bit accomplished in the remaining time he was there. About ten minutes before his appointment was due to end, someone opened the side door before turning off the alarm.

The sudden cold blast of air and the simultaneous loud alarm caused me to jump in shock, and I slid straight off the balance ball I'd been sitting on while typing notes. I had the presence of mind to protect my laptop as I fell, but that didn't give me the ability to keep my head from smacking into the desk.

Travis was by my side before I came to rest on the floor.

"Oww," I groaned as I put my hand up to my head to survey the damage and winced in pain at the touch. At least it wasn't bleeding, but I was going to have one hell of a goose egg.

"Shh," Travis soothed as he gathered me up, practically pulling me into his arms, as he examined the damage to my head. "It's not bleeding," he confirmed as he carefully ran his fingers through my hair.

My automatic response was to give a snarky, "No shit, Sherlock," but it never came out because the way he was holding me as he examined my head made me want to curl up in his arms and tell him it hurt, even if it wasn't bleeding.

He hooked a finger under my chin and gently tilted my head up toward him. "Look at me, Caleb."

I glanced up and his eyes showed nothing but concern. It was totally irrational for me to wish he'd kiss the lump to make it better. Unfortunately, having him fussing over me had my little side uncomfortably close to the surface.

I didn't resist his finger and allowed him to lift my chin farther upward. Slowly, he pulled my gaze up to meet his gentle eyes, and then he studied me carefully. "Aside from tender, how is your head feeling?"

"Do you mean do I have a headache or am I seeing double or do I feel woozy?"

Travis laughed. "You can't be *that* injured if you're so full of sass."

I shook my head slightly, careful not to move too fast, because the knot on my head really did hurt. "No, I don't have a concussion. Just a lump that's going to hurt for a few days." I brought my fingers up to my head and gingerly ran them over the bump and couldn't help flinching.

Travis took my hand from my head gently and his voice was sweet and tender when he spoke. "Don't touch it. That's going to make it hurt worse. Let me help you stand up."

41

I should have felt like an idiot. I fell off a balance ball and hit my head on the leg of the desk in front of this gorgeous and shockingly kind man. A man who'd been the star of multiple fantasies over the weekend. Yet, I didn't feel embarrassed or foolish. It was hard to feel anything but good when I was being so well taken care of.

Travis reached out and I took his hand as he helped me to stand up slowly. Before I even had a chance to get situated on my feet, he'd pulled me in, and I felt soft lips press next to the bump. I was well past the age when kisses should have made injuries feel better, but I turned into mush and heard myself let out a contented sigh as my eyes drifted closed.

"Whoa!" Dexter's surprised voice caused me to jump back from Travis and bump my already sore head against his chin.

I yelped and put my hand over the bump. "Ouch." I was going to pretend I didn't sound as whiny as I was pretty sure I had. Travis wrapped his arms around me and helped me to a chair.

"Cal, are you okay?" Dexter was looking rapidly between me and Travis. My head hurt badly enough that I was almost seeing stars and watching his eyes flick back and forth between us was making the world spin.

Travis spoke up before I could find words. "He fell and bumped his head."

"Ice, please?" I was definitely whining while also trying not to touch the throbbing lump on my head.

The request seemed to snap Dexter out of whatever trance he'd been in because he jumped slightly. "Oh, yeah. I'll be right back."

He was back not even a minute later with a cold pack that I graciously took and placed on my head. I was trying not to be annoyed with my best friend. The first time a guy wraps me in his arms and kisses my pain away, and Dexter has to appear and ruin the moment. The realization that I'd been wrapped in Travis's arms while he kissed my head after making sure I was okay came crashing down on me, and I realized how far I'd overstepped with a patient. My brain was trying to process everything, but the thumping on the side of my head was making it difficult.

Travis looked over at me. "Are you sure you're okay?"

"Yeah. Thanks. I'm sorry about that."

"You have nothing to be sorry for." He pushed the hair that had fallen into my face back slightly. "I need to get out of here because I've got an appointment in fifteen minutes, but you make sure to let Dexter know if you need something."

"Thank you for your help. As long as I keep my head away from table legs, I should be good." The stern look on his face told me I needed to acknowledge that Dexter was there if I needed him. "But if I need anything, I know where to find Dex."

Travis nodded and smiled like I'd just given him a gift. "Good. Thank you, Cal." My nickname slipped off his tongue so easily I was momentarily dumbstruck and could only nod as he left the therapy floor.

"Cal's got himself a hot man!" Dexter hissed as soon as the door closed behind Travis.

I shook my head and regretted it as the movement instantly made my head throb. "He's not my man." *But damn if I didn't kind of wish he was.* I reminded myself, for at least the hundredth time, that Travis wasn't looking for a relationship. He was so busy he'd never want a boyfriend as needy as me anyway. I had to let that idea die, or I was going to need to find a new physical therapist for Travis. We'd already crossed a line I'd never crossed with a patient before, and I could only see this ending badly.

Dexter cocked his head to the side and looked concerned. "Cal, what happened to your head? Are you sure you're okay?"

I groaned and sank back into the uncomfortable plastic chair by the small desk. "I was sitting on the balance ball, taking some notes on my laptop, when the door opened and the alarm went off. It surprised me and I jumped. I knew I couldn't let the laptop drop, so I protected it as I fell off the ball and didn't protect my head. I smacked it on the table leg." I made a face remembering how ridiculous I must have looked.

"That doesn't explain why the silver fox—"

"Travis," I corrected before Dexter could continue.

He rolled his eyes. "Fine. Travis. It doesn't explain why *Travis* was holding you in his arms with his lips pressed to your head when I came around the corner."

"Because he wanted to make sure I was okay. He was

being kind. I think we both got carried away and he just sort of… kissed the spot where I'd hit my head."

Dexter smirked. "Like a Daddy would kiss away his boy's boo-boos?"

Yes.

"No. He was just being friendly."

Lies, Caleb. All lies.

Dexter clearly didn't believe me, but there wasn't much I could do. I wasn't about to let my mind go there. Dexter didn't understand what having that—even in my fantasies—and then losing it would be like. It was better to keep my fantasies away from anyone real. My fantasy Daddy needed to be totally fictitious with no possibility of being real.

Keep telling yourself that, Caleb, because your fantasy Daddy is starting to look a lot like a sexy, older construction worker with silver hair and a great ass.

Fuck. I was screwed.

CHAPTER 7

Travis

I'd overstepped on Monday at therapy, and I knew it. I'd spent the entire day waiting for the office to call me to tell me Caleb was no longer going to be working with me. He would have been completely within his rights to do so too. There was something about him that brought out a side of me that had been dormant for years. A side that loved caring for his partner and making sure he had everything he needed.

I hadn't had a boy in my life in a decade. This was central Tennessee, not New York City. Many people in the area didn't even believe gays should have the right to marry. It wasn't easy finding a boyfriend, much less one who had the same interests as me. Yet, Caleb had intrigued me from the moment I'd met him. I hadn't been able to put my finger on exactly why until he'd hit his head and my instinct to care for him had taken over so strongly that I hadn't even realized what I'd done until it was over. The thing was, Caleb hadn't seemed to mind. He'd melted into me like it was natural for him. *Right?* Or was I imagining that?

46

The thoughts were enough to drive me crazy, but I didn't quite know what to do about them. By Thursday afternoon, I knew I needed a sounding board. Not only had I been obsessing over Caleb since Monday, I'd gone over the interaction between us countless times and I needed to talk my thoughts through with someone who would understand.

Every other Thursday evening, I met up with a group of friends from college at my dad's bar. We were a motley crew. I was the second oldest in the group. The only person older than me was Merrick and he was only a year older. We had both worked some before starting college, so we had a handful of years on the rest of the group.

Logan and Trent were best friends and had been since before I'd met them. They were already in their mid-thirties. Trent was a sheriff and Logan was one of Trent's deputies, but you'd never believe it from the chaos they still created.

Larson was a firefighter in Nashville and was far quieter than the rest of the group. He tried not to draw attention to himself. Despite his quiet demeanor, he'd become an integral part of our crew. I was closest with Dean, who at barely thirty-two, had a tendency to make me feel like an old man.

Dean was a genius and had started college at fifteen. He was in my graduate-level business class when he'd been barely eighteen and I was working on my master's degree. For as smart as he was, Dean was the most laid-back and easygoing guy I knew. He'd helped me save up to start my construction company and managed stock portfolios for all of us.

Dean had exuded confidence since the day I'd met him. I'd always attributed it to him being so much younger than his peers throughout school. He had to act confident and self-assured, even if he wasn't. That said, I'd figured out he was a Dom well before I'd heard his last boyfriend call him Daddy. Despite being social and enjoying spending time with our group of friends, Dean hadn't dated, even casually, since he'd been in a horrific car crash four years earlier.

From what Trent had been able to find out about that night, a car had crossed the center of the road and had hit the car Dean and his friend were in. His side of the car had taken the impact. It had taken Dean months to get back to some semblance of his previous self. It had taken even longer for him to feel up to coming out with us again. He still didn't seem to be himself since the accident, but I'd stopped pushing and decided to be thankful he was coming out with us at all.

That night, I didn't really care if he wanted to talk about his previous relationships or not. He was a Daddy, and I needed advice on how to handle things between Caleb and me. Since Caleb hadn't canceled our next appointment, I figured that meant he hadn't kicked me to the curb. The problem was, I didn't know how to interact with him now that he'd woken up my inner Daddy.

Telling someone I was a Daddy Dom and was looking for a boy who wanted to be babied was not as easy as saying I was looking for a submissive partner. Submission took many forms, but I was a Daddy at heart and I wanted a partner who enjoyed being my little boy as much as I enjoyed being his Daddy and doting on him every chance I got. I'd known littles in the past, but I'd mainly met them online or at a club. I'd never met a little, that I knew of, by chance. I had no clue how to bring it up with Caleb without freaking him out or coming off as totally inappropriate— even more inappropriate than I already had been.

Food came out from the kitchen before we even ordered, and I knew my mom had something to do with it. Even if she'd made herself scarce, she was back there probably driving the poor cooks insane, while she made sure we were fed. How we'd come to congregate here instead of at one of the countless other bars was beyond me, but I was glad we had.

Steve's Tavern had once been an outdated little hole-in-the-wall with a small local clientele. Over the last few years, Steve's had grown in popularity and had become somewhat of a local landmark and attracted people from every walk of life. The thing I was most proud of was the way my parents had handled becoming the unofficial gay bar of a little town in Tennessee. The evening my dad had put the rainbow flag decal on the front window had been unexpectedly emotional. Most nights, there were as many LGBT patrons as there were straight and it seemed as though my parents had managed to create one of the most inclusive bars I'd ever been to. I was proud of my dad, but also of the people of Franklin for accepting the change so readily.

As the night wound down and the others said goodbye, I

grabbed Dean's elbow. "Hey, mind if we go down the street and grab a drink?"

Dean's brown eyes showed suspicion. "We're at a bar…"

"Please?"

Dean squinted at me but nodded slowly. "Fine. You're buying though."

"Deal."

We said goodbye to the rest of the guys and climbed into our vehicles for the trip down the road to Brodrick's, a sit-down restaurant and bar that offered a broader menu than Steve's. I'd always been careful to not drink and drive, but after the amount of bread from the pretzels and the burger I'd had at dinner, I could handle another beer just fine.

Dean followed me into the restaurant, eyeing me curiously the entire way to the table as the hostess sat us. Tattoos rippled across his right forearm and disappeared under his shirt sleeve. Despite wearing clothes that were too big for him, it was clear he was well-built under them.

"What's up?" he asked as he took a seat and pulled his shirt down. It was a nervous tick he'd picked up at some point over the last few years.

I grinned. "Can't a guy ask his friend out for a drink?"

"Don't give me that shit. You didn't invite Trent, Logan, Merrick, or Larson for this impromptu drink, and we aren't at your parents' bar, so, you're trying to keep something hush-hush from everyone else."

I held up my hands in mock surrender. "Okay, okay, you got me there. *Yes* I did want to talk to you privately and *yes* I'm keeping something from the others."

Dean grinned. "Spill it."

The waiter came over and took our drink orders then left us alone. "I wanted to talk to you about Evan."

Dean choked at the name. We hadn't spoken about his ex in years and I didn't even know if he realized I still remembered his name. "What about him?" he asked when he'd caught his breath.

"I know you guys had a unique relationship. I need to pick your brain about it."

Dean's eyes widened comically at the statement. "What are you talking about?" He was doing a good job keeping the shock out of his voice, but the surprise and slight panic in his eyes gave him away.

"Dean, you're a Dom. I heard Evan call you Daddy," I said casually.

The waiter made a startled sound behind me that almost sounded like he'd swallowed his tongue.

"Good job. You're going to kill the waiter," Dean scolded me.

"Sorry," I told the young man as he set the beer glasses down in front of us.

"Uh-um." He shook his head like he was trying to clear it. "D-do you two need an-anything else?"

We both shook our heads. "No thanks," Dean managed to say while shooting daggers at me with his eyes. "You better leave a damn good tip after that one," he chided as the waiter retreated quickly.

"Now you know why I didn't want to have this conversation at my dad's place with my parents around."

51

Dean took a deep breath. "Okay. So, uh, what do you want to know? I can't see you being a boy, so are you just discovering you're a Daddy, old man?"

"Don't call me that. Merrick's older than I am and you're not *that* much younger than me."

Dean shrugged. "You're over forty. I'm thirty-two."

I growled. "If you were a sub, I'd put you over my knee for that."

Dean grinned. "But I'm not, so you won't. Now, tell me Mr. Big Bad Dom, what do you want to know about me and Evan? And remember, I have the right not to answer."

"It's not so much Evan. It's that I know you were his Daddy, so that makes it easier for me to talk to you about this stuff."

The look Dean gave me was somewhere between amused, confused, and annoyed. I guessed the annoyed part was because I was being evasive as all hell, but I wasn't entirely sure where to start. Talking about being a Daddy Dom wasn't something I did in my daily life. The last boy I'd had in my life had been a decade earlier. He'd been new to the lifestyle and we'd played a handful of times before he'd decided I was too overbearing and worked too much. He'd told me that, while he wasn't cut out to be more than a bedroom sub, he also needed more stability than I'd been able to offer at the time. The last I'd heard, he'd found a Dom and was quite happy keeping things strictly to the bedroom. I was happy for him and glad he'd found what he needed.

"I'm a Daddy as well," I started when I figured I had my thoughts organized enough. "I've known this about myself for most of my adult life. I've recently met someone, and I think there may be something there. I thought I might have fucked up big time on Monday morning, but it's looking like I haven't blown it, yet."

Dean looked like I'd just given him his every wish on Christmas morning. "Whoa, whoa, whoa. We need to backup a bit here, Trav. You can't just say you're a Daddy and not expect me to pry. And you just dumped a shitload of vague information on me. I can't help you if you don't fill me in on all of this." He leaned forward, then pulled at the back of his shirt again. I wanted to ask what he was trying to keep covered up. The tick drove me nuts, but he was an adult and it wasn't my business.

"Fine. What do you want to know?" I huffed.

Dean leaned back and crossed his arms, his black tattoos a stark contrast to his white T-shirt. "What type of Daddy are you?" At my blank stare he clarified. "Are you a bedroom, 'Spank me Daddy I've been a bad boy' Daddy? Or are you a lifestyle, 'I want to care for my boy in every possible way,' Daddy?"

"The latter." That was easy. "I need more control than just in the bedroom."

Dean scoffed. "No shit. I couldn't have guessed."

"Don't be an asshole. My ideal boy would be a little."

Dean's eyes widened and he let out a silent, "Oh." Then he found his voice and smiled. "You know, my first instinct was shock, but no, I can totally see you with a sweet little. You're right. You're such a control freak, you need that control." He paused and looked at me like I was a bug he was about to dissect. "So, what makes you think you've found a boy? Because I'm clearly missing something."

I sighed and ran my hands through my short hair. "He's my physical therapist." I explained my physical therapy appointments. Everything from the first one where I'd overheard the conversation Caleb and Dexter had had about the dragon toys, to lunch with him on Friday, and then Caleb hitting his head on Monday. "He seemed so comfortable just resting in my arms. I was so fucking hard I don't know how he didn't notice," I finished.

Dean nodded slowly as he fully processed the story. "Okay, you've got my attention," he finally said.

I didn't want to give him a chance to think too hard, so I pushed forward with my questions quickly. "Was Evan a little?"

Dean hesitated and looked uncomfortable. "Sort of. Our relationship was never perfect. He was a bit more independent than I was looking for in a boy. He was spontaneous and strong-willed. I'm too... controlling sounds bad, but that's what it is, I guess. It drove me up a wall when he'd make plans with his friends instead of coming home at night. Then he'd forget to tell me. It wasn't that he was a brat. I mean, he *was* a brat, but not in that sense. He never seemed to understand why it drove me nuts. It was to the point that punishment for those things was useless because he never seemed to put two and two together and would do the same thing the next time. Our relationship was on pretty rocky ground before the car accident. There was no way we would have survived the aftermath and all my rehab."

"Why haven't you found a boy again?" I forgot my questions about Caleb and wanted to know more about Dean.

He looked nostalgic for a moment. "Easier said than done, Trav. I'm not the same guy I was four years ago. I don't think a little is going to want a damaged Daddy."

The response concerned me, but the waiter's untimely reappearance had me forgetting to pry more. When the waiter left again, Dean turned the subject back to me and Caleb before I could pry into his statement. "So, you want a little. But aside from the dragon toys, him letting you change his drink order—that was seriously weird on your part, just so you know—and the interaction after he bumped his head, what makes you think he's a little? It can all be explained away fairly easily. There's also a chance you've found yourself a natural submissive, but *not* a little."

I groaned because Dean wasn't telling me anything I hadn't already thought about. "It's just a feeling. But I don't know what to do about it."

Dean thought for a moment, steepling his fingers in front of his face. "Okay, so this cutie likes dragons, and your gut says he may be a little."

I nodded.

"But you have no idea how to find out if he is, in fact, into the lifestyle."

"Exactly."

Dean sank back in his chair and nodded to himself. "What about getting him a dragon and asking him out?"

I cocked my head. "And how does that help me figure out if he's actually a little or not? And what if that gets me kicked out of physical therapy because I've come on to the therapist and made him uncomfortable? As much as I hate going, I need my damn ankle working right again!"

"Drop some hints tomorrow. See if a nickname gives you some insight. Boy, or baby, or something."

I wrinkled my nose. Those were terrible nicknames for Caleb. The fact that I knew that so quickly should have been a red flag that I was thinking about this too much. I'd have to think about something fitting for him, but he definitely wasn't boy or baby, I just didn't know if I knew him well enough to actually figure out a nickname. "I'll think about it."

I might not have been convinced about the nickname thing, but the dragon item was doable. I would need to get to the store and hope they had a small dragon something. Not knowing Caleb well, I didn't know what he had, so I hoped to find something that spoke to me.

"So, Mr. Barton," Dean spoke up, drawing me out of my thoughts. "Why didn't you tell me you were a Daddy Dom?"

"I could ask you the same thing."

"Nuh-uh. You heard Evan call me Daddy. It was *your* responsibility to open up to me and tell me that you're also a Daddy who wants a sexy *little* sub." His grin was pure mischief as he spoke. "If he *is* into the lifestyle—and that's a *huge* if at this point—are you going to be okay if he falls more on the ABDL spectrum and likes diapers and bottles and not just playing with toys and calling you Daddy?"

Of course, the waiter appeared with the check at that moment, red-faced and unable to look us in the eyes. I fought a laugh as he dropped the bill off at our table and hurried away without a word.

"I think you just earned the honor of leaving the tip. And yes, I'm fine with it. I want someone who needs his Daddy to take care of him. I'm fine with bottles and pacifiers and sleepers and diapers."

Dean groaned, though it was good natured. "You would spoil a boy to death, if you can stop working long enough to focus on him."

I chuckled as I got out my wallet and threw enough money on the table to cover the beers. "Yeah, if I found the right boy I'd want to give him everything. The workaholic thing is what worries me most. I've been thinking about it a lot. I think I need something to focus on. Having a boy, especially one as sweet as Caleb, in my life would give me something aside from work to focus on."

Dean fished out his wallet and threw a five on the table for the tip. "I'm glad you've at least thought about it. Being a Daddy to a little is a big deal."

I nodded in understanding. It was a huge step for any little to call someone Daddy. I had a feeling that if my gut was right about Caleb, if he ever got to the point that he could call me Daddy, it would be a huge honor. What surprised me most was that I found myself ready to put in the time needed to get to that point with Caleb. "Believe me, I know. And I think this guy may be worth it. It's just a feeling."

Dean reached out and squeezed my hand. "I'm glad to hear that. Your life has revolved around work for way too long." As he pushed back from the table he sighed. "We're going to be lucky if we're allowed in this place again."

"The waiter would make a cute little though" I said, careful to keep my voice down. "Maybe he could be your next boy."

Dean rolled his eyes. "Not looking for a boy. Those days are behind me."

"You okay?" I didn't know how he could simply leave being a Daddy behind. It was an integral part of my self-identity. Even if I hadn't played in years, I knew I'd never be truly happy in a relationship without that role being fulfilled.

He gave me a sad smile. "I'm fine. The accident changed a lot for me."

My eyebrows drew together. I was going to need to pry into Dean's life more, but now wasn't the time. We'd already embarrassed the poor waiter and were walking out of the restaurant. I needed to go to the store anyway.

CHAPTER 8

Caleb

"Pull yourself together, Caleb." Like giving myself another pep talk would help set my mind straight. I was seated at my desk with my laptop open ten minutes before Travis was due to arrive, but I'd been pushing Puff around my desk more than working.

I had to get through the next hour. Since Monday, I'd been borderline obsessed over the interaction with Travis. While the swelling on my head had subsided over the previous few days, the bruise was still there and each time my finger brushed it, I was reminded of Travis pulling me into his arms to check on me. Of him kissing my head tenderly. Of Dexter popping up and scaring me so badly I smacked my head against Travis's jaw.

Arousal mixed with embarrassment churned in my gut as I thought about the interaction on Monday and began overanalyzing the lunch I'd had with Travis the previous Friday. The feelings would then turn to frustration because I knew Travis's job came first. He'd been clear about that on the first day I'd met him and he'd reiterated it at lunch. *Then why did he have to go and be so sweet on Monday?* I wanted to scream at the warring thoughts in my head.

I was already on the verge of a minor meltdown when Dexter appeared.

"And you say they're not toys." Dexter's voice caused me to almost jump out of my skin.

"Don't sneak up on me like that!" I snapped.

He pulled a small chair up beside me and sat down. "Someone's touchy."

"I'm not touchy. I just wasn't expecting you here. Don't you have a patient or something?" I asked, looking out the door in hopes of finding an out to the current conversation.

Dexter smiled. "Nope."

"Well, I do, so you need to go."

Dexter looked at my frazzled face and read me like a book. "It's hot Daddy, isn't it? You're in here trying to pretend you're fine but you're really freaking out because you want him to be *your* hot Daddy. But you're going to pretend you don't while you spend more time playing with your dragons than working on reports or god knows what else." He picked up a dragon and put it down beside me.

"Dex, go away."

"Nope." Dexter dropped his voice and pretended to be the dragon in his hand.

I chuckled at his forced, playful voice and the way he wiggled the dragon as he talked.

"Dexter, you're going to make Caleb late for work. You

need to go." My dragon waggled just like his as it talked back.

Dexter threw his head back to laugh, but another deeper laugh came from the doorway and we both jumped to see who it was. Of course Travis was there, watching us in our animated, inanimate, argument. *Fuck.*

Dexter put the dragon down and winked at me as he headed past Travis. But he lingered in the doorway for a moment, pointedly watching me as I fumbled to set Puff back down on my desk and attempted to not die of embarrassment, again. Jesus, it was like Dexter had a sixth sense for when Travis was in the office and wanted to do everything possible to make sure I wanted to crawl in a hole and die at least once every appointment.

I stumbled with my words as I fought to control my blush. "Uh, h-hi."

"Did I interrupt?"

I shook my head. "The only thing you interrupted was Dexter bothering me. Ready to get started?" Hopefully, a subject change would help me get my horror under control. *I was going to kill Dexter.*

"Your limp is already getting better," I mentioned as we worked on stretching his ankle out some.

Travis smiled at me, but the look in his eyes was pure mischief. "You told me I had to do my exercises." There was a short pause and his voice was low when he spoke next. "I like rules and knowing what's expected."

And that statement went straight to my dick. I tripped

over my feet as I made my way to the computer to write a few notes. I heard Travis chuckle lightly as I stumbled. "First you bonk your head, then you trip over the carpet. You need to be careful."

How was I supposed to focus when Travis was saying things like that to me?

I managed to pull myself together for the rest of the appointment and kept our conversations as professional as possible. Thankfully, Travis seemed to get the hint that I didn't want to flirt, or whatever it was he was doing, and kept the conversation strictly on safe topics. Of course, all I really wanted to do was find a way to have him pull me in tight and hold me like he had on Monday.

"How's the head?" he asked as he was standing on a balance board.

I absently ran my hand over my head and nodded slowly. "It's okay. The swelling's gone down, but there's still a bruise. It's almost better though."

"Glad to hear it. You had me a little worried when you tumbled over like that."

I flushed. "Sorry to scare you. I scared myself too." The chuckle I gave was forced, but at least it sounded like I was being light-hearted about it.

"So, do you have plans this weekend?" Travis asked a few minutes later as we were doing some final stretches before he was done for the day.

Yes, I had plans, but they weren't anything I was going to talk to Travis about. My big plans involved my stuffed animals, blocks, a thick diaper, cartoons, and an early bedtime. It was probably stupid, but when I let myself be little, I made myself go to bed at a reasonable hour—*kids had bedtimes, right*? But Travis didn't need to know any of that. Not now, not ever.

"No, not really. I'll probably just hang out at home and maybe spend some time with Dexter."

Travis nodded. "You two seem so different."

I chuckled. "We are. Dexter is hyper… bouncy might be a better word… but his heart is in the right place. He's been my support system for years." I didn't often talk about my mom dying when I'd been in high school or my dad dropping me off at college my freshman year and telling me not to come back home, ever. He'd discovered I was gay over the summer and refused to have a deviant living in his house.

As much as those first few months of college sucked, Dexter was always there for me. He'd, literally, held my hand while I figured my life out. We'd lived together in the dorms all four years of undergrad. I'd spent summers at his parents' house. I rented my townhouse before I started my master's degree and Dexter moved in with me. Then when the place next door became available a few years later, he became my neighbor. And he was still my neighbor. Dexter was the closest thing I'd had to a family since my mom died.

Dexter stopped the hop-ball race with a kid he was working with and looked over at us. His face was flushed red, and I could see his freckles from across the room, but he was grinning from ear to ear. Travis continued to do the stretching exercise, but even he managed to laugh at Dexter's antics. "Well, he must keep you on your toes."

I laughed. "He's pretty awesome."

"And you two really aren't together?"

"We're close enough to almost be brothers. But there is no way I'd ever be able to date him." I shook my head trying to get the mental image of dating Dexter out of it.

"Are you dating anyone?" he asked as he tried to stretch to the balls of his feet, wincing at the movement.

"No." I wasn't really processing what he'd asked, I was more caught up in watching his facial expression for more signs of pain. "Don't hurt yourself. My job is to get you back into shape, not to have you injuring yourself more."

He grinned at me and winked. "Sorry, that's just part of my personality. I'm stubborn and strong-willed. I push myself. I don't like being told I can't do something."

I felt like I was missing something in that statement. It wasn't threatening, but it sounded almost suggestive. And the look on his face wasn't as neutral as it had been. *What wasn't I understanding?*

"Would you like to go out this weekend?" he asked as he finished the stretch.

I blinked. "Uh, um."

"Sorry, that wasn't appropriate while you're at work," Travis backtracked. "I didn't mean to put you on the spot."

"You didn't!" Dexter's voice rang out from next to us, causing us both to startle.

"Dex…" I tried to warn him.

Dexter smiled. "He'd *love* to go out this weekend. His plans were to sit on the couch and be a potato! He needs someone who will take charge and spoil him."

Dead. I was Dead. There was no way in hell this was my life. I'd entered the twilight zone, that was all there was to it. If I wasn't dead, Dexter certainly would be before the end of the day.

Travis smirked. "That's very specific."

Dexter nodded and opened his mouth to speak, but I quickly covered it with my hand. "*Enough*, Dexter." I turned to Travis and smiled. "I, um, would like to go out."

I felt Dexter lick my hand, and I said a silent prayer for patience.

"Let me give you my number." I tried to keep my expression neutral while I tried not to strangle my best friend. My hand was wet with his slobber, but I didn't dare remove it because I didn't want to know what would come out of his mouth if I did.

Travis took out his phone and unlocked it. "Do you want to enter your information?" he asked, holding it out.

I shook my head and rattled off my phone number. "I guess I'll talk with you later?" It was already nine thirty, and his appointment was officially over. "Have a good day, and be careful with that ankle," I told him as I pushed Dexter toward my office door. "I'll know if you're doing too much!" I scolded as I pushed Dexter into the office.

Travis laughed and shook his head. "Got it. Enjoy the rest of your day."

"Bye, Travis. Have a good day." I nodded as I kicked my door shut. I finally removed my hand from Dexter's mouth and wiped it across his shirt. "You are impossible! And absolutely disgusting! Do you know that? I don't need your help securing a date for myself! And you *licked* me!"

Dexter grinned. "You do need help securing a date for yourself. You were hesitating!"

"Remind me again why I put up with you?"

"Because you love me, and I'm your best friend, and you wouldn't know what to do with yourself without me. And because I have all the dirt on you, so you're stuck with me."

I peered out the window of my door to make sure Travis was gone before opening it. "I think you're blackmailing me now."

"Not blackmail, just a statement of fact." Watching an almost six-foot tall man practically bounce across the therapy room was amusing even if I wanted to kill him. It would have been more amusing if I hadn't looked over and noticed a lanyard sitting on the table at my station. I knew it hadn't been there earlier so I was curious where it had come from.

As I got close enough to it, I noticed the black and purple pattern was actually tiny dragons. The note clipped to the lanyard was impeccably handwritten and I knew who it was from before I even read it.

Looking forward to seeing you this weekend. -Travis

I smiled as I switched my name badge to the new lanyard and put it around my neck.

CHAPTER 9

Travis

It had taken me hours, and a phone call to Dean, to decide where to take Caleb on our date. After Dexter volunteered that Caleb was looking for someone to "take charge and spoil him," I was more confident in my decision to give him the lanyard. I'd left it on the table not feeling nervous, just anxious about his reaction. I still didn't know if he was simply naturally submissive or if he was a little, but I could too easily see Caleb playing with toys on the floor wearing a thick diaper under snug fitting play clothes that would show off the bulge. And that thought had brought me to a powerful orgasm in the shower that morning.

I was picking Caleb up to take him to the Natural History Museum. Dean had discovered there was a dinosaur exhibit there for the next few months. It wasn't quite dragons, but I thought going to see dinosaurs would be enjoyable for Caleb. When I'd suggested it over text the night before, his response was quick and affirmative followed by a number of smiling and clapping emojis.

As I pulled up to Caleb's address, I was relieved to find it was on a quiet street in a nice part of town. I was getting ahead of myself, but my protective instincts were already on high alert when it came to him, and I couldn't easily turn that part of myself off.

I parked my SUV and headed toward the door. I hadn't even had a chance to knock when I saw Dexter's head pop out of the door next to the address Caleb had given me.

"Just the person I was waiting for!"

I looked at the address on the door and across the porch to where Dexter stood. "Do I have the wrong address?"

"Nope, that's Cal's place. This is my place."

Their relationship was clearly more complex than I'd originally realized. "You live next door to Caleb?"

Dexter nodded as he came out of his house and met me halfway. He held out his hand and smiled. "I think you've probably gotten a bad impression of me. While I am impulsive and I do tend to lack a filter, Cal is my best friend."

I nodded.

"I was being serious when I said he needs someone to spoil him. Cal deserves it more than anyone else in the world. If you're not willing to put him first, don't even bother taking him out. Whatever you do, don't lead him on. I don't want to be picking up the pieces."

The way Dexter worded the lecture had my brain whirling about why he'd need to put Caleb back together. I didn't intend to lead him on in any way, so I didn't think we had a problem there. "You have nothing to worry about with that."

"Will you take care of him?" Dexter asked seriously.

Dexter may have come across as an untrained puppy the first few times I'd met him, but he knew something about Caleb, and he was making sure I wasn't going to mess with his best friend. I could respect his intentions, even though he might have been going about it in the wrong way. What I couldn't figure out was what exactly Dexter was hinting at.

"I'll take care of him. However, if I knew what he needed, it would be easier."

Dexter opened his mouth, but the door to Caleb's house opened and he stepped out. "I swear on all that is holy, Dexter O'Conaill, if you are embarrassing me... I know where you sleep!"

These two were hysterical. I had a hard time keeping a straight face when they got to bickering, but I feared that Caleb might actually follow through on the threat if I didn't step in. "He didn't say a single embarrassing thing. Promise." It wasn't even a lie. Dexter had not let one secret slip, even if I kind of hoped he would have. I had a feeling Dexter knew a lot more about Caleb than he liked. Dexter had a little on Caleb in height, but Dexter was lanky where Caleb was muscled and I had a feeling Caleb could take him down if he tried.

Caleb looked between the two of us skeptically. "Promise," Dexter assured him while holding up his hands.

Caleb sighed like he didn't quite believe us but had no

choice since we hadn't given him a reason not to. "I'm ready to go," he said to me as he made sure his door was locked.

"Have fun," Dexter said with a wide grin. "You're gonna love the dinosaurs!" Caleb blushed like he was uncomfortable. I wasn't surprised Dexter knew where we were going. I suspected Caleb and Dexter kept very little from each other.

There was no reason he should be having that reaction over his friend letting it slip that he knew we were going to see the dinosaur exhibit. I wanted so badly to know what Dexter knew about the cutie standing beside me.

I'd been part of the fetish community long enough that it would have taken a lot to shock me. Caleb didn't give me the impression that he was into any type of pain. His skin was so creamy and smooth, I *almost* didn't even want to spank it. I couldn't imagine it marked up by whips or floggers.

The first few times I'd met Dexter, he'd been so impulsive and hyper I'd caught myself wondering if I knew someone who could be a master for an excitable pup. I reminded myself again that I was not in the matchmaking business, and I hardly knew Dexter. Now that I was getting to know him, I wasn't so sure pup fit him that well. Despite being bouncy and excitable, I was beginning to suspect he might lean more toward the dominant side of the spectrum. I'd be overstepping more boundaries by trying to match him with a trainer than I likely was by taking my physical therapist out on a date… To see dinosaurs… Because I thought it would be a place my boy would want to go on a date. He wasn't even my boy, and I didn't know if he had any interest in the lifestyle.

Yup, totally inappropriate.

But I forgot about it when Caleb looked up at me and smiled. "Are you ready to go?"

I smiled as I reached for Caleb's hand. "Sure."

Caleb grinned and did a little hop step as we headed toward my truck. "I can't wait to see the dinosaurs," he gushed.

As we pulled onto the road, Caleb was all smiles. "I've been wanting to see this exhibit. I'm excited to finally get to."

The guy who had been nervous and anxious a few minutes ago was practically bouncing out of his seat and bubbling over with excitement. "I'm glad you wanted to see it. I know it's not quite dragons, but it's hard to find something to do with those."

Caleb laughed. "Yeah, there was a traveling dragon exhibit that was at a museum about five and a half hours from here last year. Dexter and I took a long weekend to see it. It was really cool."

"Really?" That was quite the jaunt to go see a dragon exhibit. Part of me couldn't believe they'd gone that far to see it and part of me was happy Caleb had someone in his life who was willing to do those things with him.

Caleb blushed slightly. "It was worth the drive. But, that means I've seen dragons, now I get to see dinosaurs, and they're almost as cool."

It only took a few minutes to get to the Natural History Museum from Caleb's house and I hadn't even had the chance to ask him how he and Dexter had ended up as neighbors. Being as close as they were, I was slightly surprised they didn't live together.

Caleb's eyes were wide with wonder as I paid our admission. I almost jokingly asked the clerk if he classified as a child for the day. Caleb was looking around at all the posters and glassed in artifacts the museum had on display and was so distracted I didn't even think he'd notice if I'd asked.

"Travis, look!" Caleb pulled me toward the first actual exhibit inside the museum.

A mom with three young kids looked at me like we'd done something wrong. I wrapped my arm around Caleb and pulled him closer to me. When I caught her eye over his head she was staring at us like we were from another planet. "What is it?" I asked, turning my attention back to him.

"It's a dinosaur egg. Isn't it cool?" He read the blurb about the egg and where it was found and how old it was estimated to be.

The next two hours went the same way. We bounced around from exhibit to exhibit looking at different artifacts and skeletons and reading factoids about the dinosaurs and the different time periods they'd lived in. Caleb bubbled with excitement the entire time. I was having a hard time remembering he wasn't my boy and that this was just a date—at least for the time being. I could easily see myself setting boundaries for him about running off without me or touching things without permission.

By the time we'd finished the entire exhibit, I was exhausted, but Caleb seemed to have more than sufficient energy for both of us. It was almost five though, and my stomach was telling me it was nearly time for dinner. Even if he didn't realize it, it was getting late and he'd need to have dinner soon. I started thinking about where we should go to eat as we headed toward the exit of the museum.

As we walked by the gift shop, I saw him glancing at the shelves of stuffed animals and got an idea. "Should we get something to remember this afternoon by?" I asked as I turned into the shop.

Caleb followed me in but seemed a bit more reserved than he had been thirty seconds earlier. "Like what? A Natural History Museum shot glass?" He pointed to the display of overpriced glassware.

I shrugged. "If you want. Or what about one of the dinosaur figurines?" I glanced over to see Caleb bite his lower lip slightly, unsure of the right answer. He looked intrigued, like he wanted to say yes but was holding back.

"Or," I suggested casually, "we could get one of these dinosaur stuffed animals."

Caleb's eyes widened and he looked truly excited at the idea of taking one of the green and brown stuffed animals home. There were four different dinosaurs to choose from and Caleb looked over each one as quickly as he could. It was clear he was trying to keep his excitement over the plush toys under wraps, but his eyes couldn't lie.

He sighed. "A shot glass would probably be the most practical."

"But you'd like the stuffed animal more," I countered. It wasn't a question, simply a statement of fact.

Caleb turned a beautiful shade of red, and it made me want to wrap him in my arms and help him make the decision. It wasn't my place to do that just yet though. Instead of pulling him close, I held his hand and directed him over to the plush animals. The warring emotions were clear on his face, and he leaned into me slightly.

I let him rest against my shoulder and instead of pushing him forward, I pulled back a bit. "Would you rather just get a magnet?"

Caleb shook his head.

I smiled. "You really liked the brontosaurus in the museum." The brontosaurus was also the cutest of the four stuffed animals, at least in my opinion. Caleb reached out to grab one, but my mouth was moving before my brain had a chance to stop it. "No, don't touch." The words weren't harsh, but Caleb pulled his hand back, and his eyes widened in shock like I'd smacked him. Daddy came out so easily around Caleb that my brain had totally shut the filter off.

I forced myself to soften my voice and tried not to make things worse. "Sorry. Let me." I reached out and grabbed the stuffed animal. It had a slightly dopey smile on its face and its neck was poseable.

I could have sworn I heard Caleb moan quietly, but I couldn't figure out if it was in satisfaction or horror. He smiled and nodded slightly.

I looked at the tag on the ear. "His name is Branson... Branson the Brontosaurus." Even the damn name was cute.

Caleb let out a small giggle that went straight to my dick. How an adult could make such an innocently beautiful sound was beyond me. "Well, if he has a name, we can't just leave him here." While Caleb was the one who'd done most of the convincing, I felt as if I'd crossed a major hurdle.

Getting him to open up was not going to be as easy as I'd hoped it would be. Then again, I hadn't been all that forthcoming about myself either. Maybe at dinner we could open up more and get to know one another better.

I paid for the stuffed animal with my right hand because Caleb was holding tightly to my left. The cashier looked between us for a brief moment, unsure of who to hand the bag to. I tilted my head toward Caleb and she handed the bag over. Even though I couldn't see his face, I could hear the smile in his voice as he thanked her.

After our seatbelts were buckled, I turned to Caleb. "Would you like to get dinner before I take you home?"

Caleb held the bag containing the dinosaur in his lap, unwilling to put it down. "I'd like that," he agreed as his stomach let out an audible growl. "My stomach agrees too."

"I'd say so. What sounds good to you?"

He chewed his lip while he thought for a few minutes. "I could really go for a good burger right now. There's a place down the road from here—Brodrick's—that's one of my favorites."

I forced myself to keep a straight face as I nodded. After

Thursday night, I wouldn't have been surprised to find out I was on the Brodrick's blacklist, but it was only a few minutes away, and I pointed my truck in that direction.

"Good choice. They've got the best burgers around." I didn't mention that I'd been there two nights before. Besides, I hadn't actually had any food. I'd just had a beer and traumatized a waiter.

I was relieved when the hostess didn't bat an eye when I walked through the door. She smiled politely and told us the wait would be about an hour. Though I was hungry, I could wait and it gave Caleb and I a bit of time to talk. He ended up bubbling over about the museum visit and the dinosaurs we'd seen. I enjoyed listening to him become animated and letting some of the stiffness in his body go. By the time the hostess led us to a table near where Dean and I had sat earlier in the week, we'd actually been waiting for closer to an hour and a half.

I didn't bother looking at the menu. I knew what they had, and their bacon cheeseburger was my favorite. I wasn't getting to the gym much anymore because of my stupid ankle, so I'd go with a salad instead of the fries I'd prefer. Caleb, on the other hand, took a moment to look at the menu and I took the time to watch him.

He was beautiful with long lashes and short-cropped dark hair. I'd never seen what was under his shirts, but I suspected a broad chest and firm muscles. Some Daddies preferred their boys small and twinkish, but Caleb was the perfect little for me. I always felt more comfortable with a guy I didn't have to worry about hurting, and when they were muscular and tall, it was easier.

Clearly, we'd caught the restaurant at its busiest time on a Saturday night, so I wasn't surprised when it took a bit of time for the server to come over. However, when I heard the greeting, "Hi, welcome to Brodrick's." The familiar voice made me cringe internally. I hesitated to look at the guy because I wondered what he'd think or say. Dean and I had clearly made him uncomfortable a few nights before and had left him a flustered mess. It also meant he knew a bit more about me and my interest in Caleb than I would have liked.

Caleb looked up and smiled at him.

"What can I get you gentlemen to—" His words died in his throat as I turned and smiled at him. He cleared his throat twice before he found his words again, though they were choked and slightly halting. "What can I g-get you to dr-drink?"

Caleb's brows pulled down and he looked confused at the waiter's sudden nervousness. "Do you mind if I get a beer?"

"One beer is fine. Order what you'd like." *I really needed to work on my assumption that Caleb was already my boy.*

Caleb eyed me with cautious suspicion, but seemed to relax. Was it because I didn't have a problem with him having a beer? Or was it something more? Like having a decision made for him? Or was I just reading too much into it? "Thank you," he said quietly to me. Then to the still-shocked waiter, he asked, "Could I get a Sculpin?"

When Caleb's eyes met mine, I gave him a slight nod and approving smile that made him blush and dip his head. It was an interesting reaction, and I couldn't wait to explore it further. I was also noticing I had a desire to explore quite a bit more than his reactions. His tentative smiles and bashful blushes had gone straight to my dick. I wished I could reach over and kiss all the hesitation from his lips.

I smiled at the waiter who was blushing a deep red and having a hard time looking at me. I hadn't realized how much Dean and I had shocked him, and I felt slightly guilty for it. Instead of dwelling on it, I smiled politely and asked for their beer of the month. I hadn't bothered looking at what it was, but I had faith it would be good.

When the waiter left, Caleb looked at me curiously. "Why is he so nervous around you? Do you two have a history?"

I laughed. "You could say that, but not in the way you're thinking. My friend and I were here two nights ago and he overheard a private conversation between us. I think we surprised him a bit."

Caleb cocked an eyebrow in my direction. "What type of private conversation?"

"Given that we shocked him so much he's unable to look me in the eyes without turning red and stumbling for words two days later, I think we should probably save it for somewhere outside of Brodrick's. It's nothing bad, just maybe a bit unsuitable for public discussion."

CHAPTER 10

Caleb

Dinner was the most surreal meal I'd ever had. Travis either suspected something or was just a naturally dominant guy because he'd basically taken charge effortlessly. *Or, maybe I'd ignored little Caleb's needs for so long that I was reading too much into everything he did and said.* There was no reason my heart should have fluttered when he told me that "one" beer was enough. I shouldn't have felt giddy when he suggested I have a salad instead of french fries. And, I certainly shouldn't have blushed four shades of red when I thanked him for buying me dinner and Branson the Brontosaurus.

I hadn't even minded that dinner took over two hours because of how slow the service was. I'd never known Brodrick's to take so long to get meals out, but I wasn't complaining because I'd enjoyed spending time with Travis.

I was going to blame the odd sense of giddyness for my decision to invite Travis in when he dropped me off after dinner. I'd never had a low-pressure first date. I didn't feel like he was trying to get into my pants or expected anything, yet I also didn't feel like it was a bust. Travis had been engaged and hadn't complained once as I'd dragged him from dinosaur to dinosaur. Even when his limp had become more pronounced, he'd never said anything. It was me who had finally said I was ready to go because I hadn't wanted him to hurt his ankle just to make me happy. He definitely seemed to be the type of guy who would sacrifice himself to make sure I was having a good time.

I pushed my front door open and flicked the light on with the hand that wasn't holding the bag with Branson in it. I'd been in a mad dash to clean my place up when Travis showed up a few minutes early. Since it was only ever Dexter or me at my place, I didn't normally worry much about *things* being left out. I'd found a sippy cup in the fridge, a bottle full of water that had rolled under the couch, the blanket on the back of the couch was covered in Eeyore, Tigger, and Winnie the Pooh, and there'd been a bucket of building blocks by the bookshelf. Unfortunately, I had to cut the cleaning short when I'd heard voices on the front porch. I instinctively knew if there were voices outside, one had to be Travis. I also knew my best friend well enough to know he'd been watching for my date to arrive. I only had seconds to get out there before Dexter said something that was sure to be too much information and would embarrass me to death.

Looking around my living room, I sighed silently, thankful that it appeared as though I'd gotten everything cleaned up. I smiled up at Travis. "Come on in." As soon as we were inside, I pushed the door shut quickly hoping Dexter hadn't spotted us.

The energy in the room changed once the door was shut. I hadn't realized how much I wanted to explore Travis's body and allow him to explore mine while we were out that evening, but now that desire was racing to the forefront of my mind.

Ever the gentle giant, Travis leaned forward and ran his thumb across my jaw. My knees felt weak as his forehead touched mine. "I don't know if I can keep holding back. I've wanted to kiss your beautiful lips all night."

I groaned. "Please, don't hold back." It had been years since I'd wanted to feel lips on mine as badly as I wanted to feel Travis's. He seemed so strong and confident, and I knew the kiss was going to rock my world before it even happened.

Travis tipped my chin up and brought his lips down to mine. The initial touch was the lightest brush. I could barely feel his soft lips on mine, but I felt it in my pants as my cock began to thicken as all my blood rushed south. He deepened the kiss, his lips pressing more firmly against mine, but his tongue had yet to make an appearance. My arms wrapped around Travis's neck and I dropped the bag, hoping it landed somewhere near the table by the door. He walked backward, pulling me with him, the kiss deepening with each step.

By the time the back of his legs bumped against my couch, our mouths were open and tongues were exploring.

I'd known I'd be wrecked before our lips met, but now that they had, I knew no one would ever match up to him. Wrapping his arms around me, Travis pulled me down onto the couch with him.

Travis yelped and his wide eyes met mine as we collapsed onto the couch. He reached behind him and, to my utter horror, pulled a stuffed turtle out from under him. Unfortunately, it wasn't *just* a stuffed turtle. Of course not. No, it was the turtle that held my favorite dodi—a green glittery adult pacifier with a dragon on the front. I'd custom ordered it online almost a year earlier.

The first time Dexter saw one of my pacifiers he'd asked why my "dodi" was so much bigger than any he'd seen before. I spent the next few minutes laughing more at the word dodi than being embarrassed that he'd found my pacifier. By the end of the afternoon, I'd been given a lesson in Irish folklore and had learned that kids hung their dodis on dodi trees for the siog—fairies—to take when they got too old for them.

It didn't matter how many times I told Dexter it was a pacifier, or paci, or binky, he refused to call it anything but a dodi. It had finally gotten to the point that it was easier to go with it, so I'd taken to calling them dodis as well. It was convenient, since virtually no one knew what a dodi was, so when he said something about one while we were in public, no one batted an eye.

There was clearly no way to deny being the owner of the dragon dodi. It was too big to be a child's, and it was on my couch. *Fuck.*

I sank into the far corner of the couch and buried my head in my hands. I'd never planned on telling anyone else about my little side. I'd long ago accepted I was a little. I understood it was an integral part of me. Sharing this side of myself with a boyfriend, or *potential* boyfriend, had never crossed my mind. Now I was faced with explaining my kinks to a man I'd felt an actual connection with before the end of our first date. I was waiting for the ground to open up and swallow me whole.

It would probably be immature for me to run to my room and hide, so instead, I curled in on myself and placed my face in my knees. *Because that was more mature than running away.*

Before I could think of a way to excuse myself or give Travis a graceful way out, I felt the couch beside me dip and large arms wrap around me. "Hey, Cal," I heard him say gently through the blood rushing in my ears.

I shook my head.

"Cal," he said again, this time hooking his finger under my chin and guiding my face to look at him. "Cal, it's okay."

I shook my head again and kept my eyes shut tightly. It *wasn't* okay. It would *never* be okay. He'd discovered my secret, and he was going to leave. Instead of angry words, his arms wrapped around me tighter, and I was practically scooped into his lap. "Oh, Cal. It's okay."

"H-how can it be okay?"

A soothing hand ran over my head, across my shoulders, and lingered on my back for a moment before repeating the gesture. I allowed myself to melt into his side, my legs draped over his lap. "I've been attracted to you since the first time we met. I knew there was something drawing me to you when I wanted to see you again last Friday. Then, the way you responded to me when you bumped your head on Monday… well, let's just say I was all but certain of your interests before now."

I cracked my eyes open just enough to make out his features. He was smiling tenderly at me, the way I'd always hoped a man would look at me. Could that really be acceptance and understanding on his face? Well, acceptance, understanding, and a bit of amusement as well. The relief I'd felt in that moment was short-lived when I realized Travis was probably expecting me to *talk* to him. Fuck, I didn't know if I was ready for that.

"And you're okay with it?" I managed to whisper to the floor.

"Oh, sweet boy, I'm more than okay with it."

My eyes shot up to meet his. "What?"

He booped my nose then kissed my forehead. "I love that you're a little. I love that you've got your dragons and loved the dinosaurs at the museum. I loved watching you get so excited today." He pulled me closer. "Will you tell me more about your little side?"

I stiffened in his arms. He wanted to know about little Caleb? The thought made the burger and salad I'd eaten for dinner roll in my stomach. He thought my obsession with dragons was cute, and he'd liked my enthusiasm at the museum. Hell, he didn't even seem repulsed by my pacifier. But what would he think about my toys, my clothes, the bottles and sippy cups, or worse yet, my diapers? That was a lot for anyone to take, and I knew it.

Travis was rubbing his hand up and down my back, content to wait me out. I didn't know if I was going to crack and tell him or fall asleep from his soothing touch. "This is nice," I said into his chest.

Travis chuckled. "Is it too much to talk about right now?"

I nodded lazily. "Too much."

"If I drop it now, will you tell me more soon?"

I nodded. It wasn't fair to ask me questions while I was this relaxed. I'd have agreed to just about anything to keep feeling his gentle touches.

He kissed my temple. It wasn't that late—it wasn't even nine yet—but I was exhausted. "It's okay, Caleb, honestly. You aren't going to be able to scare me away with what you tell me."

"You say that now," I said, fighting another yawn.

He chuckled. "You need to go to sleep. You've had a big day. Can I tuck you in before I leave?"

"Tuck me in?" Had I really heard that right? As in, put me into my bed, pull the covers up, and kiss me goodnight? My heart fluttered slightly. I was convinced Travis was too good to be true.

He ran his hand through my closely cropped hair, and I felt any reservations dissolve. "O-okay." I hoped he didn't

85

freak out when he saw that my room looked more like a kid's than an adult's. It was perfect for me for the times I wanted to let go for a while. Alarm bells probably should have started ringing in my head when I noticed I was considering taking him to my real room instead of the spare room I usually took boyfriends to.

Travis held up my turtle with a questioning glance around. "I'm certain this isn't the only thing you take to bed. Do you have a bottle or sippy cup you like?"

I blushed and tried to hide my face. "Mywatercupisinmybed." I mumbled quickly. I'd never even considered having to tell anyone but Dexter that I had a sippy cup filled with water in my bed—my bed that had cartoon-printed sheets and was half-covered in stuffed animals. *Fuck*. I wanted to crawl in a hole.

"What was that?" Travis asked, a rich laugh filling the room.

"I have a water cup in my bed already," I said slowly and with a bit more conviction.

I felt a gentle push on my side. "Go brush your teeth and get ready for bed."

I slid off the couch and headed for the steps that led to the two bedrooms and bathroom upstairs. Travis followed behind me and stopped as I entered the bathroom. "I'll wait out here. Let me know if you need help."

That was all he said, but it left me nodding dumbly as I stepped into the bathroom. My thoughts were swirling wildly in my brain. Should I leave the door open or shut it?

What type of help would I need? Would he just watch me to make sure I was doing everything right? Would he brush my teeth for me? Did I want that? I'd never thought of a Daddy taking care of something like that before.

My brain was conflicted, but my dick liked the idea. I gave an uncomfortable nod as I shut the door and disappeared into a six-by-ten, tiled bubble. I willed my erection to go down as I forced myself to follow my normal routine. I flossed and brushed my teeth, and then I went to the bathroom. Until that moment, I'd never wondered if I should use the bathroom or not. Would Daddy want to diaper me before bed?

"Christ, Caleb. Pull yourself together. He's not even your Daddy! It's not like he's going to diaper you tonight. He doesn't even know you *have* diapers," I scolded myself as I emptied my bladder. I blushed when I realized I was wearing a pair of fire engine briefs. They were for adults but the fun pattern had caught my eye.

Was Travis going to see my briefs? What pajamas was I going to wear?

Little me liked childish pajamas and bold patterns. But adult me usually slept in nothing more than briefs, sometimes less than that. This was getting complicated. I probably should have just told him what being little meant to me. I should have told Travis I liked cartoons and toys. It would have been a hell of a lot easier had I told him about my diapers and childish clothes. At least then he could have noped the fuck out if it was too much and I wouldn't be locked in the bathroom with a sexy man waiting for me in the hallway while I freaked out about what happened next.

Except if I really listened to the voice in my head, I knew he wouldn't have left. Travis had suspected I was little even before he'd asked me out. He'd taken me to the museum and had bought me a stuffy. A man who wasn't okay with their boyfriend wanting to regress wouldn't have done those things. *Would he?*

Even with the logical part of my brain beginning to work out Travis's understanding of my little side, I was still worried. After talking online with a few littles in college, I'd learned that coming out to others wasn't easy. Shit, being gay was easy compared to this. Being little was a bit more complicated. People didn't take it well according to most littles I'd talked to or read about. Usually, when they found a partner in the lifestyle, it was because they'd specifically looked for one on a kink site or in another place with like-minded people.

I'd gone as far as having two rooms for myself so I could keep the two parts of my life separate. I always shut my bedroom door and had taken any boyfriends to the guest room which looked like any other adult's room. When I'd invited Travis in tonight, I'd fully intended to do that if things went that far, and I still could, but for some reason, I didn't want to.

Maybe my resolve was breaking down. Maybe I was tired of hiding such a big part of me from every boyfriend I'd ever had. Or maybe it was because Travis seemed to understand me. The way he'd handled finding my turtle and dodi was a fairly good indication that he would likely understand my little side even before he'd reassured me. But could I really put myself out there like that?

"Fuck," I muttered as I washed my hands and realized I didn't have pajamas in the bathroom with me. *Why hadn't I just talked with him downstairs?* I couldn't waste anymore time in the bathroom, but I wasn't ready for Travis to see my pajamas either. At least not the pajamas I normally wore to bed if I was little. I'd tell him to wait in the hallway if I had to while I got dressed, but that seemed even more cowardly than shutting—and locking—the bathroom door while I went through my nighttime routine. If I wanted the man to tuck me in, he was going to see my pajamas.

As I fretted, my eyes fell on the oversized white T-shirt I'd hung on the hook on the back of the door while I'd been doing laundry. I'd meant to throw it away. I couldn't even figure out where I'd gotten it, but it was huge. The one time I'd put it on, the sleeves hung almost to my elbows and the hem hung low on my body. It would at least cover my bright fire truck undies.

Stripping out of my pants and shirt, I pulled the T-shirt on over my head. It was still as comically large as it had been the first time I'd pulled it on, but at least it covered my butt… mostly. Okay, some. It covered some of my butt. *Damn long torso.* I could take my undies off, but then I'd be bare-assed and that would be just as embarrassing. I wasn't ready for naked time, even if it was just to be tucked into bed. My butt was going to stay covered, even if it was in a pair of embarrassingly bright briefs.

Unfortunately, I couldn't put off opening the door any longer. I was in pajamas—if you could call a giant T-shirt pajamas—and I'd finished my nightly routine. I was stalling, and I had a feeling my resolve would break far earlier than Travis's.

I peeked my head out the door and saw Travis standing against the far wall staring at my room. I'd been in such a hurry to get into the bathroom, I'd totally forgotten to shut the door of my normal room, all but forcing me to admit it was my normal room. *Where was that giant sinkhole when I needed it?* At least the decision about which room to take him to was settled for me. I did, however, need to make it from the bathroom to the bedroom and I didn't want him to see my undies.

Travis smiled at me. He had Branson in the crook of his arm and my turtle in his hand, the green pacifier dangling from its paw like a beacon. I couldn't count the number of times I'd walked out of the bathroom to find Dexter in the same place and holding a blanket, a sippy, or a stuffy. I'd never blinked an eye at him doing it, but with Travis, it felt much bigger. Maybe it was because I actually felt something more than friendship for him, or maybe it was because tall, silver, and handsome was everything I'd ever wanted but had been too afraid to think about going after. Clearly, Dexter and I had far too few boundaries in our relationship. I was okay with letting my best friend see me little but not the man I'd just spent an amazing day with, who'd flatout told me he'd thought I was a little all along.

"Ready?" Travis asked when my head and shoulders were out of the bathroom.

"Uh, yeah. But... would you mind closing your eyes for a second?"

Travis blinked and gave me an amused, curious smirk. "Why do I need to close my eyes?"

I flushed even redder than I already was. "I... I don't have pants on!" I hoped that hadn't sounded as absurd to Travis as it had to me.

Travis was clearly amused as he fought a smile. "So, you're okay with me standing here with your pacifier but I can't see you without pants on?"

"Dodi," I corrected automatically.

"Bless you?" Travis questioned.

"No, dodi. That's my dodi." *Sinkhole, please!* I don't know why I felt the need to tell him I called it a dodi, but I had and there was no taking it back.

Travis looked at his hand where I was pointing to the turtle and green pacifier. "Your paci is called dodi?"

"I'm going to kill Dexter tomorrow," I mumbled. "Close your eyes and let me get into bed, then you can ask me questions."

Travis laughed again. "You know what? I'm going to humor you right now because I really want to learn about this dodi."

I fought rolling my eyes, but Travis closed his, and I ran

as fast as I could to the bedroom where I dove under the sheets, toppling a few stuffed animals off the bed in the process.

"Okay, you can come in," I told him uncomfortably as I arranged the sheets so I was covered to my waist.

Travis popped his head into my room and smiled. "All better?"

I nodded. "Yes, I think." My red face probably told him it wasn't, but I was going to pretend.

He took a seat beside me and handed me Branson and my turtle. "So, about this dodi…" He wiggled the pacifier at the end of the turtle's foot.

CHAPTER 11

Travis

I had to force myself to focus on Caleb and his dodi, not the way-too-baggy shirt or the tattoo he'd always had covered by his dress shirt sleeves. Even that afternoon, I'd never guessed he had a tattoo, much less a bright rainbow colored one. From what I could see, it appeared to be a hibiscus that took up all the skin I could see above his elbow.

Besides, tattoos weren't uncommon. Dodis were, and every time I heard the word I wanted to laugh. I'd heard binky, paci, soother, even dummy, but dodi was a new one. The way Caleb had corrected me so automatically, I knew I was going to have to get used to it being a dodi as long as we were together. There wasn't a question in my mind that we were together—I needed to find out if he felt the same way—and the next few minutes could make or break our potential relationship.

The pink shade Caleb had turned when I'd asked him to explain where the name came from was adorable. "Dexter," he'd said on a sigh and I couldn't help but laugh. I didn't know either of them that well. I knew Dexter even less than I knew Caleb, but for some reason, the word dodi seemed like it would have come from his redheaded best friend.

"I don't know *why* the Irish call them dodis," Caleb said, his voice small and bashful. "But apparently, they have these trees called dodi trees and when kids get too old, they tie them to the tree for the fairies to take them. It's some old folktale or something. Oh, I guess I should tell you that— surprise, Dexter is Irish. His parents are from Ireland, but he was born here so he doesn't have much of an accent. Though, trying to talk with his mom and dad can be quite a trip!"

Okay, so I understood that the Irish called them dodis, and I knew why Dexter called it a dodi. What I didn't fully understand was why Caleb also called it a dodi. Their relationship was fascinating. It didn't seem as though they kept anything from each other, hell they even lived next door to each other. I couldn't figure out how to ask why Caleb used the same word for pacifier as Dexter did. Thankfully, I didn't have to because Caleb began talking again before I could figure out the best way to ask the question.

"When Dex found my… pacifier," he choked out, clearly embarrassed to be having this conversation. "He told me I should have hung my dodi from the tree a couple of decades earlier, and it surprised me so much, it made me forget about being horrified he'd found it. He'd already found out about my… interests… before then, so it wasn't much of a surprise. I think he was more surprised it was for an adult. Since then, it's just been known as my dodi." Once the admission was out, Caleb sighed and yawned.

I reached over and ran my hands through his short hair. "I like that story, and your dodi's perfect for you." I pointed to the dragon on it and smiled. "And I love the glitter. It's a hint of surprise, like the bright tattoo you keep hidden under your long sleeves."

I felt Caleb lean into my touch as I spoke, and I wanted to wrap him up in my arms and hold him all night. He wasn't ready for that though. He was still barely ready for me to see him in his bed with brightly colored sheets and the pile of stuffed animals on the side. On the pillow beside him was a bright blue, zoo-themed sippy cup. I picked it up and noted the weight—there was plenty of water to get him through the night without a refill.

"Alright, you're ready for bed. We can talk more later. Please text me in the morning when you wake up."

He nodded slowly. "Mm-hmm. I'm tired."

I placed a gentle kiss on the top of his head and heard him sigh. "I know you are. Let me get you tucked in so you can get some sleep. I'll let myself out."

Caleb began to wiggle his way down in the sheets, so I lifted them slightly to ease his struggle. As the sheets fluttered up, the bright fire truck print on his briefs was visible. Now it made sense why he was so shy about me seeing him running from the bathroom to his bedroom.

Looking around his room, I could tell Caleb was clearly comfortable being little, but apparently that comfort didn't extend to me seeing him that way, despite my assurances that I understood and expected it. I needed to figure out how to get him to open up a bit more, I just didn't know how to go about that.

I smoothed the sheet around him and pulled the blanket up to his chin. He'd already found the dinosaur we'd bought at the museum, and it was tucked into his arm. I settled the turtle close enough to him that he wouldn't have to look for his dodi when he wanted it.

"Night, sweet boy," I whispered. "Sleep well."

"Night," Caleb yawned in return. I flicked off the light as I left the room and headed toward the front door. Looking around specifically for things to hint at his interests, I saw a box tucked on a shelf that appeared to have some blocks in it as well as a colorful blanket folded on the chair. I was sure if I looked hard enough, I'd find out most of his interests, but from what I'd seen so far, I thought Caleb might be the perfect boy for me.

If only I could get him to open up.

I let myself out, making sure to lock the door on my way out. I wished I had a key to lock the deadbolt, but the door lock would have to do.

"Did you have a nice day?" a curious voice asked from the other side of the porch, causing me to jump. I turned, willing my racing heart to not give out on me, and saw Dexter sitting on a chair near his front door drinking a glass of wine.

"I think he enjoyed himself. I know I did." At least that was an easy question to answer.

"Where's Cal? I've been texting him."

I smiled at his curious nature. "He's sleeping. I tucked him in before I left."

Dexter's eyebrows knitted together. "You tucked him in?"

I nodded. "He was tired. We had a busy day."

Dexter didn't know how to respond, which surprised me quite a bit. The few times I'd seen him, Dexter had never lacked for words. He seemed to be trying to figure something out in his head.

"What did you think of that gray comforter on his bed? I keep trying to tell him it needs to be replaced."

It was my turn to look at him in confusion. "His comforter was red, not gray."

Dexter's eyes went up in shock and he grinned. "Holy shit! Cal let you see *his* room? Oh, damn! Come in! We gotta talk!" He was out of his chair so fast I didn't have time to tell him no. The door was open and he was ushering me inside. "I'll get you a drink. What do you want? Water, beer, wine, soda?"

"A beer would be great. What do you mean his room? What other room would I have seen?"

"The gray one." The way he said it was like it should have been obvious.

I tilted my head in question. "I never saw a gray room."

Dexter's eyes widened comically, and his legs bounced

excitedly. "Cal showed you *his* room!" It wasn't a question. It was almost a squeal of delight. "Oh my fuck, he *likes* you!"

"Dexter, you're not making sense." I wanted to be annoyed with him, but there was something about him that was impossible to be mad at. "Why is him letting me see his room so special?"

Dexter grinned. "Because he's never let anyone, besides me, see his room."

"Why?" I was starting to feel like we were talking in circles.

Dexter's expression changed from excited to almost melancholic. "Because he's convinced no one will ever understand him. He's special, he knows exactly what he likes and wants, but Cal is certain no one will accept him for him. So much so that he won't even try to find someone who gets him."

"Gets him? As in his stuffed animals and sippy cup and dodi?"

"Just to name a few things, yes." My words must have caught up with him because he clapped and his eyes sparkled with joy. "You saw his dodi and didn't flip out?"

"I sat on it first, but yes."

Dexter opened his mouth, thought better of it, stopped, appeared to gather his thoughts, then started talking again. "How much do you know about him?"

"Not as much as you, clearly." Neither of us were willing to give much away, unsure of how much the other knew about Caleb's personal life. Each time I spoke with Dexter, I gained a bit more respect for him. He might have lacked a filter, but his loyalty to his friend was impressive.

"You've seen his room—again, seriously huge deal there—and his stuffies, and the damn dodi."

I laughed. "Yes, the dodi that you named."

"I told him it was time to hang it from the dodi tree." *Ah yes, the dodi tree.* "I sometimes hide it in the fairy garden out back." Dexter's smirk was devious. "I tell him the fairies are going to take it for someone who needs it. I think the fairies have decided he needs it though. It keeps finding its way back to him."

One of us needed to crack and tell the other what we knew or we'd be there all night talking about dodis, trees, and dodi fairies. "None of that bothers me," I said when Dexter took a breath.

Dexter nodded in approval. "I didn't think it would. Especially after you left him that dragon lanyard yesterday. He smiled every time he looked down at it, by the way. Would more bother you?"

Ah-ha! The in I'd been looking for. "What do you mean more? Like, if Caleb told me he wanted a Daddy? Or that he uses a bottle and likes to wear diapers?"

"Damn, he's found his pot of gold," Dexter smiled in triumph. "You don't care about that, do you?"

"That he might want that stuff?"

Dexter nodded encouragingly.

"Honestly? No, I don't. I had a suspicion he might be at

least open to the lifestyle since last week. After yesterday, I was pretty convinced. Today, even though he never said anything specific, I could see how much he wanted to let go. I don't care. In fact, I like it. I like when my boyfriend needs me... needs Daddy, I guess you could say... to take care of him."

"You'd spoil my Cal?"

I couldn't help but laugh. Dexter seemed so happy, there was very little I could do but nod in agreement. "I'd love to, if he'd open up to me."

"When's your next date?"

I chuckled. Dexter was certainly persistent. "I was hoping to make him dinner tomorrow night. He fell asleep before I could ask him though. I'll have to touch base with him tomorrow morning."

Dexter leveled me with a piercing green glare. "You won't dick him around, will you? Like you aren't going to get his hopes up and then decide he's too much work, right? Because he keeps telling me he's too high-maintenance and no guy will want him. And he keeps telling me you're too devoted to your job. I know there's the perfect guy out there for him somewhere. If you don't want him just as much when he's demanding your attention as you do when he's a twenty-seven-year-old physical therapist, then you need to walk away now. I can fix the disappointment of losing you after one night. I don't know that I'd be able to put him back together after a month or a year."

I respected the hell out of Dexter in that moment. He was just as good a friend as Caleb had told me he was. I shook my head. "I do work too much. Since I've met Caleb, I'm beginning to think I work so much because I don't have someone who needs me. I have no intentions of leaving him because he's too needy. Truthfully, I like feeling needed."

Dexter got a far-off, dreamy look in his eyes as he sighed. "Ah, you'll be the perfect Daddy for Cal. Now, about dinner tomorrow."

"What about it?" That was a stupid question, but it was dinner. What did I need to know?

"You've got the person who knows more about Caleb than anyone else sitting across from you. What are you planning on making?"

I'd already been planning out a meal in my head, but he was right, I had his best friend sitting across from me. I might as well use the time to plan out exactly what Caleb would like so it would be perfect.

CHAPTER 12

Caleb

I wanted to die of embarrassment when I woke up Sunday morning and remembered the night before. Travis had tucked me in and had seen my dodi, that was still between my lips, and he hadn't seemed to freak out. But what did he think about it after he'd left? By all accounts, I felt like Travis had the potential to be my Daddy, but there were still so many questions. And finding out your date has a pacifier and stuffed animals isn't something most people would take lightly.

My worries about what he thought once he had time to process everything quickly faded when I checked my phone.

Travis: *Do you have plans today? I was hoping to make you dinner tonight.*

I read the text at least five times before I convinced myself I'd read it correctly. Instead of texting Travis back, I sent a quick text to Dexter.

Me: *Travis wants to make me dinner tonight!*

The response was almost instant.

Dexter: *I know. Full disclosure, I was on the porch when he left your place last night. He told me he wanted to see you again today.*

Me: *Dex… how much did you embarrass me?*

Dexter: *I didn't say anything to him that he hadn't figured out on his own. You've got to give him a chance… a* real *chance.*

I didn't know if I wanted to know what they'd talked about. But if Travis had talked with Dexter and still wanted to make dinner for me, it clearly hadn't scared him away. And given the 11:35 p.m. timestamp, I knew he'd talked to Dexter before sending the text. Hell, part of me felt better about Dexter paving the way—steamrolling might have been a better word if I knew my best friend—for me. I finally sent a text back to Travis.

Me: *I'd like that.*

I hadn't expected my phone to buzz in my hand with his response before I'd even managed to roll over enough to swing my feet out of bed. My bladder was screaming for relief, but it was cold in my room that morning. *Why don't more people wear diapers to bed?* I chuckled to myself at the thought while I unlocked the phone to check the text.

Travis: *How does 4:30 work?*

Me: *That works well.*

Travis: *Great, I'll be there then.*

Well at least I didn't have to worry about what to make for dinner that night.

By late morning, I was sitting on the living room floor building with a set of wooden blocks while Dexter lazed about on my couch and the TV droned on in the background. We were watching an action flick, but my blocks were a lot more interesting than a movie I'd seen so many times I had most of the lines memorized. Occasionally, I'd look up at the TV when a scene caught my ear, or Dexter and I would begin talking about something going on that week. For the most part, I was focused on the blocks I had spread out across the patchwork quilt Mrs. O'Conaill had made for me after my mom died.

The blanket had been on my bed for years, but when I'd moved into my townhome, it had found a place in the living room. I tried to keep my toys on it. That made clean-up easier and I didn't worry about something being forgotten if someone was coming over.

Dexter and I had been talking about going to the bar later in the week when he'd gone quiet and began tapping furiously at his phone. The guy had the attention span of a gnat. I'd gotten used to it over the years, so I turned my attention back to my blocks. I was halfway through building a fort to keep an army of attacking soldiers—the tiny cylindrical blocks—from attacking a castle. I'd long ago given up trying to figure out how my mind came up with these ideas, but I could see the battle clearly in my head and I needed to get the walls in place before the army arrived. If Dexter was going to text, I was going to take the time to fortify the defenses around the village and castle.

"Travis is going to be here in twenty minutes," Dexter said as he set my phone on the coffee table. *When had he picked up my phone?*

104

I dropped the block in my hand, causing the precariously erected wall to crumble. "What?" I gasped, looking around at the mess that surrounded me. My dodi sat next to me, still attached to my turtle, blocks littered almost every inch of the blanket, a half-empty sippy cup of juice was on my other side, and while I was wearing jeans, my T-shirt had a diapered teddy bear on it. I'd gotten it for free when I'd ordered a case of diapers a few years earlier. It was cute and the closest to little clothes I wore around Dexter.

Dexter stood up from his spot and stretched. "He's leaving his house now. I told him it was fine to come over."

"Why didn't you at least *ask* me? And why is he coming over *now*?" I was not whining... I was just strongly questioning. "He wasn't supposed to be here until later. Help me clean up!" I snipped at him as I started to grab blocks from across the blanket.

Dexter crouched down beside me and ran his hand down my back. "When I saw his name on the screen, I figured you wouldn't want to miss it, but I didn't want to pull you away from your toys. He decided he wanted to make you lunch and dinner so he could spend more time with you. I didn't want him to just walk into the house and totally freak you out."

I blinked up at Dexter. Why did he have to be so damn understanding, even when he was driving me nuts? "Well, then help me clean this up."

"You don't have to clean it up, Cal. Travis isn't going to care. You know that, right?"

Logically, I *knew* that, but I still shook my head. "It needs to be cleaned up."

Dexter sighed and pulled the block bucket from beside the couch. "Alright, let's get it cleaned up." At least he was placating me. In just a few minutes, we had the living room basically cleaned up and had taken my cup back to the kitchen to wash it out.

As I was drying it off Dexter came over and put his hand on my shoulder. "You're making me sad right now, Cal."

The cup slipped from my hand and bounced across the floor. "What? Why?" I didn't rush to get the cup, more worried about what I'd done to upset Dexter.

"You're dooming this relationship before it even gets off the ground. Travis wants you just the way you are—shy, confident, embarrassed, scared, little, big."

I huffed. "Dexter, how the fuck do you know that? You've talked to him a handful of times! I love that you don't see my little side as some big thing, but Dex, it's not that easy! There's a chance—a *small* chance—that Travis will make a good Daddy, but I don't think that I'm ready for him to totally see that side of me. I don't know if I ever will be. I find it hard to believe that the perfect Daddy is going to just hobble his ass into work one morning and all of a sudden I get my happily ever after."

I hung my head and Dexter walked around me to pull me into a hug. "Caleb, if you'd just give Travis a chance, I really think he might be the guy you've been looking for. You just have to believe it." There was a knock on the door and Dexter gave me a tight squeeze. "Pull yourself together for a minute, and clean up your cup. I'll get the door."

"Thanks," I whispered into his shoulder.

He kissed my cheek. "Anytime." Then he turned and bounded through the living room toward the door.

I grabbed the sippy cup off the floor and the lid from the counter and tossed them into the cupboard where I kept all my little, kitchen-appropriate stuff. I'd only had time to take a few deep breaths before Travis walked into the kitchen and saw me standing at the kitchen sink staring at the wall.

Two paper grocery bags were set on the counter beside me seconds before strong arms wrapped around my body. "What's wrong, sweet boy?"

I didn't *mean* to step back into his embrace, and I didn't *intend* to let him turn me around so he could hug me tightly, yet I did both.

"Nothing has to happen that you don't want to happen today. I brought a few things as a surprise for lunch, but if it's too much for you they'll stay in the bag."

I didn't want to ask, I *really* didn't want to ask. "What did you bring?" *Shit, I asked.*

Travis grinned. "Oh, apparently my boy is curious?"

I nodded, liking the way he called me his boy.

He shrugged. "I'll see if I think you're ready when it's time for lunch. Go to the living room and hang out with Dexter while I get everything ready."

"I can help you," I offered quickly. Having someone cooking in my kitchen while I sat around seemed weird.

"You can help by going to the living room. Dexter looks lonely. Go keep him company." Travis stepped to the counter and began pulling things out of the bag. "I bet you've got some toys somewhere you could play with if you wanted to." I blushed and bit my lip causing him to chuckle. "That's what I thought. Go, sweet boy."

Was it weird that I liked when he called me sweet boy? I sighed but headed toward the living room where Dexter was sitting on the couch with the remote in his hand.

"I shouldn't have meddled, but I thought if I didn't do something, you would hide forever. However, you are still managing to hide." At least he had the decency to look a little sheepish about using my phone.

I sank back beside Dexter. "Thank you. You may be right. If you don't push me some, and if Travis doesn't push me some, I might never actually open up."

"Blocks?" Dexter questioned with a grin glancing at the bucket beside me. "We can set them up again."

I nodded slowly. "Get the blanket. I'm going to go upstairs and change my shirt."

Dexter rolled his eyes but humored me, and I hurried up to my room, taking the steps two at a time. I stripped out of my teddy bear shirt and replaced it with another black shirt. I hoped Travis wouldn't notice the wardrobe change. He hadn't said anything about the shirt, so I hoped he hadn't noticed it. It was simply too much for me at the moment. I was back downstairs not even a minute after I'd gone up. In that time, Dexter had managed to lay my blanket on the floor and had restarted the movie on the TV.

108

Looking at Dexter, I had a feeling my warring emotions and confusion were clear on my face. He got off the couch, took my hand, and pulled me down to the blanket with him. "It's okay, Cal. All you have to do right now is be here. Let your man take care of lunch and you."

I looked at the bucket of blocks, over toward the kitchen where Travis was already working on lunch, and back to Dexter. My mind was a jumbled mess of thoughts that I couldn't sort through. Play? Be big? Be little? Sit there like a stone? I didn't know what to do. Dexter seemed to know what to do because he picked up a block and thrust it into my hand.

"Today is all about you getting to be little Caleb." He turned up the volume on the TV a little, situated himself so he managed to block my view of the kitchen despite his smaller frame, then picked my turtle up and held the dodi out to me. I held it in my hand for a moment before finally pushing it into my mouth. Dexter reached out and rubbed his hand over my head and it made the category five hurricane in my stomach settle to a tropical storm.

I had to remind myself that I'd wanted this for as long as I could remember. If Travis couldn't handle little Caleb, I'd be hurt, but it was better to find that out now than in a few months when I'd become more attached to him. I tried to smile at Dexter, but I could feel how wobbly it was.

"You've got this."

He didn't say anything else as he began handing me blocks. I decided to start rebuilding my fortress. Having

Dexter supplying blocks to me and blocking my view of Travis allowed me to slip back to the place I was before I'd found out Travis was coming over early. The increased volume on the TV drowned out any noise from the kitchen and before long, I'd forgotten anyone else was in the house. By the time Dexter stood up, I'd rebuilt the fortress and the villagers were getting ready to defend the castle from the advancing army and our movie was over. Dexter grabbed the remote and changed the channel to an older cartoon I'd seen countless times.

"I need to head home," Dexter whispered and my body tensed. "None of that. You need to let Travis see little Caleb. He'll know exactly how to take care of you. He already does." He pushed at my dodi to keep it in before I could drop it to protest. "I'm next door if you need me, but I know you won't. Get comfortable before lunch is ready. I'll check on you later."

I growled from around the pacifier he was holding tightly to my mouth. I glanced into the kitchen and noticed that Travis was engrossed in his work and wondered how much time had passed so far. I didn't think it had been that long, but I'd purposely kept clocks out of my living room so I didn't worry about time when I started playing. I'd gotten in the habit of setting an alarm on my phone and didn't worry about the time until it went off.

I huffed and Dexter smiled, but turned to head out the back, through the kitchen. I heard a whispered conversation, but it was so hushed I couldn't make anything out over the TV.

Not even a minute later, the door shut and Travis and I were left alone. While part of me wanted to cry for my best friend to come back, a larger part of me was ready to see where this led if I could only give it a chance. It wasn't going to be easy, but I wanted it. I had already shown Travis pieces of little Caleb last night. I just needed to let him in enough to show him the rest. I decided to take Dexter's advice and tried focusing my efforts back on my toys.

I must have done a decent job because when Travis came to get me for lunch, I yelped in surprise and dropped my dodi.

"Sorry about that, sweet boy," he apologized. "Lunch is ready." He held out a hand for me to take as I got to my feet. The villagers had mostly defeated the attacking army and, only a few enemies remained. He looked over my blanket with the little wooden blocks toppled over. "What's going on there?" he questioned.

I wanted to be embarrassed, but his question showed nothing but pure interest in my creation and it made it hard to be embarrassed. Until that moment, I never thought there would be a man who would be interested in what my mind came up with when I allowed myself to be little. "The army was trying to invade the village and take over the castle." I pointed to each piece of the setup.

"It looks like it was quite a battle," Travis murmured as he led me to the kitchen.

I nodded, looking back at the blanket. "It was. The villagers have almost won."

111

"Well, maybe after lunch you'll have time to go back to it." The statement was so offhand, like it was the most natural thing in the world to tell me, it made my throat constrict and tears prick the back of my eyes.

I couldn't speak for a moment, so I forced out a nod as he walked me to the table. A place was set for me with a brand-new divided plate and a sippy cup that matched. Sucking my bottom lip into my mouth, I let my eyes fall to the chair where the triangular bib I hid in the back of the cupboard was now sitting. It looked a lot like a bandana once on, but it was definitely a bib. However, it was another part of my little persona I'd kept hidden from everyone, including Dexter.

My plate was a rectangle divided into four large sections piled up with food. Since the cup had dinosaurs on it, I figured there would be dinosaurs below the food too.

In the first section, Travis had placed a pile of macaroni and cheese that appeared to be homemade, another had chicken strips—from the smell in the kitchen, I figured they were also homemade—with ranch dressing in the corner of the section. Dexter must have told him what my favorite dipping sauce was. In the third container were steamed carrots and broccoli, and in the last appeared to be strawberry yogurt. Everything looked amazing, I hadn't had to lift a finger, and my kitchen was clean. I felt some of my stress melt away.

"Thank you," I managed to get out as he pulled the chair out for me. I was beginning to question everything I'd thought about finding a man who would both understand and accept every part of me. Travis seemed to break the mold of every guy I'd ever dated. The real question weighing on my mind was if I was okay with calling anyone Daddy after spending my entire adult life *certain* I wouldn't find a man who understood my desires?

Except, Travis really did seem to *get* my needs. He seemed to understand what I wanted, and apparently wanted the same things, just like Dexter had tried to tell me.

Fuck, I hated when Dexter was right.

As I took a seat, Travis fastened the bib around my neck. It was unnecessary, yet it was another thing that showed he accepted me for me. It was another thing that made me feel emotional and hopeful in a way I'd never been before. I didn't know how I felt about that though. I didn't want to get my hopes up and have him decide I was too much work, yet he was making me lunch, holding my hand, and fastening a bib around my neck. I had to take a deep breath before I was able to grab the fork that matched the plate.

My hand was shaking as I tried to get the macaroni onto the fork. I felt a strong hand rest over mine. "Hey," Travis's voice soothed. "What's going on in that brain of yours that has you shaking?"

How did I even start to answer that question? This was such a huge moment for me, and as I tried to figure out what was bothering me so much, I suddenly realized it was because I wanted this so badly. I'd never understood how hard it was to keep my little side away from previous boyfriends. Little Caleb was so much a part of me that it wasn't surprising I'd never had a long-term boyfriend. I never felt like I'd found a guy I could be little around. I was scared Travis could be that guy.

"What if you leave?" It probably wasn't the best sentence, or starting place, and fuck if I didn't sound needy as hell, but there was no taking it back.

Travis looked around the room. "And go where?"

I sighed. "I mean. You're here. And this lunch... Y-you don't know what this lunch means to me. If I let you see me, see little Caleb, I'm afraid I'm going to get too needy and scare you away. You've already told me your job is basically your life. I know it's ridiculous, but I don't want to be second place."

A rich laugh filled the kitchen. "Oh, I think you probably need to worry about me being too overbearing and pushing you away. I'm pushy and controlling, and I like to have things a certain way. I like routines and I have expectations. And you're right, I have prioritized my job for years, but I've never had someone in my life who makes me want to randomly go out to lunch either."

A tear slid down my cheek. I could understand why those things would make some guys feel smothered, but to me it sounded... perfect. "Wh-when I'm little, I'm needy. I know that. Ask Dexter, he knows it too. I like attention, and I like to feel important. I could sit here and tell you that my need to be little stems from my mom dying when I was in high school or my dad disowning me because I'm gay. But I knew I liked regressing way before those things happened. I didn't understand it until after high school, but I knew it was part of me." I took a shaky breath and closed my eyes. I was on the verge of becoming an emotional mess.

Travis looked at my plate. "We don't have to figure everything out before we have lunch. Eat before it gets cold. I'm here today, for as long as you'll have me. We'll have plenty of time to talk after you finish your lunch."

I nodded. Now that the dam had opened, there was a lot I wanted to say. It would probably be a good idea to take the time while I ate to organize my thoughts. I stabbed a bite of the macaroni and managed to get it into my mouth. It was, hands down, the best macaroni and cheese I'd ever had and I let out a little moan of pleasure as I chewed.

"Like it?" Travis asked with a smirk.

"It's amazing! If everything you make is this good, I think I'll keep you around." The strange thing was, it wasn't hard to see me spending a lot more time with Travis, and that was a new feeling. I didn't just *like* him. I felt something a lot more than that toward him. Knowing that he understood my need to be little Caleb as much as big Caleb made me want to spend even more time with him.

"How about you wait to try the rest of your food before you make any crazy declarations."

There was no knife for the chicken, so I chose to pick the pieces up with my fingers and dip them into the ranch dressing as I ate. They were just as good as the macaroni, and the smile on Travis's face made the experience that much better.

"I've never let anyone see me when I'm completely little. Not even Dex." The admission surprised even me. I'd thought it and it had come out just as quickly.

After swallowing his own bite of macaroni and cheese, Travis probed me for more information. "When you say little, what does that mean to you?"

I felt heat creep up my face. I stabbed a few carrots with my fork and brought the bite to my mouth. At least chewing would give me a moment to organize my thoughts and possibly figure out where to begin.

When I'd chewed the bite to the point that it was evident I was stalling, I swallowed and drew circles on the table in front of me with my finger. "Blocks and my plates and cups are just some of what I have."

Travis nodded, but blessedly didn't push me. He had probably already figured out I was hiding a large part of what I was looking for. "I'm sorry I'm being vague. This is just something I don't know how to talk about. I've only told Dexter, and there wasn't as much at stake when I told him."

When I froze up, Travis seemed to realize I was going to need some encouragement and began talking. "I was about twenty the first time I learned about D/s relationships. I was taking a women's studies course in college, looking for an easy A. The class hit on numerous random topics. Honestly, the professor was a bit of a nutcase, but one day, sexuality came up in class. It escalated from sexual identity to alternative lifestyles pretty quickly. By the end of the class, it had turned into a full blown BDSM discussion. That was the first time I'd heard of Doms."

"I'd have died of embarrassment right there on the spot."

"I was too curious, honestly. I went back to my dorm that evening and started down a very interesting path on the internet. Nothing near as comprehensive as what's out there now. The internet was still pretty new at the time and information was spotty at best. But as I researched Domination over the next few weeks, I discovered Daddy Doms. I liked the idea of being able to dominate someone with love instead of whips and restraints. Don't get me wrong, those can be fun, but I've never wanted someone to kneel for me."

I shivered. Whips and restraints made me nervous. I had a boyfriend who decided he wanted to try restraints one time. He'd barely had the leather cuffs fastened around my wrists when I'd freaked out and wanted out of them. Needless to say, that relationship didn't last long, and I'd not tried anything like that since.

"About ten years ago, I met a guy who wanted to explore age play. I discovered then that I loved being a Daddy to a little. I liked the trust and dependency of the relationship. I liked being able to focus everything I had on my boyfriend and his needs—schedules, baths, diapers. I liked it all. Unfortunately, he felt smothered and our relationship fell apart rather quickly. I haven't found another man who was into that lifestyle since."

"Won't have that problem with me." My eyes widened, and I gasped slightly when I realized what had come out of my mouth.

Travis grinned like he'd just won the lottery. "Does it help you to know what I'm into? Do you think our interests will align?"

I nodded to both questions but was unable to figure out what else to say. I did know that my appetite was gone. I'd eaten most of my lunch, but between the admissions and my nerves I wasn't hungry anymore. At least with most of the food gone, I could see each of the four different dinosaurs decorating the plate. They were just as cute as the dinosaurs on the cup.

"All done?" Travis questioned as I pushed the plate away from me.

I nodded. "Yeah. It was very good. Thank you."

He beamed. "Thank you. Let me get you cleaned up."

Travis got up and used the corner of my bib to clean a spot on my face where, apparently, I had a bit of ranch dressing in my light beard. I didn't even bother trying to hide the blush that spread across my face. It was such a Daddy thing to do, and apparently, I wasn't capable of eating without getting food on me. My dick stirred in my jeans at the thought of having a Daddy to take care of me, yet I wanted to hide my face in shame because I apparently needed someone to look after me.

"I'll be right back," Travis murmured after placing a gentle kiss on the top of my head.

I managed a stiff nod before he headed toward the sink. I couldn't even force myself to watch what he was doing, but I heard the water run for a few moments, then heard the squishing sound of a washcloth being wrung out. Travis was back at my side a few seconds later, rubbing the warm cloth over my face to get anything he'd missed. Then he took each of my hands in turn and washed them carefully. As he unvelcroed the bib from my neck, I let out a yawn I wasn't expecting.

"You've had a big morning. How about you go play for a few minutes while I clean up the last of the lunch mess? We'll go upstairs and tuck you in for a nap afterward."

"I can help clean up," I volunteered automatically. Sitting on the floor playing while someone cleaned my kitchen felt strange.

Travis gave me a stern look that made me feel weak all over and made me thankful I was still seated. "You may go play or clean up your toys while I finish up in here. It will only take a few minutes."

I found myself yawning again as I headed back to the living room. It really had been a long morning.

CHAPTER 13

Travis

I heard another yawn as Caleb made his way back to the living room. A few seconds later, the unmistakable sound of blocks being dropped into a bucket could be heard. Lunch hadn't been exactly what I'd expected, but I could tell it was exactly what he'd needed. He hadn't come right out and told me the details of his interests, but when I'd told him about me and my interests, not only had he not recoiled, he'd assured me he didn't have a problem with anything I'd said. There were layers to Caleb and it was going to be fun exposing each one of them in time.

Watching him lose himself in his building blocks while I'd made lunch for him had been telling. He'd not taken the pacifier… dodi… out of his mouth until I'd surprised him. I hadn't intended to sneak up on him, but he'd been so lost in his play that he hadn't heard me coming, and it had been hard to bring myself to interrupt him.

The look on his face when he'd seen the bib I'd found in the cupboard was a priceless mix of anxiety and appreciation. I'd found three bibs, all the same style, but I'd picked out the white one covered with blue stars. It didn't look like a traditional bib and was more of a triangle, but it fit Caleb's style well. I thought of heading to Pride with him that summer with a rainbow bib around his neck. Most people wouldn't even realize it was a bib because it looked so much like a bandana, but it would be a constant reminder that he was my boy. I had to be careful to not get ahead of myself. We hadn't even discussed if we were actually going to try dating and I was already planning for months down the road.

The look of longing and relief he'd given the bib when he'd seen it made it clear he wanted to submit and let everything go, yet he was stubbornly holding back. I hoped I'd be able to help him learn to let go. He struggled with giving up control, even though I could tell he wanted to. Not helping me make lunch had been difficult for him, and the way he'd stiffened when I cleaned him up made it clear he wasn't used to letting someone else take care of him.

Caleb was beautiful when he blushed, but I wanted to see him free enough that he didn't have that reaction every time I did something for him. I could see in his eyes how difficult it had been for him to relent and let me clean the kitchen, but he'd done it. Seeing how stressful it was for him to not be helping, I'd finally told him he could clean up his toys and I wasn't surprised to find that was what he'd done. For now if it made him feel better to be doing something, I was going to let him. He would need to clean up what he had out before playing with other toys, anyway.

I'd cleaned up most of the lunch dishes before I even let him know lunch was ready, so the only things left were the plates and silverware we'd used, and it didn't take long to rinse them off and put them in the dishwasher. The bottle on the top rack hadn't escaped my notice when I'd been cleaning up earlier. It also meant I didn't hesitate to fill a bottle I'd found in the cupboard with apple juice I'd found in the fridge.

Before going to find Caleb, I reached into the bag for the last surprise I'd brought with me. I'd spent the morning at the store looking for dragon things but had come up mostly empty-handed. I'd settled on the dinosaur divided plate with matching cup and silverware since I knew he liked dinosaurs. On the way to the register, I'd passed an endcap with small stuffed animals and one was a black dragon with rainbow glitter wings. I'd quickly grabbed it and now, right before naptime, seemed like the right time to give it to Caleb.

I was only slightly surprised to see his dodi in his mouth as he finished cleaning up the blocks. In the whispered conversation before Dexter left, he'd warned me Caleb preferred it whenever he was in a little headspace, but given how hesitant he'd been to let me see him little, I found myself thankful he was comfortable enough to put it in.

Even around the pacifier, I could see him fighting yawns. "Naptime, sweet boy. You're going to fall asleep on the floor if we don't get you up to bed."

He nodded slowly and stood up, though he halted slightly when he noticed the bottle of juice in my hand. I

122

gave him what I hoped was a reassuring smile. "I saw your bottle in the dishwasher and found a few others in the cabinet. I'm guessing they help you relax."

Caleb nodded stiffly, and when he pulled his dodi from his mouth, he volunteered information without prompting. "I like to take them to bed. But no one's seen them before. I don't even let Dexter see me with them, though he knows I have them."

"I'm not Dexter. And I want to take care of you. If you like having bottles at bedtime, it's my job to make sure you get them."

"Oh, okay…" The way he trailed off, I could tell he was still processing what I'd told him. Apparently finished processing, he gave a small but confident nod. He was the sweetest boy I'd met in, well, possibly ever.

I took his hand and led him up the steps. There was no hint of a diaper under his jeans and we hadn't even talked about them, so I decided to play it safe. "Do you need to go to the bathroom before naptime?"

His cheeks turned a rosey shade of red, but he nodded.

"Okay, hand me your dodi. I'll be waiting for you when you're done."

Caleb closed the door slowly, and I spent the next few minutes looking forward to the day he opened up to me about all his desires. The day that I'd be able to lay him down on the bed and change his diaper before naptime. There would come a time when I'd push him to let me into those closed off parts of his life, but our relationship was still too new. He needed to figure out on his own that he wasn't going to scare me away. If keeping little pieces and parts of himself hidden away helped for now, then I'd let him keep them undisclosed.

I heard the toilet flush and the water turn on as he washed his hands. I resisted the urge to praise him as he stepped out, looking slightly embarrassed that I'd waited for him to be done in the bathroom. He was going to have to get used to my need to micromanage. I'd decided over a week ago that I liked him, and by the time I'd tucked him in the night before, I knew he was going to have to be the one to tell me to leave if he ever got tired of me. I just needed him to understand that nothing he said would surprise me or push me away.

Walking into his room, one side of his bed was still covered with stuffed animals, but thanks to the light of day and the fact that he hadn't made the bed that morning, I caught a glimpse of the wooden bed rail that lined his side of the bed. Looking around, I noticed most of his room was neat and tidy. The closet was shut, and there were no clothes or clutter on the floor. If it weren't for the brightly colored bedding, the pile of stuffed animals, and the safety rail, I'd not easily pick up on the less adult items unless I was looking. I was curious to see what the closet and drawers held, but I needed to get him ready for bed.

There would be time to discover what lay inside his drawers and closet in the future. For now, the yawning boy in front of me needed out of his jeans and into his bed.

I set the bottle on the nightstand and turned my attention to Caleb. "Time to get those pants off," I told him as I took a step closer. He tensed for a second but seemed to relax each time I asserted myself and took decisions away from him. However, I didn't like the stiff set of his shoulders as I approached him. Walking close, I held his turtle out. "You can have your dodi while I get you ready."

Caleb's mouth opened instinctively as I held the nipple toward his mouth. As soon as the guard rested against his lips, they closed around it and I could see him beginning to work it with his tongue. Some of the tension left his body as he settled into a steady sucking rhythm. I gave him a few seconds before I hooked his belt loops with my index fingers and pulled him close.

"Alright. Let's get you undressed." It wasn't a question, but I looked at his eyes for any sign of resistance. The only response I got was a jerky nod of his head. I worked on unbuttoning his jeans and eased the zipper down.

As I pulled the fly open so I could slip them down his legs, I saw the way his body tensed again. Taking my time, I exposed the front of his underwear, which turned out to be race-car-patterned training pants with bright green piping around the waist and legs. "You are so perfect," I mused as I took in the sight before me. It wasn't a lie. He was perfect—from his strong leg muscles to the brightly colored training pants to his shy smiles.

The words caused Caleb to blush, but his body relaxed slightly as I let the jeans fall to the ground. Taking his hands,

I helped him step out of his pants before scooping them off the ground and tossing them on the armchair near his bed. When I bent over, I felt the stuffed animal in my back pocket and smiled. The jeans landed on the chair and I watched as it swayed slightly back and forth. The slight movement, that extra little attention to detail, drove home how much Caleb needed the time to be little and let go of the stress from his daily life.

I patted the bed. "Alright, naptime." I pulled the small dragon out of my pocket and handed it over to Caleb whose eyes went wide.

"You got me a dragon!" He reached for the toy automatically but pulled back slightly. "May I hold him?"

He was so perfect. "Of course. He's yours afterall."

Caleb took it and smiled brightly as he held it near. He watched as I adjusted the blankets so he could climb in. Big eyes looked at me questioningly as I pulled the blankets up for him. There was only one stuffed animal, a dingy brown thing that looked like it had gone through a war, on his side of the bed. It wasn't hard to figure out it was his special bear, so I made sure he had it before I flipped the rail up and heard it click into place. As he realized what I'd done, Caleb buried his face into the pillow and seemed to burrow even farther under the blankets.

I ran my hand over his short hair, hoping to sooth his uncertainty away. "Think there is room for me in there with all your stuffies?" I hoped the question would bring him out of his worry before he completely shut down on me. He'd seemed to be relaxing as he'd gotten tired and I didn't want him to clam up.

I got a nod and a mumbled reply that I was going to take as a *yes*, so I went to the other side of the bed and moved a handful of stuffed animals, including Branson, to the ground. As I bent down, I saw a few packs of diapers under his bed. Just like that, another piece of the puzzle fell into place.

I slipped into the bed beside Caleb and reached over him for the bottle of juice before I got us both settled. When I was resting on my side, my head propped up with a few pillows, Caleb still had his back toward me. I gently grasped his shoulder and maneuvered him so he was facing me. As he rolled over, he seemed to naturally gravitate toward me, resting his head gently on my chest while I pulled him closer to my body with the arm that was now trapped under him.

I tugged gently at the turtle and Caleb allowed his dodi to slip out of his mouth. Setting it on my jean-covered hip, I picked the bottle back up and placed the nipple to his mouth. He didn't seem to want to open for a moment, but as I ran the nipple over his lips, he finally parted them and pulled it into his mouth. At first, he seemed hesitant to actually suck at all, but eventually, natural instinct took hold and he found a steady rhythm. As the bottle drained, so did the tension in his body.

As he drank, Caleb's eyes became heavier. A few times, I thought he'd fallen asleep because the sucking would stop completely for ten or fifteen seconds before he'd start again.

By the time he sucked air instead of juice, his eyes were closed and his bear was pulled to his chest.

I kissed the top of his head as I pulled the bottle away. I'd forgotten how peaceful and soothing it was to hold a bottle for a boy as he drifted off to sleep. "Stay?" he mumbled while a hand lazily searched for something in the bed. As he patted my chest and the pillow, I realized he was looking for his dodi.

I picked up the pacifier and guided it to his mouth. "I don't plan on going anywhere." As soon as it was situated, Caleb was out and his steady deep breaths pulled me under not long after.

CHAPTER 14

Caleb

As the world came back to me, I couldn't help but curl a bit closer toward the warmth beside me. It wasn't until the warm pillow pulled me closer that I remembered I'd taken a nap. Dexter had no problem curling up in my bed with me to nap, but I knew instantly that the body next to mine was not my best friend's. It was too big and solid and smelled of sandalwood and something altogether different than Dexter. In my sleep-addled state, it took me a moment to remember Travis tucking me in and giving me a bottle of juice before I'd drifted off snuggled into his side.

I had no clue how long I'd napped, but the sun was still bright so it couldn't have been that long. It had been long enough that I felt rested and ready to be awake. I also became aware of my erection pressing firmly against Travis's leg. I wanted to slink away, but Travis was clearly awake and had almost certainly noticed my arousal.

I felt his chest move up and down with silent laughter. "What's got you so tense over there?"

I shook my head, unable or more likely unwilling, to form the words needed to express the thoughts in my head. Surprisingly enough, my embarrassment didn't seem to be affecting my dick in the least. If anything, I was getting harder the longer I stayed silently hiding in Travis's shirt. The urge to thrust against his leg was getting harder to ignore as well. I couldn't remember the last time I'd been so turned on. Then again, I couldn't remember the last time I'd been with anyone who seemed to understand my desires on any level... not that I'd been all that open or honest about those desires in past relationships.

I felt a hand slowly trail down my side and rest on my hip, and the feeling caused me to groan. Of course, the noise coming from me also reminded me that my damn dodi was still in my mouth. I was fighting the urge to play ostrich and hide my head in the proverbial sand more and more as the day progressed. Even though I knew Travis understood, it wasn't like a magical switch had been flipped and I was suddenly able to accept that I didn't have to be embarrassed about letting someone see me at my most vulnerable.

Pushing the pacifier out with my tongue, I forced myself to ignore my insecurities and focus on Travis and the hand that was rubbing up and down my stomach, alighting nerve endings I never knew I had. I finally gave in and moved my left leg over his in order to grind my cock into his hip. As my thigh settled across his legs, I could feel his erection pressing against his jeans, the impressive length snaking down his leg. He clearly wasn't turned *off* by what he'd seen so far, and it helped boost my confidence and make me feel less unsure of myself.

I tilted my head upward, looking into Travis's eyes for the first time since before I'd fallen asleep and saw nothing but passion and desire reflected in them. A wicked smile crossed his face as he angled his head downward, locking his lips with mine. Unlike our first kiss the night before, there was nothing slow or tentative about it. It was lips and tongues and, yes, teeth clashing as we nipped and sucked at each other.

As Travis broke the kiss, taking the nips down my jaw and over my throat, I threw my head back. "Trav, shit," I moaned into the quiet room. My head fell back onto the pillow as his hands snaked under my T-shirt, slowly lifting it up and over my head. His fingers trailed up my sides, almost a ghost of a touch, yet enough to drive me wild. I was squirming and writhing by the time the shirt had been removed from my body.

Travis's lips found my skin again. First the pulsepoint, then working down until he reached my nipple. At first, he simply licked around the already sensitive bud before he plucked it gently with his teeth. My nipples had never been a particularly erogenous area of my body, but whatever it was that Travis was doing was driving me insane. My back arched off the bed, and I screamed out in pleasure and frustration as he released my nipple.

I babbled willing to do just about anything to feel his

mouth on my body again. "No, no, no, no please. Don't stop."

A deep chuckle filled the room as his head bent down again and he blew gently over the tender skin of my wet nipple. Goosebumps covered my stomach and arms. "Fuck!" *More. Less.* Shit, I didn't know which. I just knew I needed something.

"You're being so good," he whispered into my chest before slipping over to the other nipple.

As if the torture on my nipple wasn't enough, Travis cupped my heavy balls and began massaging them through my underwear. I was already too far lost to care that he was rubbing me through a pair of training pants instead of a pair of my sexier briefs I usually wore when I thought there was a chance someone would see them. I didn't have many, but I kept a handful around for just these occasions. I was at the point that, if he didn't care, I certainly wasn't going to either. All I cared about was more stimulation.

Once both of my nipples were hard peaks atop my chest, Travis began licking and kissing his way down my stomach. I wasn't a gym rat by any stretch, but I had a nice set of abs I'd managed to keep even after graduating college and not making it to the gym as often as I would have liked. His tongue ran along the valleys of my stomach muscles and caused my cock to twitch. I could feel precum dampening the inside of my briefs but knew it wouldn't be noticeable through the thick panel. It didn't stop me from thrusting my hips upward. If anything, the thick fabric around my cock gave even less than a normal pair of underwear and increased the friction on my dick.

"Please," I whispered as he kissed down past my belly button.

I felt his breath near the waistband when he responded. "Do you like this?"

Nodding frantically, I searched for the right words, but my brain seemed to be done for the moment because I wasn't able to string sounds together into intelligible words.

His nose was buried in the fine line of hair running from my belly button. "Do you want more?"

Fuck yes, I wanted more. I wanted anything he'd give me. I wanted everything possible. I opened my mouth to beg but words didn't come out. "Mmm... Ung... Mmph."

Travis laughed. "Words."

I fisted the sheets on either side of me and forced myself to take a deep breath. "Then stop tormenting me!" I snapped.

The sexy man between my legs seemed to find my outburst amusing. He leaned up, hands on either side of my body, his face hovering over my stomach and turned his head to look at me. "I stopped," he smirked. "Do you have words yet?"

My muscles finally loosened and blood began flowing back into my brain. "So much more. Please."

Travis didn't wait for more words, he was back to the waistband of my underwear—I was definitely not going to think of them as training pants while Travis was looking at me like I was a dessert buffet. His hands snaked around the waistband and grasped the elastic band at my hips. I lifted my hips from the bed as he began to tug them down and freed my trapped erection from the snug fitting material.

Lying naked in front of Travis, I felt vulnerable, and as his eyes took in my body for the first time, I had to fight the urge to cover my dick with my hands. The feeling only lasted a few seconds though, because once his lips brushed the head of my cock, I couldn't think of anything but the pleasure I was feeling.

As he patiently kissed and licked every inch of my cock and down to my balls, I knew without a doubt, he was the perfect Daddy. He was patient and kind with a downright wickedly naughty streak. He was in absolutely no rush, seemingly content with his slow exploration. I, on the other hand, was not so patient and felt myself fighting to remain still while he licked and kissed along my shaft.

"Fuck, please, please," I chanted. I had no clue what I was begging for at the moment. It must have been something more than he was giving me because I didn't know how much longer I could restrain myself from either fucking up into his touch or cumming without anything more than kisses.

I felt a finger begin to slide down my crack and my legs rose up and back automatically. My hole fluttered when his finger touched the sensitive skin. He didn't even attempt to penetrate me, but it made my body light up and my back arch up off the bed.

I reached under my pillow and grasped the small bottle of lube I kept there—*because, seriously, dry jack-off sessions were uncomfortable*. Once the bottle was in my hand, I tapped Travis on the shoulder with it. He looked up, surprised at first but when he saw what was in my hands, he smiled and took the bottle. The squelch of lube leaving the bottle filled the room and caused me to squirm in anticipation. Then came the feel of the lube drizzling onto my hole, cold and shocking at first, but Travis's finger reaching down and catching it seemed to erase everything else. The bottle cap clicked shut at the same time a large finger breached my outer wall of muscle causing my dick to jump so violently it smacked my stomach and left a smear of precum just below my belly button.

"Oh, oh, oh holy…" my voice trailed off again as I writhed beneath him. He seemed to enjoy torturing me because I was certain I heard him chuckle when his mouth closed around the head of my dick at the same time the finger playing with my ass pushed all the way inside me.

"Shit!" I screamed and pounded at the bed. I staved off cumming too soon by biting my lip so hard I tasted blood.

The finger inside my ass began twisting around, clearly trying to ready me for a second, but his mouth and tongue were working magic on my dick at the same time. I wasn't sure if the warring sensations were bringing me closer to orgasm or holding me off. I certainly had no clue where to focus or where the next electric touch was going to come from.

Every gasp or buck of my hips had Travis adjusting either his mouth or finger. I wasn't sure how he was managing to do such vastly different things to my body at the same time and be so damn good at both.

As he pulled his finger out of my ass, I thought I was finally going to get a break long enough that I might be able to form a coherent sentence to adequately describe how good I was feeling. I only had time to gasp in a breath before two fingers were pushed inside me, creating a delicious burn. It didn't hurt, but the stretch was enough to remind me there were two fingers in my ass, stretching me and grazing my prostate. The touches were never enough, always brief and soft, enough to drive me insane, but not enough to help me find release.

As he scissored his fingers in my ass, sending another wave of pleasure-pain up my spine, my cock hit the back of his throat and I found myself torn by conflicting feelings again. Did I scream in pleasure and let my orgasm finally overtake me, or were Travis's scissoring fingers enough of a distraction to keep the orgasm at bay?

I knew when Travis's third finger joined the other two inside my ass because I suddenly felt full and it was almost impossible for one of the fingers to *not* nudge that bundle inside me with each movement.

"Fuck! Shit! Travis!" I called out, the first words that had escaped my lips in close to five minutes. "Fuck me, please, please fuck me!" I begged.

His fingers stilled and my dick fell from his lips. At first, I thought I'd said something wrong. "Are you sure?" he asked after a moment. "I don't want to rush you."

I shook my head violently from side to side. "No, no rushing. Want you… inside… me." I wasn't too proud to beg at that point.

"Do you have a condom?" he asked, fingers still in my ass.

I nodded then groaned. "Bathroom." There was no reason to have a condom in this room because I'd never had a man in this room before. At that moment, the bathroom might as well have been a million miles away.

Travis looked between me, the bathroom, and his hand before finally coming to a decision. He seemed reluctant, but he pulled his fingers out, and the loss of pressure in my ass was almost unbearable. I groaned as he reached behind him and pulled his wallet out of his back pocket and fumbled with it for a moment before finally pulling a condom out of it.

"I know, Cal," he soothed. "Just a minute and I'll take care of you. I've got to get undressed first."

I'd been so wrapped up with the feelings of his fingers in my ass that, until he'd fished his wallet out, I hadn't realized he was still wearing all of his clothes.

He was going to take care of me. *Daddy was there and would make it all better.* It wasn't hard to see Travis as Daddy and that made me even more turned on and slightly emotional. I didn't know if I was ready to accept having a Daddy. I still worried about letting him into my life in that capacity only to have him change his mind. Even though the logical part of my brain knew Travis wouldn't do that.

He reached behind him and tugged his form fitting T-shirt over his head, allowing me to see his bare chest for the first time. He was gorgeous. His wide chest and defined abs were clearly well-earned from years of hard work at his job. The smattering of gray and black chest hair turned me on even more, and I reached up to run my hands through it as he unbuttoned his jeans.

With the fly undone, Travis slipped his jeans and briefs down and shimmied out of them. I wasn't paying attention to him undressing any longer. I was gawking at his thick cock swinging heavily in front of him. I gasped at the sight, wondering how he was going to fit inside me and if three fingers had actually been enough prep.

Hooking his finger under my chin, he pulled my gaze up to meet his. "We'll go slow."

I nodded, my ass already tensing at the thought of having something that large inside me. He was definitely bigger than anything I'd ever taken before—toy or real.

He picked the condom up off the bed before sitting back on his heels and ripping the package open using his hand and teeth then carelessly tossing the foil wrapper to the side. By the time he got it opened, it appeared as though his patience was beginning to unravel. He was sheathed quickly and picked up the bottle of lube again. The snick wasn't as loud this time, and the cold sensation on my ass never came. I looked down to find him slathering his condom-covered cock with what he'd poured out into his hand. Once he was satisfied, he spread the extra over my hole, slipping two large fingers in with ease. Apparently, he was confident that I'd had enough prep because he pulled his fingers out and lined his dick up with my ass.

I keened when I felt the blunt head of his dick press against my hole. It didn't matter that I'd been thoroughly stretched. I was going to feel it no matter what. I slowly let out my breath and encouraged my body to relax. As he breached the outer ring of muscle, my body screamed at the intrusion, but just below the surface was a desperate aching need to feel more.

He was attentive and slow, allowing my body to adjust to his size. Despite feeling his legs shaking with the desire to thrust forward, he watched me closely. I pulled my legs back and the new angle seemed to open me up enough that he was able to make it past the firm second ring of muscle and, despite the burn, pleasure rocketed through my body. I felt like I was being split in two but in the best possible way. It was like Travis had ripped my insecurities and uncertainties out of me and was putting me back together with each inch he pressed into me.

By the time his balls hit my ass, I was pleading and begging for more. I wanted everything he'd give me. "Please." I heard myself begging as he pulled out. I felt the tip of his dick almost come out of me before he pushed back in. This time it was faster, causing my plea to turn into a moan of pleasure.

"You're so tight," he marveled as he began moving his hips quicker. Large hands gripped my hips and pulled me closer and my hips higher off the bed. It was the exact right angle that on his next thrust, his cock hit my prostate, and I screamed loudly enough I knew Dexter had probably heard. I didn't have more mental energy to put into that thought as Travis leaned forward, placed a hand on either side of my head, and dipped his head to kiss me roughly.

I moaned into his mouth and rocked my hips to meet his thrusts. We could have stayed that way for seconds or minutes, I had no idea. All I knew for sure was I wanted more. More kissing, more attention, more sex, more of anything Travis was willing to give me. My ass involuntarily clenched around him sending sparks up my spine.

"Shit," Travis moaned as he leaned back up. "Do that again, Cal. Jesus, do that again," he begged as he gripped my right hip with his left hand and wrapped my dick in his other. He thrust faster.

Forcing myself to focus on his instruction and not allowing my mind to get lost in the feel of his warm hand wrapped around my throbbing erection, I clenched my muscles and Travis screamed out. "Cum, Cal," he demanded.

I hadn't realized how close I was until that moment. Maybe it had been that I was holding back waiting for the right moment—the permission, the demand—to cum. Whatever the cause, I felt my dick twitch and my muscles contract, and I came all over Travis's hand and my stomach.

140

Rope after rope of thick, creamy cum shot from my dick. Travis's hand continued working me until the pleasure was gone and my dick was overly sensitive, despite me feeling his cock pulsating in my ass as he filled the condom.

Eventually, I twitched as he played with my spent cock and he let it go. He leaned down and kissed my chest while he eased himself out of my ass. The loss made me wince and I felt cold as he got up.

"I'll be right back," Travis assured me as he walked out of the room. A few seconds later I heard the water running in the sink and he was back not long after that with a warm cloth. He cleaned me up gently, first wiping my chest and stomach and eventually working his way to my soft dick, wrapping the cloth around me and cleaning me thoroughly. When he was satisfied, he tossed the washcloth into the hamper and climbed back into bed, wrapping my body in his strong arms.

I would feel it later, but for now, I was too exhausted to care.

CHAPTER 15

Travis

Caleb drifted in and out of sleep for almost half an hour before seeming to finally be awake enough to get out of bed. I was in no hurry to be anywhere but with him. It was only a bit after three, so I didn't have a problem letting him drift for a while. Having a snuggly boy curled up to my side was enough to make me happy to stay in bed all day.

I felt Caleb yawn and begin stretching before his eyes finally cracked open and he looked up at me with a bashful smile. "Sorry, I think I fell asleep."

I rubbed his shoulders. "It's okay. You needed the rest."

He stretched again and scratched his stomach, wrinkling his nose up. "Eww, dried cum."

"Sorry. I tried to clean you up, but you were quite covered."

He sighed. "I guess I should shower."

"What about a bath?"

The question caused him to stiffen in my arms. "A bath?" he asked tentatively.

I didn't know what was so worrisome about a bath, but Caleb clearly had reservations, so I broached the subject cautiously. "If you want. I'd love to give you a bath and get you cleaned up."

His breath seemed to catch in his throat as he stuttered out a response. "O-oh... uh..." He stopped, sighed, and I felt his shoulders square up slightly when he finally made a decision. "I-I'd really like that."

I'd figured he would, but I wasn't going to say that. Instead, I settled on a reassuring squeeze to his shoulders. "Let's go get you cleaned up and you can play for a bit afterward." I slid out of bed, grabbed my discarded clothes, and hastily redressed. I walked around to his side of the bed to put the rail down. Once it was tucked away, I held my hand out and he took it, his face flushing a beautiful pink.

Clearly, without me around, Caleb was confident about his likes and desires. He had toys, blankets, and everything he needed to help him sink into his role. Despite knowing that I was okay with it, Caleb still had trouble opening up about what he wanted. My conversation with Dexter from the night before came back to me. Caleb was so convinced no one could understand him and his likes he'd never even thought about discussing this vital part of himself. I was going to have to move slowly and prove to him that I was here, no matter what he wanted to share with me. I knew a patient approach would make the first time he called me Daddy that much sweeter.

We walked to the bathroom hand-in-hand. Judging by

the rest of the house, I'd have been shocked if there weren't toys and bubble bath somewhere in the bathroom. I'd barely stepped into the bathroom when I noticed a large bucket of bath toys on a shelf by the toilet and multiple bottles of bubble bath next to the bucket. I smiled to myself knowing the toys would provide enough of a distraction for Caleb that he'd relax while the tub filled.

I pulled the bucket down and set it on the bathmat. "Look for some toys to play with in the tub while I get it filled," I instructed.

Caleb sank to his knees, following the direction without hesitation, and began digging through the bucket. I marveled at how natural submission was for him. He followed commands easily, but questions tended to make him overthink. I was going to have to keep that in mind.

I started the tub and allowed the water to warm while I looked over the bottles of bubble bath. Finally deciding on the strawberry-scented bubbles, I returned to the tub to pour some in. As I returned the bottle of bubble bath to the shelf, I watched Caleb as he sorted his toys into two piles. Some of the toys he'd look at more carefully and others he would put down quickly. I couldn't quite decide if there was a rhyme or reason to the piles. Some boats made it into one pile, some into the other. Two fish made it into the pile on the right, three into the pile on the left. The same went for foam blocks, sea creatures, and other toys. Eventually, as the tub was almost full, he dumped the larger pile back into the bucket and started the process over again with the smaller pile. Finally, the smaller pile was whittled down to about eight things and everything else was put back into the bucket.

"Put the toys in the tub and get in." I'd *almost* asked him if he was ready to get into the tub but caught myself before the question could escape. He seemed to have found a peaceful place where he was okay letting me see him naked and little-ish. I knew he wasn't showing me his full little side, but he was showing me enough that I was willing to count it as a win.

Caleb quickly tossed the toys into the tub before standing up and climbing in. His dick was soft and hung gently against his leg. I moved the bucket of toys back to the shelf and watched Caleb climb into the tub, noting that his earlier nerves seemed to have receded. As he lowered himself into the bubbles, he was already reaching for the two boats he'd put into the water. My instinct was to help him, but I knew it would be better to let him relax into his role without me hovering.

Instead of sitting close by, I sat on the closed toilet seat and watched as he zoomed the boats through the bubbles and sent little divers searching for fish that had sunk to the bottom of the tub. It was easy to lose track of time while watching Caleb play in the water, but as the bubbles faded, I knew it was time to get him bathed. Part of me hated bringing him out of the space he was in, but I was interested to see how he responded to me now that he'd been playing in front of me for the last fifteen minutes.

I stood up and grabbed a washcloth off the stack in the cabinet where I'd found them earlier and knelt beside the tub. My ankle protested the movement, but I wasn't about to let the moment pass.

Unfortunately, Caleb saw my slight wince as I got down onto the ground and his eyes widened. "Don't push yourself so hard!" he scolded as I adjusted my leg so I was comfortable.

"I'm okay," I assured him. "We need to get you washed before the water gets too cold." I hoped changing the subject back to his bath would put him back into the headspace he'd been in while he'd been playing.

Caleb looked unconvinced about my leg but nodded hesitantly. His carefree demeanor was mostly gone, but he hadn't built up the walls he normally did when we began to talk about anything on the ABDL spectrum. Instead, he watched as I dunked the washcloth into the water and poured some of the body soap he had on the side of the tub into it, working it into a lather.

As the pleasant aroma of lavender filled the bathroom, Caleb seemed to relax even more, and by the time the cloth made contact with his back, he leaned into me. I slowly worked the soap across his back in large circles, allowing him ample time to sink back into that space where nothing else seemed to matter to him. When his back had been washed from the water-line to his neck, I moved the cloth toward his front and repeated the process. Caleb clearly enjoyed the sensations because he would occasionally let out a small sigh or his body would lean closer to me as I worked. It would have been difficult to make the process take much longer, but it was worth it to see him finally beginning to relax.

I washed both of his arms, his sides, and under both arms before finally admitting to myself that it was time to wash the parts of him that had been covered by water until that point. I said a little prayer to any deity that might be listening to keep him from shutting down completely when I asked him to sit up for me so I could clean him.

"Lean up for me, Cal." The nickname rolled off my tongue effortlessly and I liked how it sounded especially when Caleb was little.

Caleb's eyes looked confused for a few seconds. "Huh?"

"You're not all clean yet. Please get up so we can finish getting you clean and get you out of the tub." Caleb's eyes darted around nervously, as though he was expecting someone to walk into the bathroom at any moment. "It's okay, I'm going to finish getting you cleaned up, then we'll dry you off and get you dressed."

Caleb finally tucked his legs under him and sat up so he was out of the water. I ran the soapy cloth around his waist and above his dick. He was still soft, but as I wrapped my hand around his dick to make sure it was clean, I felt it twitch and begin to come to life. At least he wasn't *too* nervous. I finally moved to his backside and cleaned each of his butt cheeks before slipping into his crack to make sure any residual lube was washed away. As soon as my fingers grazed his hole, I felt him clench and his face contorted slightly.

I ran my left hand over his stomach. "I'm sorry. Was I too rough with you?"

Caleb shook his head. "It's a good hurt," he assured me with a bashful smile. The fact that he didn't blush or hide his face told me he was completely sincere. It didn't make me feel any better that I'd made him uncomfortable.

"More prep in the future." I hoped he caught on to the fact that it hadn't been a question. I was planning on being around for a lot more than just an afternoon.

That time, a blush did spread across his face, and Caleb ducked his head as he nodded in agreement.

"Alright, pull the plug. You're all clean." I stood up, careful to not tweak my ankle, and headed toward the cabinet to grab a bath towel. Even Caleb's towels were brightly colored, and I smiled as I pulled out a bright red bath sheet to wrap him up in.

Caleb had pulled the plug and was gathering his toys and setting them on the side of the tub when I returned with the towel opened in my arms. A flash of surprise crossed his face when he realized I was waiting to dry him off, but a look of relief quickly replaced the surprise and apprehension.

He climbed out of the tub and shivered when his wet skin hit the air-conditioned room. I gathered him in the towel as quickly as I could. It took a few minutes, and he giggled and squirmed as I dried under his arms and between his legs, but eventually, he was dry and I wrapped the towel around his body.

"Head to your room. We'll get you some pajamas and then go downstairs for a snack and some cartoons."

Caleb climbed up onto the bed and pulled a dinosaur throw blanket over his legs to keep warm while I walked over to the dresser. "Where are your pajamas, Cal?"

"Middle drawer," he answered as he searched for something on his bed.

I turned around and found the drawer with pajamas in it. He had quite a selection to choose from. I was figuring out Caleb fairly quickly and the discovery didn't surprise me. There were union suits and brightly colored two-piece sets in both long and short sleeve varieties. I sorted through the drawer for a moment before coming across a dark-blue pair of pajamas with rainbow-colored stars and orange cuffs. They were bright and fun, and I could easily see him playing on the floor with a thick diaper underneath.

"Where are your undies?"

He pointed to the top drawer of the dresser and nodded when my hand landed on it. There were even more selections of briefs than he had of pajamas. There were brightly patterned adult briefs as well as bold training style briefs like he'd been wearing earlier. I'd already seen him in the training pants, so I didn't hesitate to grab a pair with dinosaurs on them and head over to Caleb.

He seemed to be getting more comfortable with me because he didn't hesitate to stretch out his legs and let me slip his briefs up them, nor did he blink when I pulled them up over his half-hard cock and tucked him safely inside. Without hesitation, Caleb lifted each of his legs—using my shoulders for support—to step into his pajama pants, then waited patiently while I pulled them up his legs. We repeated the same process as he let me help him with his shirt. A grin spread across his face once I'd gotten him fully dressed.

"Snack?"

He nodded eagerly and hurried toward the door, waiting for me at the top of the steps. Even though Caleb was clearly becoming comfortable being little Caleb around me, he watched me carefully as I headed down the steps, one at a time, occasionally commenting on how I was stepping or how to navigate the stairs in a more efficient manner to avoid strain on my ankle. Apparently, he had trouble turning off his physical therapy brain like I had trouble turning off my Daddy instincts.

Once we made it downstairs, though, Caleb seemed to be back into that *almost* carefree space where it didn't matter that he was walking around with a pacifier in his mouth and childish pajamas on. He looked between the TV, the kitchen, and me, trying to figure out where he should go.

"Snack?" I asked again.

He nodded, the turtle attached to his dodi comically flopping around as he moved his head, and followed me into the kitchen. He sat down at the table without hesitation or question. There didn't appear to be any toys in the kitchen, unsurprising since he had to cook, but I was already making a mental note to find some toys to keep in there for him while I was cooking.

Thankfully, we wouldn't be in the kitchen long. I just needed to make him a snack to get him through until dinner. I found applesauce pouches and peanut butter in the pantry and celery sticks in the fridge. It wasn't a huge snack, but setting them down in front of Caleb and seeing his face light up was worth it.

He was on his second celery stick when the door lock on the back door began to jiggle and was eventually unlocked. Caleb didn't even flinch as the back door opened and Dexter walked in.

"I heard you guys had fun earlier," he announced as he shut the door. Looking over Caleb's attire and his snack, Dexter seemed to soften. "And it appears as though you're already ready for bed."

Caleb grinned at his best friend and readily leaned into the hug Dexter offered. It was fascinating to watch the two of them together. Dexter's exuberance never fazed Caleb and Caleb's cautiousness didn't annoy Dexter.

The most fascinating thing about the friends was that the two of them seemed to be happy no matter what they were doing. I could see other men being jealous of their relationship, but I could also see just how in tune they were with one another. Nothing remotely sexual passed between them. Even the kiss Dexter placed on Caleb's forehead when neither thought I was watching was chaste and brotherly.

CHAPTER 16

Caleb

By the time Travis left my house on Sunday, I couldn't wait to see him again at his physical therapy appointment on Monday morning. I didn't have to worry so much about what I said around him, though I did have to make sure we kept things professional. At least mostly professional.

I saw him Mondays and Fridays and Travis made an attempt to make it out to lunch with me at least a few times a week. It was nice when we were on our lunch breaks because I got to spend time with Travis when he wasn't in over-protective mode. He still watched me like a hawk and he seemed to want to hold my hand if we were walking anywhere. I didn't mind the things that made him feel good about his role in our relationship. The things that made him feel good also made me feel cared for. Even how he preferred to order for me didn't bother me. Aside from those things, which were minor in my view, our time together was spent getting to know one another outside of our naturally Dominant or submissive roles.

As much as I enjoyed getting to know Travis outside of the house, I still loved our time together when we were at home. As hesitant as I was to open up about my little side, Travis was strong and steady and continued to show me he found joy in taking care of me in any way I'd let him. I could snuggle up with him and watch cartoons in my pajamas just as easily as I could sit on the floor and play with my toys.

When Travis was around, I noticed I didn't worry as much about biting my tongue when I was tired or frustrated either. I'd always been one to watch what I said and how I acted. It changed when Travis was around, though. When I was tired, I had a tendency to want to be closer to him. When I was in a bad mood, I tended to be more obstinate.

One of the first times I'd had a bad day while Travis was around, I'd been grouchy and didn't want to clean up my toys before bed. It was ridiculous, and even at the time I'd known it, but I didn't want to put my blocks away. I wanted them there after work the next day so I could continue playing. I'd pouted and grumbled as Travis tried to get me to clean up. After a number of failed attempts, he'd finally put his foot down.

"If you don't clean up your blocks, you may find yourself over my knee. If that happens, you're still going to have to clean them up, but your bum is going to be tender while you do it."

My eyes had grown wide at the threat, and I quickly cleaned my toys up. The more my brain had processed that thought in the bathtub later, though, the more I had liked the idea. My dick, especially, loved the idea. Every time I thought of being across his lap with my ass on full display while he reddened it, my dick took notice.

The idea had grown over time to the point that I was thinking about it almost obsessively for the next two weeks. And that is how I ended up in my current predicament while I waited for him to arrive.

To tell Travis or not to tell Travis.

His *take charge of any situation* personality had a way of making me putty in his hands. I'd never considered myself a brat, and I was sure a true brat would tell me I wasn't one.

There was just something about the way Travis got growly and dominant when I didn't do what I was supposed to do—be it cleaning up toys, getting ready for bed, or just taking too long to get ready to go out. Each time he showed that assertive side, I became more curious. I'd never wanted to push someone to the point they got frustrated, and even as I pushed limits with Travis, he seemed more amused than annoyed, so I began to feel more comfortable being a bit more… playful… naughty… bratty.

What I didn't understand was why the idea of having Travis put me over his knee was sounding more and more like a reward than a consequence.

After turning the words and possible scenarios over in my head until I'd almost gone crazy, I'd decided I *wanted* a spanking. I just didn't know how to *ask* for one. I'd started doing the only logical thing, willfully disobeying. The only problem was, I couldn't push myself to be bratty enough to actually earn the spanking. The thought of purposely doing something bad enough to disappoint or frustrate Travis enough that he'd actually spank me soured my stomach. So, every time I pushed the limits, I relented before I really upset him.

Dammit, being a little was hard work. Or, maybe just being me was exhausting. I wanted to open up about liking diapers, but I didn't see how it was possible for someone, even Travis, to be okay with it.

I wanted a Daddy, but I was afraid to open up about it and be hurt if he left.

The idea of being spanked was hot, but I didn't want to disappoint my *not* Daddy.

My head was a frustrating place to be at the best of times, but lately it had taken a turn for the infuriating.

To top it off, when Travis had left for work that morning, he'd told me not to touch myself. He'd wanted me horny and needy when he got home. Well, I was horny and needy, but I was also a jumbled up mess of undisclosed desires too. I needed to find a way to put my nerves and confusion to the side for the evening. At least until I got to cum, then I could let all the doubt and uncertainty creep back in.

"Cal, my sweet boy, what's wrong?" Travis's voice brought me back to reality. I'd totally forgotten he'd set up my quilt and toys and turned the TV on for me while he made dinner in my kitchen. I'd been sitting on the floor with a block in each hand, not moving, and not paying attention to the TV for long enough that the end credits were rolling and Travis had definitely noticed I hadn't touched anything else on the blanket.

I looked up at him and knew my face was flushed, but I shook my head to dismiss his concerns. "Just got lost in thought." I wasn't going to lie and tell him nothing was wrong. It would make him upset that I wasn't telling the truth. And that brought me right back to the beginning of my worries. *Fuck.*

Travis sat down beside me with his back against the couch and scooted me farther back so he could wrap his arms around me. "You honestly look like you want to puke." He tried to make it sound like a joke, but I could tell he was concerned.

I pushed my face into his shoulder and took a deep breath, relishing the smell that was so uniquely Travis. It was masculine yet calming at the same time. He'd clearly showered before he'd come over because I could still smell the soap through his shirt. I sighed and closed my eyes. "I'm overthinking," I finally admitted.

Travis chuckled. "Your knuckles were white on your blocks and you haven't moved in almost half an hour. Can you tell me what you're overthinking about?" A strong hand ran up and down my side as we sat.

"What's for dinner?" I questioned.

"Not working, Cal. It's in the oven for the next thirty minutes. It could stay in there longer if we're not ready to grab it."

Well, at least he wouldn't burn dinner. I'd feel even worse if he ended up burning our dinner because of my insanity. I didn't know if I had it in me to actually voice everything running through my head. Could I possibly come right out and say, "I want you to bend me over your knee and spank me"? *Why couldn't I be more confident like Dexter?* He'd be able to flat-out say what he wanted, whether he meant for his desires to be voiced or not. Dexter didn't seem to understand why some people had a hard time accepting or understanding kink and sexual desires, so he was an open book for the most part. I still couldn't figure out what, if anything, he was into, which was strange.

"Cal," Travis poked me in the side gently. "Are you okay? You seem to have checked out."

I giggled at the sensation and squirmed a bit. At least I could answer that question honestly and more easily. "I started thinking about what Dex is into."

Travis laughed. "Well, that's a random thing to be thinking about when you were so lost in your own head a few minutes ago."

I shrugged. "Well, it started by thinking about how Dex would just be able to say what he was thinking without any hesitation. It wouldn't even cross his mind that what he wanted might be a bit outside the box and might even turn the person he was with off. He'd just say it anyway."

I felt Travis nod above me. "So, you want something outside the box and you're afraid I'm going to react badly to it."

Fuck. I'd said too much.

I hedged. "It's not *that* outside the box."

Travis was quiet for a few seconds. It didn't make me nervous, and he was still holding me close and was back to rubbing my side gently. If he was at all concerned about what I'd let slip, he was doing a very good job hiding it. "You know, you going mute every few seconds is beginning to worry me."

"Sorry," I mumbled into his shirt. "I just can't seem to find the words to make the thoughts in my head make sense. I'm having a hard time finding a way to voice them."

"I can understand that." He didn't put pressure on me to say more, and he didn't seem turned off by the fact that I wasn't vocalizing more of my thoughts. "I can't think of much you could tell me that would scare me away though. I've gotten to know you pretty well this last month or so, and there's nothing about you I don't like."

I may have melted a bit more into his side at those words. Travis was everything I'd ever wanted in a man, but I'd never allowed myself to believe existed. And he *really* did like me. "I don't want to disappoint you," I finally managed to blurt out.

"I don't think you could."

I groaned at myself. I clearly hadn't used enough words. "I-I mean, I don't want to upset you to the point that you're mad at me. *Shit!* I'm screwing this up."

"Language," Travis warned. He usually reminded me to watch my words around him when I started to curse. There

158

was something about it that made me go weak in the knees every time. I'd finally gotten to the point that I was accepting it was because it was close to having Daddy remind me to be good. My body definitely liked that thought.

"Yes, that… I mean, not *that* but close." I closed my eyes and hung my head. I needed to get myself together.

"Take a minute, find the words, and try again. What you're saying isn't making a lot of sense. We've got plenty of time, and dinner can wait if needed."

I nodded and tried to pull myself together. I was an intelligent guy who had excelled in every English course I'd ever taken in school. I knew I had the words, I just had to find them.

Finally, things seemed to fall into place, a bit like Tetris pieces coming together to form a perfect four-row block. "I don't want to be a bother or a disappointment to you. Ever. But when you get all demanding and take charge when I'm not doing what I should be doing, it makes me want things."

I had to get the word out. Spanking fetishes were almost vanilla thanks to all the crazy reality TV shows with too-rich women oversharing every detail of their lives. It didn't feel vanilla or small in my head though. It felt big and scary, but I wasn't about to chicken out at this point.

I felt Travis inhale a breath like he was about to ask me to go on, but I didn't want to make him prod me more or question my sanity any more than he already was. I forced myself to continue before he could start speaking. *At least I wouldn't interrupt him.* "You told me you'd put me over your knee if I don't behave and it confused the hell out of me at first. My first thought was that I didn't want that at all because it would hurt. Then I started thinking about it and something about the idea of being put over your knee makes me really excited… turned on, I guess. But, when I think about pushing so far you have to punish me, it's not exciting anymore. It's a major mood killer."

Travis pulled me into him so tightly I finally found it easier to just wiggle my butt onto his lap and lay my head on his shoulder. In that position, both of his arms were wrapped around me. At least my bumbling, fumbling admission hadn't freaked him out. Once it was out in the open, it was easier to look at the big picture and see that wanting to be spanked probably wasn't something that would be a deal-breaker for him.

"First and foremost, Caleb, you've never done anything close to disappointing me. However, I can understand your fear in that regard. I think I can ease some of that concern for you right now. If there is ever a time that I am truly upset with something you've done, I promise I will never spank you. Spankings are not something I'd give out of anger. They really are supposed to be fun, and many people actually find them relaxing."

Hearing Travis explain his views so easily made the worries and fears swirling in my head and stomach settle. Spankings weren't a punishment, and they were supposed to be fun. What I didn't know was how to proceed from where we were.

Being a bit bratty or disobedient was kind of fun, but I didn't know if I could manage it when I knew the end goal was to earn a spanking. Thankfully, I didn't have to think too hard about it, because Travis addressed my concerns before I could voice them.

"I have an idea. How about tonight, if you get your toys cleaned up after dinner, you can have a spanking as a reward?"

I thought about it for a few seconds. "Reward spanking?" I knew my words were hesitant, but this was all new territory for me, and I didn't know what to make of it all.

"I want you to experience a spanking without any pressure or concern. I think it would be good for you to have your first one as a reward. In the future, you might decide to push the limits in order to get a spanking, but for the first time, let's just make it no stress. You can earn your spanking by simply cleaning up your toys. All two blocks sitting on the blanket." He laughed as he looked over the blanket at the spot where I'd dropped the blocks from my hands when he'd pulled me close.

Travis was silent for a few moments then he added, "But, if you don't clean up your blocks, you're going to earn a timeout. You decide which you want more. Timeout *is* a punishment, just in case you're wondering."

I shivered. I didn't like the idea of being punished, but I knew I wanted to be spanked. I'd wanted it for almost two weeks, and Travis was giving me an easy way to get what I wanted.

"Okay," I agreed just as the timer on the oven started going off. It looked like I was going to have to make it through dinner first, and I had a feeling it was going to be the longest meal of my life.

CHAPTER 17

Travis

Maybe I shouldn't have told Caleb I'd spank him after dinner. He didn't seem to know what to do with himself. He was clearly turned on because he'd wiggled and squirmed in his chair and even the few times he'd managed to keep his attention on eating and not nervously fiddling with his fork, he still rocked his hips back and forth.

His bumbling explanation of what he wanted had originally worried me. No matter how hard I worked at showing him I meant it, nothing he could tell me would change the way I felt about him. When he finally fumbled his way through telling me he was afraid of disappointing me, I couldn't help but gather him in my arms. Reminding myself that Caleb had never trusted another boyfriend with his little side helped to remind me that he probably hadn't ever explored some of the more common aspects of the lifestyle.

I knew his fear of losing someone he trusted ran deep within him. I told him frequently that the only way he was going to get rid of me was to tell me to leave. Words didn't seem to be enough for my sweet Caleb. He would likely struggle to accept that I wasn't going anywhere for a long time. I would have to continue to show him I was in this for the long haul.

Thankfully, once he'd managed to vocalize his concerns, I knew there was a way to put part of his anxiety to rest. Just because I'd never spank anyone out of frustration or anger, didn't mean Caleb innately knew that. I *thought* that telling him I'd spank him as a reward would help him feel at ease. Apparently, the thought had only served to increase his arousal and distract him from his dinner. He'd been so lost in thought, he'd managed to miss his mouth completely with more than one bite, and his chin and the bib I'd fastened around him before dinner were dotted with food.

I'd learned Caleb got quiet when he was nervous or anxious so the silence didn't bother me. I was enjoying watching him trying to focus on his meal while his mind wandered elsewhere. His hands and face were both going to need to be cleaned before he could get his reward, but I suspected it would help him sink into the proper headspace for a spanking.

"I don't think I can eat anything else," Caleb finally admitted when he'd eaten almost everything on his plate.

I pushed my chair back and grabbed both our plates as I stood up. "You ate well. Though, you may be wearing as much as you got into your mouth." The statement caused him to blush. "Stay there, and let me get a rag to clean you up."

Caleb, as always, waited patiently for me to come back. I used the cleanest part of his bib to wipe the cheese sauce from his light beard and then used a wet washcloth to clean his face and hands. The way he held each hand out, fingers spread, with a smile on his face, let me know he enjoyed this as much as I did. As I took his bib off him, I looked to the living room. "Can you go fold your blanket for me and put your toy bucket back on the shelf while I wipe down the table?" It was getting harder to not refer to myself as Daddy, but I knew it was still too soon for my cautious boy.

Caleb nodded and hurried off to the living room as I finished up the last few things in the kitchen. Before I left the kitchen, I grabbed one of his bottles out of the cupboard and filled it with water for later. I was in the living room with Caleb not even four minutes after I sent him to clean up. He was standing by the couch looking nervous as I entered. There was no reason for him to be concerned about how he'd cleaned up because nothing was out of place, so that just left his nerves at what was coming next— the unknown.

"You did a very good job in the living room. Thank you for doing what I asked."

Caleb looked at the bottle in my hand as he nodded his head, but didn't say anything in response.

"Let's head upstairs, Cal. I think we'll both be more comfortable in your bed."

Caleb reached out and took my free hand, then followed me upstairs to his room. Seeing how stiff he was, I knew we

165

needed to take a few minutes to talk, no matter how hard it would be on him. Instead of heading to the bed, I placed the bottle on the nightstand and headed to the chair that sat along the wall and took a seat. "Come sit down with me for a few minutes." It was a place we'd found ourselves many nights, usually shortly before bed if he was having a bottle.

Caleb looked worried, but took a few uncomfortable steps my way before he reached the chair and folded himself into my lap. "If you're unsure or not ready, there's nothing wrong with that." Of course, my dick didn't feel that way, but this wasn't about me, it was completely about Caleb and making sure he got what he needed.

He shook his head back and forth with more conviction than I was expecting. "I-I want this." Even though the words were quiet, they were clear. "I just, I just don't know how it's going to go."

"Well, we should probably start with safewords. Do you have one?"

He shook his head. "I've never needed one before. If I had to pick one, though, the traffic light system seems the easiest to remember."

Well that was one conversation we didn't have to have. Caleb was aware of and understood safewords. "I like that system. It's easy to remember and use. It also gives you something other than 'stop.' You can let me know if we're approaching what you're comfortable with without having to say much."

Caleb nodded as he picked at a button on my dress shirt. "I agree."

"Good. So, we'll use the traffic light system. That includes for tonight. If something gets to be too much, use your safewords. They're there for a reason."

"Okay, safewords. It's okay to use them."

"Do you have any other questions or concerns?"

Caleb shook his head this time. "No, no more. I think it's all practical experience now."

"Well, then in that case, stand up so I can take your pants off. Spankings need to be on bare skin, not through clothes."

Caleb bit his lip and hesitated a beat before nodding once and standing up. He didn't even try to reach for the pajama pants he was wearing. He stood in front of me and waited patiently as I sat forward in the chair and hooked the waistband of his dinosaur printed pajama bottoms with my fingers and worked them down his legs. Caleb automatically stepped out of them once they were at his ankles, and I tossed them onto the bed. I didn't know if I'd put them on him again after his spanking or not, but I wanted them nearby if I decided to.

My breath still seemed to catch each time I saw him wearing his training pants. They were such a sweet addition to any outfit he wore, be it pants or childish pajamas. I debated on pulling his training pants all the way off, but I thought having them wrapped around his thighs would add a little something extra to the experience, and I'd enjoy looking at them hugging just below his perky ass as I turned it red.

167

I reached behind him and squeezed each of his ass cheeks through the thick padding of the briefs. "I think we'll both be more comfortable on the bed," I mentioned as I stood up.

Caleb followed closely and climbed in after I did. He sat on his knees and watched as I propped some pillows up behind me. Once I was comfortable, I patted my lap. "Across my lap, Cal. I think you've earned a spanking tonight."

It was Caleb's turn for his breath to catch. "I-I thought... I thought undies had to be down too?"

I smiled as I guided him over my lap. "Don't worry. I'll get them down when it's time. For now, you lay across my lap. Remember, you have safewords, use them if it gets to be too much. This is meant to be fun, but, I don't want you to cum from this. You need to tell me if you get too close."

His head shot up and his eyes met mine, going wide with surprise. "Cum from a spanking?"

For being so confident in his role as a little, Caleb seemed almost naive when it came to anything involving other forms of kink. "Spankings can be a lot of fun, sweet boy. Just make sure to tell me if you're going to cum."

His nerves seemed to be mainly focused around when his *reward* would begin and far less on the possibility of getting so much pleasure from it that he came. I squeezed his butt again as he got comfortable and allowed my fingers to trail along the leg bands of his briefs, from his hips inward and as far as I could reach between his legs. I felt his legs open slightly, silently begging for my hand to go low enough that I'd graze his balls. I forced myself to stop and move my hand the other way, back up toward his hips. I gave him a light pat on the back, hardly enough to feel through the layers of his training pants, but his ass still arched up off my legs slightly as he chased the feeling.

I grabbed the waistband of his undies and began pulling them down, moving slowly over his thickening cock, until his ass was fully exposed and the waistband rested a few inches below the round globes. With Caleb laid across my lap, exposed and waiting, it was hard to not jump into the spanking quickly, but I forced myself to trail a finger along his upper thigh and allow him time to relax.

The slightest touch caused his back to arch off the bed and shivers to run down his spine. Caleb was so sensitive to touch, I knew he'd love sensory play of any sort. I couldn't let myself go too far down that rabbit hole at the moment because I had a needy boy on my lap who was finally beginning to relax as my fingers ran over his tender skin.

Once I felt like he'd relaxed enough, I squeezed his right cheek and quickly brought my hand down on the same spot. It wasn't a hard smack by any stretch of the imagination, just enough for him to feel it. It wouldn't even leave a mark if I stopped there. But I didn't intend to stop.

Despite his surprised gasp, Caleb's ass arched off my lap slightly, almost chasing the pleasure. I started the process over again, rubbing along his left side for a few seconds, squeezing his cheek, and then spanking the same spot I'd

169

just squeezed. Caleb, for his part, repeated his reaction, ass arching up, a little moan, and finally settling back onto my lap. I continued my slow exploration and pace until I'd lost count of the number of soft smacks I'd given him. It had been enough that a faint pink had bloomed across his entire backside.

"How are you doing, Cal?"

He nodded. "Green... so much green."

I chuckled but went back to playing with his cheeks, squeezing and kneading before finally beginning to pick up the pace. The next spanks were faster and harder. I didn't give him much time between each one, but I could feel his cock, thick between my legs, each time he arched off my lap.

I'd slow down for a moment or two, kneading and rubbing, enjoying the beautiful sounds of pleasure coming from him as he experienced each new sensation before I'd deliver a few harder spanks to his ass. I could tell he was getting desperate when I slowed down to examine his flushed skin and he wriggled his ass and began pleading with me. "Green, please, green."

I chuckled at his rapid words. "Remember, you can't cum."

He nodded frantically, but I noted his body was free from the tension that had filled it at the start. "Green," he repeated. His ass was a beautiful shade of red that would fade over the next several hours. My goal wasn't to leave lasting marks, it was to let him find a place where every doubt and uncertainty that had plagued him about our relationship and my intentions faded away, even if it was just temporarily.

I teased my hand over his skin. "One day, you're going to beg for me to let you cum as I spank your ass," I told him before I brought my hand down again.

Caleb was so lost in the pleasure, he didn't hesitate before nodding frantically.

"You're going to be so beautiful all draped over me while you hump my leg. I can already hear those beautiful little pleas to let you cum."

His whisper was almost breathless. "Yes, want that."

My heart clenched. I'd been trying hard not to get ahead of myself, Caleb had reservations about me being his Daddy, and I had to respect that. But in my head, I could hear his little whimpers for Daddy to let him cum and it blurred that line in my head just a little more. I was Caleb's boyfriend, but I wasn't his Daddy yet. I hoped at some point he'd be ready to cross that line in the sand he'd created. I knew I would be ready for him to accept me as his Daddy whenever that happened.

I squeezed his right cheek in my hand and he moaned loudly. Before I continued my thought, I smacked the spot where I'd just grabbed and Caleb whimpered beautifully.

"You're being so good," I told him, lost in the fantasy but careful to not let him know I was fantasizing about being his Daddy.

I spanked him a few more times, harder and sharper than the earlier spanks, and while Caleb moaned, he didn't writhe or beg for more. He'd found that place where nothing—not even his raging erection—mattered. After sinking into that fuzzy, floating space, I knew it would be easy for him to think he could take more than he really could, so I slowed down, again rubbing his reddened cheeks gently, gradually lessening the intensity of the slaps until I was simply massaging his skin.

I let him lay across my lap, his erection persistent but completely forgotten, as he floated. I gave him about five minutes before I finally grabbed the bottle of water I'd brought upstairs and maneuvered him up to the head of the bed so he could rest in my arms. I couldn't help but smile when I realized he'd found his dodi at some point and was sucking lazily on it as he cuddled into my arms. His eyes only opened for a brief second as I tugged gently on the plush turtle.

"I've got a drink for you," I told him quietly before he finally released the pacifier. His eyes closed again, but his mouth remained open until the bottle's nipple finally touched his lips. As he pulled the bottle into his mouth he hummed softly and my heart melted just a bit more.

CHAPTER 18

Caleb

My eyes cracked open, but I didn't remember falling asleep. What I did know was my ass was deliciously sore and my cock was painfully hard. Slowly, events leading up to my unintentional nap began coming back to me. As I remembered being laid out across Travis's lap, my ass being bared, and then being spanked for the first time, I felt a strong arm pull me tighter.

"Are you back?" Travis's deep, steady voice questioned.

I nodded slowly, noticing my dodi was in my mouth. I finally forced my eyes all the way open and looked around the room. It was later than I'd expected it to be, but I didn't know if that was because I'd napped for a long time or if the spanking had taken longer than I'd realized. Either way I didn't have enough functioning brainpower to care.

"How do you feel?" His voice was measured and even, but I thought I detected some nerves as well.

I nodded slowly again.

Travis chuckled. "I need words, sweet boy."

I reached up and pulled the dodi out of my mouth before I spoke. "Good. Really good." It wasn't a lie, despite the tenderness of my backside. I felt cared for in a way I couldn't remember feeling before. "Really horny too," I added with a rock of my hips into his still-clothed hip.

While I knew he'd been anxious to hear my thoughts, I hadn't realized how nervous he'd actually been until his grip on me loosened slightly and tension flowed out of his body like a dam being opened after a heavy rainfall. "Are you sore?" he asked as I wiggled around, my undies having found their way back into place at some point after the spanking.

Telling him no would be a lie, but telling him yes would be too. Yes, I *felt* the tenderness, and yes, I was a little sore, but it was even better than the tenderness after a rough round of sex. "Only in a good way." I hoped that was enough of an assurance for him because I didn't know if I had a better way to explain what I was feeling physically.

Travis ran a hand along my side causing me to squirm. "I'm glad I didn't hurt you. I wasn't expecting you to slip into subspace."

"Subspace?"

I felt Travis's head nod up and down. "That place you went to where the world kinda faded away."

I nodded. "I liked that." It probably wasn't enough, but it was all I had. After having Travis pull my pants down and redden my ass while I writhed, moaned, and begged for more, I didn't feel so worried about opening up some. "But I didn't cum."

"No, you didn't cum. You were a very good boy."

I nodded. "Did I earn a reward?" It was one of the first times I'd felt the desire to add "Daddy" to the end of the sentence. Something was beginning to change inside me, I just didn't quite know what to make of it.

Travis's wandering hand moved lower toward my hip. "Why yes, I think you did. Good boys who follow instructions do earn rewards."

I hummed in agreement. I definitely liked the idea of earning an orgasm, especially after not having one this morning.

His large hand slid to the front of my briefs and I whimpered slightly when I felt him trace the outline of my hard-on through the thick fabric front. While I loved my training pants, getting hard in them was not always the most comfortable experience because they were so constrictive. This was one of those times where the fabric hugging tightly to my dick and balls was both infuriating and maddeningly erotic.

Travis took his time, cupping my balls and rubbing his hand up and down my shaft. If it weren't for the numerous layers of fabric on the front, I knew the front of my undies would have been soaked with the precum I could feel dripping from my slit.

"Please," I finally begged when I felt like I couldn't take more without cumming. It wasn't going to take long for me to reach an orgasm no matter what. Between not cumming that morning, the wildly erotic spanking, and the attention

Travis was giving me, I was only a few strokes away from an orgasm.

Travis took pity on me, freed my erection from the confines of my underwear, and wrapped his hand around my cock.

He slowly worked his hand up and down, gathering more precum each time his fingers slid over the tip. My slit was leaking enough that it never felt uncomfortable or rough. At a certain point—somewhere between the time his hand that had been holding my back snaked between my legs and began massaging my heavy balls, and the time the hand on my dick started working faster—I realized I was doing my best to hold off my orgasm.

Like he could read my mind, Travis whispered into my ear, "You don't need to wait for permission. Cum when you need to."

That was all the encouragement I needed, and I felt my balls draw up tight to my body as pleasure radiated up my spine and my focus narrowed to his hands on me. I came with a shout, my head thrown backward, as rope after rope of milky white cum painted my chest and abs.

Travis milked my dick until it became too sensitive, and I gasped as his thumb and forefinger squeezed the last droplets of cum from me. He brought his hand up to my mouth and leaned up for me to suck it clean. It felt naughty, dirty, and oh-so-right as I licked him clean of my release. When he was satisfied with the job I'd done, he pulled his hand back and scooped a puddle off my chest with two fingers and slowly brought them to his mouth before licking them. *Hottest. Thing. Ever.*

I moaned and my dick twitched, but that was all that happened and I finally settled back onto the pillow behind my head. Travis leaned over and gave me a kiss. "You taste really fucking good," he told me as he pulled back.

"Language," I teased before I felt a blush try to cross my face, but I suspected I was too tired for it to actually be noticeable.

Travis laughed heartily. "I guess I deserved that."

I giggled a little and curled into him. I could only blame the fuzzy, tired, relaxed feeling in my brain for the next thing out of my mouth. "Thick diapers would provide enough padding so my butt wasn't tender."

Travis stilled and my brain caught up with what I'd said. Before I could even try to backtrack, Travis was speaking. "One day, I'd love to put you in a diaper. I wouldn't care if it was after a spanking or not. But if they would make you feel better after being spanked, I'll get you one now."

I shook my head rapidly. "Not now. But… someday."

"I like someday." He was quiet for a moment before starting to speak again. "Are diapers something you want to have as part of your little play?"

Me and my big mouth and lack of filter. I wasn't quite sure how to respond. "Would you mind?" Answering a question with a question probably wasn't the most mature response.

A chuckle filled the room. "Oh, sweet boy, I wouldn't

177

mind. First, I already know I like my partner to wear diapers. Second, even if I didn't already know that, I would make an exception for you, and I know I'd enjoy it."

"Oh." It was good to know Travis didn't mind diapers, but this was such a huge topic in my head.

"You have diapers." It wasn't a question.

I nodded.

"And you like them."

Again, it wasn't a question, but I nodded an affirmative, though it was slow and hesitant.

Strong arms wrapped around me and a kiss was placed on the top of my head. "I look forward to the day you trust me enough to see you in them."

I felt my face flush, but being wrapped in strong arms made it hard to get too worked up. Or maybe it was the pull of sleep that was rapidly taking over my brain. I was exhausted.

Exhausted and covered in cum.

One of Travis's arms released from around me and I heard Travis open the packet of wipes I kept by my bed. My muscles contracted when the chilly wipe touched my overly heated skin, but I was drifting off rapidly. I had two thoughts before the world went dark. *Ohmygod, I told Travis I like diapers* and *Shit, Travis didn't cum.* Before I could think more about either thought, I was pulled under by exhaustion.

*****

My alarm went off at seven thirty-five, just like every other morning, and just like every other morning, I burrowed my head into my pillow and groaned. Unlike every other morning recently, my alarm didn't turn off, and a big arm didn't wrap around me and pull me close. I also felt tenderness across my backside that wasn't normally part of my morning wake-up.

Since the first time Travis had spanked me, I'd gotten more used to feeling his marks on my skin for a few hours. The night before, Travis had to spend the night at his house, one of the first times we'd been apart at night in a few weeks. I hadn't been happy about going to sleep without him there, but Travis had assured me he had a way for me to remember who he belonged to.

His idea of reminding me who he belonged to was draping me over his lap and spanking me hard enough that I'd begged him to stop and had even been close to using my safeword before his hand finally stopped landing on my backside. The resulting tenderness had been more intense than I'd ever remembered another spanking being.

Opening my eyes, I knew Travis wasn't there, but I certainly remembered him thanks to the tenderness on my ass. The feeling wasn't unwelcome and I was happy he'd thought about it.

I also remembered the conversation that followed. The one where he'd confessed that he was looking forward to one day being my Daddy. I'd heard him and I almost wanted to call him Daddy right then, but I knew I wasn't ready. The sweet words, and the promises he made to be here for me whenever I needed him, and the declaration he'd made to care for me as long as I'd have him had gone straight to my heart... some had even bypassed my heart and made their way to my dick. I'd fallen asleep with a raging erection, and I'd also woken up with one.

Unfortunately, my painfully hard dick was going to have to be ignored because I remembered Travis telling me to leave my cock alone. Apparently, Daddies controlled orgasms sometimes, and if I wanted him to be my Daddy one day, he was going to control my pleasure as much as he would take care of all my other needs and wants.

The fact that I'd been instructed not to cum didn't matter anyway, because I had to be at work earlier than normal, and I hadn't given myself enough time for a shower jerk-off session when I'd set my alarm. Okay, more accurately *Travis hadn't given me enough time when he'd set my alarm.*

I was still going to curse the early mornings we both had that day because I'd woken up to a tender ass and a cold half of the bed. Though I'd begrudgingly admit, if pushed, that feeling his marks still on me made the strangeness of not waking up with him rubbing my back a little less annoying.

It was strange how I'd slept alone for the vast majority of my life, but after only six weeks of spending most nights with Travis, it felt weird to not wake up next to him. I tried to ignore the feeling of melancholy accompanying the coldness on the side of the bed I'd begun to think of as his.

I was halfway through my shower when I remembered it was Thursday, and I'd promised Travis I would go out to dinner with him and his closest friends. He talked about them like they were his family and had assured me that none of them would care that I was a number of years younger than they were, but it still made me uneasy to think that he was going to introduce me to the guys that meant so much to him. Beyond that, they always met at Steve's Tavern, a bar about twenty minutes from my house that his dad owned and both of his parents managed. I knew his parents knew about me, but going to Steve's probably meant that Steve, and likely Delilah were going to be there, meaning I'd meet his parents *and* his friends on the same day. I didn't know if I was ready for that, but I also knew I couldn't back out.

I spent the rest of my shower, as well as the rest of my morning routine, thinking about how the night was going to go. I didn't even realize I'd forgotten to leave my dodi in my room until I got to the kitchen to find Dexter sitting at my table eating a bowl of cereal.

"Make sure to take that out of your mouth before you go to work," Dexter mentioned between bites.

My hand went to my mouth and I chuckled realizing I'd forgotten to leave it upstairs. Tossing it onto the counter, I began filling my coffee mug. At least Dexter had the decency to start the coffee. "You know, you have your own kitchen with your own food. I'm starting to regret giving you a key," I teased.

"I'm out of milk. Besides, I haven't seen you in what feels like forever!"

I rolled my eyes, despite my back being toward him. "You saw me at work yesterday!"

"But that's not the same. You're always with Travis now. My baby bird has finally flown the nest, but I miss him."

Even though the line was corny, I knew Dexter was being sincere. I couldn't remember a time since elementary school that I'd gone so long without spending excessive amounts of time with him. I took a sip of my coffee, then realized Dexter had known Travis wasn't at my place that morning. "Hey, how did you know Travis wouldn't be here?"

"His truck isn't in the lot."

I took my cereal bowl to the table and sat down next to my best friend, looking into his bright green eyes. "I'm going out to dinner with Travis tonight," I admitted as I poured milk into the bowl.

"This is news why, exactly?"

"At his dad's bar... With his friends."

Dexter's eyes brightened. "Seriously? Damn, when are you finally going to drop that wall you have built up?"

"What wall?"

He shook his head like he was sad for me. "You haven't even let Trav see you fully little yet. I also know you haven't let him be your Daddy."

"How the fuck do you know that?"

Dexter flung his spoon through the air, splattering milk

against the wall, but he was too distracted to notice. "I know you well enough. I dare you to tell me I'm wrong."

Crickets. I couldn't deny it. "What if he leaves?" I asked my cereal.

Dexter sighed sadly. "Oh, Cal. He's not going anywhere. Have you seen the way he looks at you? Fuck, if I could find a guy who looked at me like that, I'd be putty in their hands! When are you going to see he's here for the long haul? He wants you to meet his friends and possibly his parents. What is he going to have to do before you believe he loves *all* of you."

"He doesn't love me. It's too soon." I was going to ignore the rest of what Dexter said because I, logically, knew he was right, I just wasn't ready to really think about it.

The spoon was jabbed in my direction, dripping more milk onto the table. "You're hopeless, Caleb. That man has seen you every single day for over a month! Even when it's out of his way. He showed up to take you to lunch last week because he was 'around the corner' but then you told me he'd been working on some big bathroom remodel in Kingfield all day. Did you think about that? Kingfield is a half an hour from here, Cal. He wasn't anywhere near 'around the corner.' You're so clueless."

I chewed my cereal slowly while I thought. I was starting to think I really was as clueless and hopeless as Dexter said I was.

"Cal, you're going to go to dinner with his friends tonight and see how okay it really is. Travis is a great guy! I swear to you. You need to open up to him." He shot me a pointed stare that would have made me cower if anyone other than him gave it to me, but from Dexter, I could see the care and compassion in it. "And you need to get out of here, your first appointment is in twenty minutes."

"Fuck!" I grumbled, shoveling the last few bites of cereal into my mouth before tossing the bowl into the sink. "I swear to you Dex, if I find dried milk on my wall, floor, and table this evening… well, I know where you sleep and I have a key to your place too!"

I rushed out of the kitchen to put my shoes on and heard Dexter laughing maniacally. "Clean up the fucking milk!"

"I'm going to tell Travis you're using bad words."

I smirked as I shoved my feet into my Chucks. "I can cuss all I want." *For now.* I opened the door and grabbed my keys and phone off the table. "Travis isn't my Daddy!"

I was going to pretend I didn't hear the, "Yet. He's not your Daddy, *yet*," that followed me out of the house as the door shut. Unfortunately, I couldn't ignore the shocked look from the middle-aged woman who lived in the townhome on the other side of me. I gave her an uncomfortable smile and small wave as I rushed to my car.

CHAPTER 19

Travis

I couldn't seem to shake my feelings of unease about the night ahead. Caleb was a fixture in my life and it felt wrong to prevent him from meeting my friends, but at the same time, I didn't want him to be subjected to the Barton family insanity before he was ready. I'd finally decided to let him make the decision. Caleb wasn't as shy and awkward in his adult life as he was when he was little.

When I'd brought it up the night before, Caleb had smiled and agreed quickly, but as the night wore on, I could see his nerves beginning to set in. Even the spanking I'd given him before bed hadn't seemed to be enough to get his nerves to totally settle. I'd told him he didn't have to go, but he continued to assure me he wanted to. I had to trust that Caleb wouldn't do anything he wasn't comfortable with just to please me.

I suspected he was more concerned about being the new guy in a group of men who'd known each other for over a decade. Or it might have been that he would likely meet my parents. My dad was easygoing, but my mom could be a bit intense. It wasn't that she tried to be meddling or anything else, it was more that her mothering gene had taken hold and she wanted to make sure that everyone I'd ever brought around was taken care of. It didn't matter if it was a friend or a boyfriend.

My friends had gotten used to it long before, but Caleb was wishy-washy when it came to family. He talked openly about his mom's death when he was a teenager, but he was tight-lipped about why he didn't speak to his dad. Dexter would only tell me that there was bad blood and maybe someday, Caleb would tell me about it. Since Dexter wasn't as loose-lipped about the fallout as he was with almost every other aspect of Caleb's life, I knew it was something that would probably piss me off.

Given that I was a forty-one year old man living in central Tennessee, I'd been lucky to have parents who accepted me regardless of who I was attracted to. If anything, my mom probably went a little overboard with inclusion. She'd quickly become the woman wearing "Free Mom Hugs" shirts at Pride. She'd actually gone to Pride before I ever got to go to one.

My dad had always been a man who believed that it didn't matter what you did behind closed doors as long as it was safe, sane, and consensual. He could have been a walking billboard for a fetish club, honestly.

Things got a little crazy when the first out country singer met his husband at my dad's little, no-name bar after a tour stop in Nashville. After that, Steve's had become a landmark and the closest thing the area had to a gay bar. Amazingly enough, there had never been a problem, and while I didn't advertise that my dad was Steve, I was proud of how he'd handled things since the bar had become somewhat famous. My dad never treated any customer any differently than he'd treat me or one of my friends.

I knew they'd be accepting of Caleb, regardless of our age difference. I worried most about them overwhelming Caleb with their laid-back acceptance of anything thrown their way, especially if his family situation was as bad as I suspected it was.

I'd spent most of the night before and most of the morning thinking about how to help Caleb feel less pressure about the evening. I still hadn't come up with any brilliant ideas when I pulled my truck to a stop in front of my newest client's house and found Ben standing on the porch waiting for me. I knew he and his boyfriend shared a car, and I often picked him up when I could, but that morning, he'd insisted he would meet me at the house.

"Haven't been waiting long, I hope," I said to him when I joined him on the porch.

"Nah, only a few minutes. You probably passed Ash on your way through the neighborhood."

I knocked on the door of the brick home. "Will Ash be done with school before the end of the day?"

Ben nodded. "Yeah. It's his long day, but he'll be done around four forty-five. He's going to swing by the office and pick me up on his way home."

As we waited for the client to answer the door, my mind finally landed on an idea to help Caleb feel more at ease with tonight's dinner. Ben had come out with me and the guys a few times, but Ash had never been able to join him. Maybe if they could join us at dinner, some of the pressure would be off Caleb because there would be two new people at the table.

The door opened before I could ask Ben about his plans for the evening. As soon as we greeted the potential client, my focus was only on work. Ben had quickly become my shadow while I met with clients, drew up plans, and worked on estimates. I was happy to have him around because there were days I spent hours alone in the truck driving from client to client, and he was not only a great employee but also good company. It also meant I'd gotten to know Ben pretty well and had learned a lot about his boyfriend.

As we climbed into my truck for the twenty-minute drive back to the office, I remembered my thought about dinner. "Hey, would you and Ash want to come to dinner with us tonight?"

Ben shrugged. "I'll text Ash and ask. I don't know if we have plans or not."

"Great. I'm bringing Caleb to meet everyone, and I'm afraid he's going to be overwhelmed by the guys. Or, you know, my parents."

Ben laughed. "Your parents are great, Travis."

"They are," I agreed. "But you're also not my boyfriend. You've never seen my mom when I bring a guy around."

"I've seen her when you bring co-workers and friends around. That's enough for me. But she's awesome. From what you've said about him, Caleb should fit in well with everyone. I have a feeling you're overthinking this."

Ben was right. I was probably worrying about nothing. Then again, I couldn't remember the last time I'd brought a guy around who I actually cared about.

My mind still wasn't fully settled when we got back to the office, so I slipped into my office and shut the door. I pulled out my phone and called Dean.

"What's up?" Dean asked as he answer the phone. I could hear his fingers flying across his keyboard as he worked.

"Sorry to bother you in the middle of the day." I pulled up my email to at least pretend I was working.

Even with the rapid-fire typing coming through the phone, I knew I had Dean's full attention. "Caleb's coming to dinner tonight."

The typing stopped. "Seriously? I can't remember the last time you brought someone to dinner, aside from Ben."

I ran my hands nervously through my beard. "I know, I know. Shit, Dean, there's something about Caleb that I can't get enough of."

Dean chuckled. "And you're scared either Trent, Logan, or your mom will scare him off."

"Fuck. Yes. You know how intense all three of them can be."

"And he's a sub. He's used to being around one Dom,

189

he's not used to being around multiple dominant personalities… and Delilah Barton."

I laughed. "Exactly. My mom is overbearing enough for you guys. Can you imagine what she'll do to Caleb?"

"Valid concern. I'll try to keep Trent and Logan in check tonight. You work on your mom. Maybe your dad can keep her busy?"

I groaned. "That means I have to give them a heads up that I'm bringing someone. Dad will spill the beans in a heartbeat. I'll wait until closer to the time we plan to show up. With any luck, Mom will be off tonight."

"Ha! Right. Because she doesn't work on nights we're going to be there. Wishful thinking, Trav."

There was a knock at my office door and I groaned quietly. "I've got to go get actual work done before I have to fire myself for slacking off."

"See you and your man tonight."

We hung up, and I opened my door to find Ben standing on the other side smiling. "Sorry to interrupt your call. Just wanted to let you know Ash is excited to come to dinner."

"Awesome." I meant it too. Not only were Ash and Ben closer to Caleb's age than the vast majority of the group, but their relationship fascinated me. Ash had a submissive vibe about him, but Ben didn't seem to be a Dom at all. While I couldn't figure out *how* their relationship worked as well as it did, it was clear the two loved each other. I'd caught myself wondering, more than once, what it would have been like if I would have found the man I was supposed to be with in my early twenties.

Until Caleb had come along, I hadn't thought there was a person I was meant to be with. But that had changed the first time he aimed his bashful smile at me. I'd already found myself planning a spare room redesign so he had a place that could truly be his in my house. Though, if he was more comfortable having all of his stuff in the master bedroom, I wouldn't hesitate to change my gray and white room to bright and bold in a heartbeat.

Now, I just needed to make sure no one scared him off.

CHAPTER 20

Caleb

Regardless of the excessive worrying I had done that morning, my day flew by and, before I knew it, I was standing outside Travis's office, trying to talk myself into going in. There was no real reason I was uneasy about the evening ahead. Logically, I knew it was because Travis's family and friends cared about him and his happiness far more than my own family had ever cared about mine. There was something intimidating about walking into a situation where I knew people were going to be genuinely interested in the man I was and judging me as their friend's boyfriend.

Travis's parents were another hurdle. They were *accepting* of Travis. From what he'd said, they didn't care that he was gay. All they wanted for him was happiness. I'd never had a chance to come out to my mom before she'd died, but to say my dad hadn't taken the discovery well was an understatement.

Parents made me nervous.

As I stood leaning against the hood of my car and staring

at the building, a young guy bounced by me, practically skipping. He hardly looked old enough to be out of high school, but he was grinning from ear to ear. He stopped and cocked his head to the side, studying me like a curious puppy. It was hard to feel uncomfortable under the scrutiny because he looked like Dexter when he was getting an idea.

"You coming in?" the guy finally asked.

I sighed. "Working on it."

He scrunched up his face, not helping to erase the puppy image I had in my mind. "What's up?"

I must have looked like an idiot staring at the building like it was going to spontaneously combust at any moment. If I could tell any stranger that I was trying to work up the nerve to go in to meet my boyfriend, it would be this one. He practically had rainbows dancing around him and the light blue, glittery tennis shoes he was wearing were like a billboard announcing his sexuality to the world. "I'm meeting my boyfriend for dinner."

"Oh? Does he work here too?" Then the young guys eyes went wide like he was putting pieces of a puzzle together. "Is your boyfriend Travis?"

I nodded. "Um, yeah?"

The kid bounced slightly. "Oh! Ben's talked about how much happier Travis has been lately! Come on. Let's go!"

Ben was Travis's right hand man. Travis had talked frequently about how indispensable the guy was to him. Any remaining reservations I had about the guy began to melt away. He knew Ben well enough that Ben had been talking to him about Travis.

"Oh!" the guy exclaimed a second later. "I'm Asher, Ben's boyfriend."

I felt myself smile. He was like a younger, brown-haired Dexter. "Caleb."

"Nice to meet you!" Asher began heading toward the door and I followed him. "Wait, you're going out with Travis for dinner? Are you guys going to Steve's too? I thought Ben said Travis was going out with us."

"Yeah. We're heading out with some of his friends."

"Awesome." It appeared as though I'd already made a friend. More accurately, it seemed Asher had adopted me as a friend, but I'd take it. "At least now I'll know someone there. I'm kinda freaking out."

Asher laughed. "The way you were looking at the building like it was going to swallow you up, I kinda figured you were nervous about something."

"That obvious, huh?"

He laughed. "Just a bit. Hey, Ben!" he said as the door shut.

Ben was older than Asher, but not by much. Ben was, however, far bulkier and looked skeptical about something.

"Hi, Ash. Are you bothering clients?" he questioned as he looked at me.

Asher shook his head rapidly. "Nooo. He's not a client! He's Travis's boyfriend."

Ben groaned. "That's even worse. Don't bother my boss's boyfriend, Ash." The exasperated tone in his voice reminded me so much of how Dexter talked to me I

194

couldn't even be mad that they were talking about me like I wasn't there.

A head popped out of an office down the hallway. "Did I hear someone say my boyfriend was here?"

I couldn't help the smile that split my face as Travis appeared. "The one and only! At least I'd better be the one and only," I joked.

"Believe me, there's no one else. Come here. I'm stuck on a conference call, but I want to see you."

I felt my cheeks flush but headed back toward the office. I barely got into the room when he pulled me down onto his lap so I was straddling him, the chair rocked backward and hit the wall before we could tumble over. "Hi." My voice came out slightly breathless once I was sure we wouldn't land on the floor.

"I missed you this morning," he told me with a kiss to my neck. The feeling sent goosebumps running through my body. "How was your day?"

Sitting on his lap, his arms wrapped around my body, it was hard to remember why I'd been anxious a few minutes before. "It was good." It was also hard to not call him Daddy. He was the perfect Daddy for me. Dexter was right. I just wasn't at the point in our relationship that I was ready to call him that, and I knew in his office, with his employee only a few feet away, was not the right place to say it—especially not for the first time.

Dexter's words had bounced around in my head all day. It was time for me to start seriously considering where I saw our relationship going. I'd opened up enough that I'd let him see *parts* of me, but not all. For sure not all, but a lot. Far more than I'd ever shared with another boyfriend and I'd been fairly comfortable with that from the very beginning. Travis had been patient with me, never pushing for more than I was willing to give, even if I was beginning to think I needed that push. Dexter was right—as much as it killed me to admit it—it was time for me to open up to him and reveal the final pieces I'd kept hidden.

"What's got you so tense?" He was paying more attention to me than to his conference call, and I felt guilty about it.

"Nothing. Just got lost in thought." I forced a smile that I hoped he'd believe. I wasn't ready to talk about what was going through my head at the moment. But I was close.

His arms tightened around me, and I let my cheek rest on his shoulder, soaking up all the attention I could from him in that moment. It didn't escape me that I was still straddling his lap, but he'd gone back to talking with the people on the other end of the line, and I zoned out.

There was a chance I drifted off to sleep for a bit before I finally felt the chair move and heard a laptop shut. "Sorry about that," Travis apologized as I sat up. "But, I'm glad you got a few minutes sleep. You were so comfy there, I almost fell asleep too."

"I think I was tired."

Travis grinned. "I think you've overthought how tonight will go all day long and you've exhausted yourself."

196

I nodded bashfully. "Possibly."

Travis placed a soft kiss on my forehead. "Come on my little worrywart. You'll see. It's going to be just fine. I'll introduce you to Ben and his boyfriend Ash."

"We've met." I chuckled.

We walked out of his office and Ben was sitting at the reception desk inputting something on the computer while Asher was perched on his lap. In front of him was a box of crayons and a coloring book page with construction workers and the logo of Travis's company across the top. A quick glance at the waiting room told me it had come from the children's area.

While I was thankful to have had the time with Travis in his office, part of me wished I would have stayed out in the waiting area so I could have colored with Asher. Travis leaned close and whispered in my ear. "Next time, sweet boy. I have some crayons in my office already."

The way he said it let me know he understood and wasn't judging me. It was like it was natural for his boyfriend to want to color.

"Maybe I could hang the picture you color on my filing cabinet?" And damn if his voice didn't sound a bit hopeful.

"I'd like that," I agreed. "Next time, though. We're supposed to be going to dinner."

Travis nodded. "Ben, come on. We're getting out of here. That's enough work for the day. If I'm late again, the guys are gonna have me by the balls. I'm always late to dinner."

Asher quickly put his coloring page on Ben's desk and returned the crayons to the children's table as Ben shut down his computer. In a matter of minutes, Travis was locking up the building.

"Are you okay driving separately?" Travis questioned as we approached our vehicles. "We can go straight to your place after dinner tonight. It's closer than my house anyway."

"Yeah, that's fine. I'll follow you." I wasn't as confident as I sounded, but I wasn't going to let him know I was still nervous. Thankfully, I was no longer freaking out and my nerves were manageable. Being curled up in his lap and resting for a few minutes had settled a lot of the unease that had coursed through me all day.

Besides, if I drove separately, I could escape if things went south. Not like Travis would let me, and I knew that, but it was a nice thought.

Asher and Ben climbed into the late-model car Asher had driven up in and backed out. They were out of the parking lot before I had even put my car in reverse. I watched as Travis eased his truck out of his parking space then waited patiently for me to do the same.

Pulling into the parking lot of Steve's Tavern, I realized I'd been there a number of times with Dexter. I couldn't figure out how I'd never put two and two together, but Travis hadn't been lying when he told me the bar was a welcoming place. Steve's was one of my favorite bars because I had always felt welcome. It was definitely refreshing to know there was a place in central Tennessee that was inclusive. Of course, if his parents were anything like Travis, it would have been hard for them not to be kind and accepting.

The realization that I'd been here a number of times helped to calm my remaining nervousness. I'd probably met both of Travis's parents before and hadn't even known it. I'd never been one to drink to excess, so I knew I'd never made a fool out of myself and didn't have to worry about them remembering me for some ridiculous drunk antics.

"Shit," Travis grumbled as he met me at my car. "Merrick, Dean, and at least Logan are already here. I hope Trent and Larson aren't here yet."

I giggled at his distress. It was so rare to see him ruffled. "What's the big deal?"

Travis put his hand on my back as we walked toward the door. "The big deal is, I'm *always* late. It's become somewhat expected. I was trying to be here early today, but that damn conference call."

"So, who all is going to be here again?" I asked, looking around the packed parking lot.

A warm smile spread across Travis's face and lit up his eyes. Knowing his friends evoked such a reaction in him made the remainder of my nerves settle. They couldn't be bad people. And dammit, once again, Dexter was right.

"Well, clearly Merrick is here. He's the oldest of our group. I met him in college. He's definitely the most no-nonsense one of us. Which is funny because Logan and

Trent are both in law enforcement. Anyway, Merrick's a business consultant. Specifically for restaurants. I guess it plays into his demeanor, but when I met him, he was fresh off being a flair bartender in New York City for a few years. He's mellowed a lot with age."

"Dean's not much older than you," he continued without a break. "He's only thirty-two now. He's… assertive."

"Is that a nice way to say he's an asshole, or just a more vanilla way of telling me he's a Dom like you?" I was surprised I'd asked the question, but I couldn't take it back once it was out.

Travis's rich laughter filled the parking lot causing Ben and Asher to look at us from outside their car. "It's a nice way of saying he's a Dom."

"Okay so one of your friends is broody the other is a Dom. What else do I need to know?"

"Trent and Logan have known each other since high school. They're trouble, great guys, but trouble. Trent's a sheriff nearby and Logan is one of his deputies, but watch out they can be a handful."

"Noted."

Travis tapped his chin in thought as he opened the door. "Larson's a firefighter in Nashville. Don't be offended if he doesn't say much to you. He's a pretty quiet guy."

I didn't have a lot of time to respond because we had walked into the crowded bar and Travis was ushering me toward a table with four men seated around it. They were watching the four of us and grinning widely as we approached the table.

"Well, you beat Lars here," Merrick laughed. He seemed to be in good spirits. I wondered if that was because of the almost empty beer glass in front of him, because he definitely didn't seem broody at that moment.

Travis looked properly chastised as he smiled and shook his head. "Yeah, yeah, yeah. At least I'm not the last one here tonight. I got held up on a conference call."

"Sure you didn't get held up with your man?" the tow-headed blond asked.

The dark-haired guy who sat next to him smacked him upside the head hard enough that I heard the crack over the music. "Don't be an ass. We don't even know the guy yet! Excuse Logan, he doesn't have any manners. I'm Trent," he smiled warmly as he held out a hand for me to shake.

I managed to shake his hand before Travis pulled me into his side like he had to protect me from his hodgepodge of friends. "So, you've met Trent and Logan." Travis's tone was sharp and had it been aimed at me, I would have been cowering, but Logan grinned mischievously. "Also, this is Merrick," he pointed to the first guy who'd spoken, confirming my assumption. "And this is Dean," he said with a grin in his voice.

Dean nodded in acknowledgement. "It's good to finally meet you. Trav has been talking about you nonstop for weeks." He winked at Travis and when I looked up, I noticed my boyfriend was looking uncharacteristically bashful. He'd been talking about me to his friend and was embarrassed to be outed.

I didn't have time to tease Travis about Dean's revelation because Asher stole my attention as he wiggled his way toward the table and chose to sit on Ben's lap instead of the chair beside him. The two seemed to fall into an animated conversation.

"Everything okay over there?" Travis asked after a few minutes of whispering back and forth.

Ben nodded. "Fine. Ash is just happy."

"Oh?"

Ash bounced excitedly on Ben's legs. "It's great! Ben told me on the way here we got the apartment we applied for last week!"

"Finally?" Travis asked, looking pointedly at Ben.

Ben grinned sheepishly. "It's taken a bit to save up enough, but yeah. We can pick up the keys this weekend."

"Let us know if you need help," a deep voice asked from behind me, causing me to jump.

"Sorry," the guy chuckled. "Didn't mean to sneak up on you."

Travis nodded. "Hey, Lars."

Larson held his hand out to me. "Nice to meet you," he said as we shook hands.

"Where are you from, Caleb?" Dean asked me as Larson got settled in a seat between Logan and Ben. I felt Travis's arm tighten around my shoulder in a possessive, yet comforting way.

"I'm only a few minutes from here, actually. I guess you could say I'm a local boy, born and raised."

"Trav has been coming to work from the opposite direction most mornings," Ben noted.

Thankfully, Travis answered for me with ease. "He's got quite a comfortable bed." No mention of the fact that it was far easier to sleep at my house because all my toys, my dodi, and my bottles were all there. He tucked me under his chin and held me close. I didn't know if the other guys could see the possession in his hold, but I certainly felt it.

"It is pretty comfy... especially when you're in it," I teased.

After that, conversation progressed to more mundane topics, but even when it turned my direction, his friends tended to rib Travis more than probe into my life. As we finished our burgers, Larson looked over at me and grinned. "You got the old man moving around better. He's almost back to normal. I don't know if it's the physical therapy at the office or at home, but whatever you're doing keep it up."

Dean and Trent both choked on their beers, and Travis's mouth opened and closed a few times in shock. Finally, Travis shook his head and responded to his friend. "It could be a combination of both."

"Touché, Travis, touché," Larson bowed his head and laughed.

CHAPTER 21

Travis

I knew Caleb had been nervous about meeting my friends, but so far, the night was going well. Ben's boyfriend was just as talkative and energetic as I expected. Caleb was relieved to let Ash take most of the attention from him while he figured everyone out. Caleb had finally relaxed and was all smiles, and the tension in his shoulders was already easing.

"You know, Trav, it's really good to see you with someone again," Merrick mentioned quietly as Caleb was lost in a conversation with Trent about a video game I didn't understand.

I smiled because I couldn't help myself. Since Caleb had come into my life, work was no longer my highest priority. I was taking evenings and weekends off, and the business hadn't fallen apart. I was curious, though, because something had changed that evening, and I didn't know what exactly. Caleb had seemed even more relaxed than normal, like some invisible thread of worry or stress had finally snapped.

"Thanks, Merrick," I answered quietly while my fingers ran through the buzzed, short hair on the back of Caleb's head. I swore he purred every time I did it, and he melted into me a bit more than he had been before. "It's about time for you to find someone."

Merrick shook his head in amusement. "I'm forty-two. I think I'm getting a bit old to be finding love."

"Jesus, don't talk like that. I'm only a year younger than you. You make it sound like I should be digging my grave, not planning a weekend with my boyfriend." I'd almost said *lifetime* and it wouldn't have been a lie. I didn't think Merrick, or anyone else, would understand how deeply I felt for Caleb.

I looked to the other side of Caleb and found Dean taking in the surroundings, watching Ash and Ben with an almost wistful look on his face. He'd been single so long, I was beginning to think he'd forgotten how good it felt to be in a relationship. The truth was, though, for being a bunch of men in our thirties and forties none of us had rushed to settling down, and with the exception of me, no one else seemed near that point.

Hell, I doubted Logan would ever settle down. I'd lost track of the number of women he'd dated. Trent was out but not openly gay, it had always remained on a need-to-know basis, and I didn't see that changing. Merrick had resigned himself to a life of solitude for whatever reason, and Larson wasn't much better. He always seemed too busy with work to worry about dating anyone. Dean had always been a long-term relationship guy before he'd been in the car accident, but since then, he'd refused to even think about dating. I still needed to get to the bottom of whatever that was about.

Now that Ben was around with his boyfriend, I wondered if Dean's seriously dormant sex drive was waking up again. He already knew Caleb was a little, and the way Ash seemed to radiate sub, it was likely his Dom instincts were on full alert. Honestly, if Ben and Ash weren't so clearly head-over-heels in love with one another, I'd have introduced Ash to Dean. Dean would do well with an excitable sub like Ash.

We were packing up to leave when I saw my dad's head poke out from the kitchen and look in our direction. *Shit*, he'd seen us. There was no way around introducing Caleb to my parents now. It would look highly suspect if we rushed out.

"My dad saw us," I whispered into Dean's ear.

"And that's my cue to get the fuck out of here. Love your mom, but I'll gain ten pounds if she has a chance to get out here with more food."

"Thanks, asshole," I joked as Dean grabbed his ballcap and pushed it onto his head.

Logan and Trent also grabbed their hats, though theirs were well-worn Stetsons, and both scurried out the door making excuses as soon as they saw my mom's head come through the door that separated the bar and storeroom.

Merrick leaned over and spoke into my ear. "You're on

your own for this one." He was laughing as he dragged Larson away before he'd had a chance to finish the last of his drink.

I shook my head. "She doesn't bite!" I called to my friends' retreating backs.

Ben and Ash jumped up as both my parents headed toward the table. "She's more like an anaconda, she'll squeeze you to death with love… or she'll kill you with food! Come on, Ash I've got to be at work early tomorrow." Ben grabbed Ash's hand and started pulling him away from the table.

Asher began complaining that he wasn't ready to go but a quick whispered word and he relented. "Nice to meet you," Asher pouted slightly as he told us goodbye. "I don't know why food is such a bad thing, though," he began complaining as he followed Ben to the front door.

"Why'd everyone run out of here so fast?" Caleb questioned looking at the now empty table.

"Because no one wants to be around when my mom realizes you're here. Not that it's going to be bad," I tried to reassure him. "She's just going to be incredibly excited. Oh, and she feeds them all so much they end up waddling out of here."

Caleb laughed and squeezed my hand but didn't have a chance to say anything because my mom was already to us.

"Well, you'd think they'd seen a ghost the way they all hurried out of here!"

I groaned. "My mom's a bit… intense. Her heart's in the right place, but she can be a bit overwhelming."

I smiled at her and my dad who was behind her and looking frazzled. "Sorry!" he mouthed.

"Hi, Mom." I pulled Caleb into my side a bit protectively. My smile was probably forced, but I had no clue what would come out of her mouth.

"How are you?" The question was aimed at me, but she was looking directly at Caleb.

"Doing well, but we were just leaving."

"Sorry," my dad apologized quickly. "I didn't even tell her you were bringing someone."

"You *knew*?" she shot my dad an incredulous look.

I jumped in quickly. "I called right before we got here and asked him not to tell you because I didn't want you to feel pressured to be at the bar if you weren't already here." The lie fell off my tongue easily, and I felt Caleb move a half-step closer to me.

"I'm Delilah," my mom said, ignoring my attempts to usher Caleb out the door.

Caleb straightened and smiled as he held out his hand. "Caleb. Nice to meet you."

My dad's head cocked slightly to the side, and his eyes narrowed like he was trying to figure something out. "I've seen you here before," he finally said.

Caleb nodded. "I come here with my friend for a drink from time to time."

My dad's eyes lit up in recognition. "The redhead!"

"That would be the guy." His laugh was genuine, and I felt some of the tension leave my body.

My mom seemed to know who he was talking about. "Oh, the guy who makes me keep Bertha's Revenge in stock!"

Caleb laughed and nodded. "Yeah, that's him."

"He's so sweet!" my mom gushed. Her brows turned down and she looked between Caleb and me. "I always thought you two were together. Did something happen? You guys always looked so happy."

"Ma!" I scolded.

Caleb put his hand on my forearm. "It's okay," he assured me. Then he turned back to my mom to answer her. "Most people think we're together, but we're just friends."

Despite Caleb's reassurances that it was okay and his relaxed body language, I was on edge. My mom was too nosy for her own good. She wasn't malicious, and I knew she had the best intentions, but she lacked an understanding of boundaries.

She turned a quizzical eye on me. "So you two?"

I nodded. "Caleb and I have been dating for over a month now."

My mom's eyes widened comically, and I saw Caleb bite his lip to keep from laughing at her reaction. "What would a cute young guy see in an old fart like you?"

"Hey, watch who you're calling an old fart. If I'm old, what does that make you? If memory serves, you just turned sixty-five this year!"

My mom smiled at me. "Oh sweetheart, I just keep getting better with age."

I wrapped an arm around Caleb. "And these are my parents, Delilah and Steve."

To my dismay, my mom pulled out a chair and I knew we were going to be there for a while. All I wanted to do was get my boy back to his house, curl up in bed, and have a nice quiet evening, but that wasn't happening anytime in the near future. I pulled a chair out and pulled Caleb down onto my lap, much the same way Ash had perched on Ben's lap all evening.

My dad looked at us and sighed. "I'll go get a round of shots."

"No," I snapped more forcefully than I'd intended. Caleb had already had two beers that night and he was driving. "We both have to drive back to Caleb's place tonight," I amended. "And we both have early mornings." I might have made the last part up, but I hoped it would keep my mom's *meet the boyfriend* interrogation short.

My dad shrugged, and I swore he mumbled something about this being far more comfortable with alcohol. While I didn't disagree, I needed to make sure we were both safe to drive.

"A month, huh?" my mom asked curiously once my dad had taken a seat.

Caleb spoke before I could. "I'm his physical therapist."

My dad laughed. "Well, that explains why he's still going to PT."

The statement caused Caleb to laugh, and I finally relaxed, thinking this conversation might not be as bad as I'd thought it would be.

CHAPTER 22

Caleb

As I drove back to my place, I couldn't help but chuckle to myself. Travis had been so uptight and tense as soon as his parents made an appearance that I'd worried it was going to be absolute hell. Once we finally got through the first few awkward moments, I'd found Delilah and Steve to be funny and welcoming. Delilah actually reminded me a bit of my mom, and she gave me hope that maybe my mom wouldn't have reacted as terribly about my being gay as my dad had. Steve was the comedic relief and always had a quick-witted quip or funny response. For as tense as Travis's mom made him, his dad relaxed him just as much.

Of course, it was now past nine and we'd been at the bar an extra two hours. I was getting tired as I drove through the streets near my place. I'd worried myself almost sick that day for nothing and now it was catching up to me as I yawned repeatedly. I couldn't remember the last time I'd been so glad to see the parking spaces by my townhouse when I pulled around the corner. Travis's headlights pulled in behind me a few seconds later, and I could feel myself relax just knowing he had followed me and we were almost home.

He was parked beside me by the time I had my car turned off, and he waited for me while I gathered my work clothes. I'd thrown them haphazardly in the passenger's seat earlier in the day after I'd changed before leaving work.

As I joined him on the sidewalk, he pulled me into a tight hug and kissed my temple gently. "Sorry my parents ambushed us tonight."

I tilted my head upward and pressed my lips into his. "It's okay, really. They weren't bad, and your dad is funny."

"I was hoping to get through the evening without seeing them."

"Is there a reason you didn't want them to meet me?" I'd never gotten the impression that he wanted to keep our relationship quiet, but the way he'd been fretting about his parents meeting me had me overthinking.

Travis pulled me in for a tight hug. "Oh, Cal, it's nothing like that. I just know family is stressful for you. My mom can be a one-woman Pride fest and sometimes doesn't realize how overbearing she's being."

"She really wasn't that bad tonight. Right now, all I want to do is go inside and relax for a little bit before bed." I interlaced our fingers and tugged Travis toward my door. Travis waited patiently as I unlocked the door and turned on some lights.

I'd cleaned my toys up before we'd gone upstairs the night before, so the living room was still clean. "Drink?" I asked as I headed toward the kitchen.

"I'll get them. You take a seat," Travis told me. I knew what that meant before I sat down at the table. I wouldn't be getting beer or wine, and whatever I got would be in my sippy cup or a bottle. I was just fine with that. My turtle was sitting on the table, and I grabbed it automatically, flipping it around and looking for the dodi that had been there that morning.

When I realized there was nothing attached to any of the feet, I knew instantly where it was. "I'm going to kill him," I growled as I stood up and headed toward the door.

"Whoa, Cal! Where are you going and who are you going to kill?" Travis asked as he stepped back from the fridge and followed me out the back door.

I didn't bother going to pound on Dexter's door because I knew right where he'd put my dodi, again. As we walked to the middle of the small yard we shared, I approached the giant oak tree that dominated the yard and crouched down toward the left side.

"Cal, sweetie, what are you doing?" Travis asked as I opened the little door at the base of the tree.

I reached in, my tongue poking out of my lips as I concentrated. "Getting my dodi back." My fingers felt around inside the small, hollow space in the base of the tree until I found the cup Dexter had put it in. "Ah-ha!" I announced triumphantly as I grasped the container and pulled it free.

Travis stood looking down at me, completely perplexed. "Care to explain?" he asked with a chuckle.

"Dex was at my place for breakfast this morning. I left my turtle on the table when I left. He took my dodi and put it here so the fairies would take it tonight."

I realized Travis hadn't grown up with the O'Conaill family and not everyone had fairy gardens or gave things to the fairies. Travis probably thought I was nuts with the way I was going on about fairies taking a pacifier. I walked over to him and snuggled up to him before I pulled my phone out of my pocket and turned the flashlight on, aiming it toward the base of the tree.

"This is Dexter's fairy garden, Tír na nÓg. Also known as *The Land of Youth*. It's a fairy tale and he thought it was a fitting name for the fairy garden." I gave him the condensed version of the dodi trees and Irish folklore. It was too cold to stand out there much longer dressed as we were. I had my dodi back and, in the end, that was all that mattered.

I felt Travis's chest begin to vibrate with laughter before it finally bubbled out of him and became audible in the still evening. "I remember Dexter telling me about this one time. I didn't quite believe that he actually took your dodi and hid it in the tree."

"Well, he does."

Travis pulled me closer. "I can't think of anyone who needs their dodi more than you do. Is this something he does often?"

I shook my head. "Only sometimes, when he's being a butthead." Probably not the most mature word I could come up with, but fitting nonetheless.

"I may have to have a chat with Dexter about leaving your dodi alone. Besides, I don't think there are many sparkly green ones with dragons on them."

I shook my head.

A gentle kiss was placed at my neck and I melted into Travis's arms even more. "Let's get you inside and ready for bed, my boy. You've had a long day and look like you're about to fall asleep."

I moaned. I didn't mean to, but I couldn't stop it. Travis had never called me *his* boy—sweet boy, yes, but never *my* boy—and the possession and care I heard in his voice did funny things to my insides. Paired with my rapidly shifting feelings, my brain was starting to short circuit.

I was his boy. Travis had said it so easily, I couldn't help but wonder if he'd even realized he'd said it. It seemed so natural for him to call me his boy. That stupid protective wall was crumbling quickly.

"Let's go in and get your dodi cleaned off and I can finish getting your bottle ready and then we can head up to bed."

"Yeah, that sounds good," I agreed. Getting out of the backyard and away from the emotions pushing down on me was exactly what I needed. We were upstairs only a few minutes later.

Travis had become comfortable in my space, and likewise, I'd become comfortable with him in my space. He didn't even ask as he shuffled through my drawers, looking for a clean pair of undies and pajamas for me that evening. I finally allowed myself to wonder what it would be like to have him grab a diaper instead of my training pants for bed. With Travis and I spending so much time together, I hadn't worn a diaper in over a month. Longer than I'd gone without wearing one in years, honestly. The idea wasn't wholly unpleasant—just another piece falling into place.

He turned to find me sitting on the bed, and my expression must have seemed off as I processed everything going through my head. "Are you okay, Cal?" he questioned as he set the clothes down.

I blinked a few times. "Sorry, I got lost in thought." Looking down at the pile of clothes, I smiled. It had been a while since I'd worn my spaceship pajamas. Leave it to Travis to also find the undies that matched them.

A thumb ran across my cheek. "Are you sure you're okay?"

I nodded. "Promise. Just getting tired."

It seemed to appease him because he reached for the buttons of my shirt and began popping each one open. I always got shivers when he started undressing me. The tender care and full attention he gave me always made me want to squirm. My nerve endings always seemed to catch fire as his rough fingers grazed over my skin as he worked my shirt off my shoulders. His hands were thick, so each time he grabbed my waistband, they would press against the tender skin of my stomach and my dick got excited each and every time. It never seemed to understand the difference between bedtime routine and sexy times.

"You know," he began as he worked on my pants. "I want you to be comfortable, Cal."

I nodded. "I'm very comfortable."

He kissed my lips gently. "You make me happy. I'm happier with you than I can ever remember being in my life."

His words made my breath hitch slightly.

"I think I've always let this be assumed and as such, it's gone unsaid. I want to make sure that you know, when you're ready, I'd be honored to be your Daddy."

A tear leaked from my eye and I nodded sharply. "Thank you." I wanted to say more but my words were stuck in my throat. He'd always been clear that he was a Daddy, his every action told me he was the right Daddy for me, but to hear him say it settled something I hadn't known was amiss.

He hugged me to his chest and whispered quietly. "It's okay. It doesn't have to be tonight, or even anytime this year if you're not ready. But I want you to know, I'm not going anywhere."

I nodded again. "I-I want that too. When I'm ready, I want that."

"I'm glad to hear that." Travis pulled back slowly and kissed each of my cheeks, then my nose, and finally my lips. "Thank you."

I blinked. "For what?"

"For being you and for letting me be me."

I couldn't figure out what to say to that, so I leaned forward and kissed him. I hoped it conveyed how much his words meant to me, and how much I cherished them.

217

He finally got back to undressing me, stripping my pants off me, and leaving me in just a pair of puppy dog printed briefs. I didn't feel the slightest bit shy or uneasy being seen in them. Travis's dark brown eyes gazing over my body made me feel sexy. It was just another piece of the puzzle clicking into place. He'd been telling me since the beginning I was going to have to be the one to get tired of him and kick him to the curb before he left, but I hadn't been ready to see that before now.

Travis slid my briefs down my legs. He was focused on me getting to bed. His Daddy instincts had kicked in, and he knew I needed bed more than sex. I was trying to convince my erection of that as he knelt to slip the spaceship training pants over each of my legs before pulling them up and into place. With a little adjustment, he had me tucked securely into them. The training pants hid my erection almost as well as a diaper would have, and aside from a little bulge in the front, it would easily be out of sight and out of mind for the rest of the night. Travis slid my pajama pants up my legs and they hid my arousal even more.

I was beginning to feel tired by the time my shirt had been pulled over my head. "Now, let's get you into bed sleepy head."

I nodded and scrambled up to the top of the bed, waiting as Travis clicked the safety rail into place. The first time he'd found it, I'd been mortified, but now it was part of our routine, and I always felt better once he clicked it into place. I waited for Travis to strip off his clothes and climb into bed next to me.

He grabbed the bottle of milk off the nightstand as he climbed in, and I found a comfortable position with my head on his left arm and my body tucked tightly to his. I felt safe and protected there and wondered how it was I'd spent my life without this. The bottle made it to my mouth seconds later, and I began the steady sucking pattern I knew would lull me to sleep before it was gone.

"Would you like to spend the night at my house tomorrow night?" Travis questioned as I relaxed.

I nodded. I liked Travis's house. It was so much bigger than my townhome, we just tended to spend more time at my place because my stuff was at my house. I fell asleep wondering what it would be like to have my things at Travis's.

CHAPTER 23

Travis

There was a lot to do to get ready for Caleb to spend the night at my house. I had things I wanted to buy for him, but I also knew he had things he would not be able to sleep without. He would definitely want his dodi. We also needed to pack his pajamas, undies, and a change of clothes. As he showered on Friday morning, I packed a bag making sure to toss the necessities in it—his bear and dodi were my top two priorities.

By the time he got out of the shower, there was a bag packed and sitting at the top of the steps. The morning felt incredibly domestic as we ate breakfast then left the house together. I ended up following him to the physical therapy office since I had a scheduled appointment. Thankfully, my ankle was finally starting to feel more like it had pre-injury. If it hadn't been for getting to see Caleb two extra times throughout the week, I probably would have stopped going a while ago.

I tried to put in a half day at the office, but Ben was getting frustrated with me by lunchtime.

"I don't know where your head is today, but it definitely isn't here," Ben chastised me after catching a third mistake on the estimate we were working on.

I ran a frustrated hand over my face. "My mind definitely isn't on work today. I've got about four hundred other things running through my head right now."

"Get out of here. This estimate isn't due until next week. I'll finish it up this afternoon, and you can review it when you're thinking clearly on Monday."

I hated to admit it, but Ben was right. I was probably just holding him up at that point. "Alright, fine, I'll go. Call me if anything comes up."

He nodded and waved me out of his space. I didn't allow myself to think too heavily about leaving, because if I did, I'd probably end up talking myself out of it.

I quickly packed up my bag and headed out to the truck. I resisted the urge to call Dean for advice on what I was going to do that evening. While I knew Dean would be happy to help out, I didn't want to overshare about Caleb and have him feel as though I'd betrayed his confidences if he ever found out. I did make a mental note to open up to Caleb about Dean's past and interests. Sharing Dean's history with Caleb would give me someone to talk about how to best encourage Dean to get back into the dating world. Hopefully, it would also let Caleb know there was someone else in my group of friends who understood our relationship. Someday, I hoped Caleb would be comfortable enough to finally call me Daddy. If he knew Dean understood our relationship on that level, I hoped it would ease stress while we were out with the guys, especially if he ever slipped up and called me Daddy in front of him. I already thought of Caleb as my boy and I hoped he would soon open himself up to letting me really be his Daddy in both relationship and name.

I ended up driving directly to a big-box store where I could find everything I needed in one place, including groceries. I'd been spending so much time with Caleb at his house, even my milk had been expired the last time I'd looked in my fridge. I pulled into the parking lot a few minutes before one and jumped out of my truck. I had four hours before Caleb would be arriving, and I still needed to figure out dinner.

I headed straight toward the children's department. I started in the feeding section, picking out a few bottles, sippy cups, plates, and silverware, before moving onto the bedding section where I found a bed rail similar to the one Caleb had on his bed. I'd decided the rail helped him feel more secure at night because he never got near it in his sleep—he was usually curled tightly against me while he slept. I still wanted to have one for my house because he needed to know I wanted him there. I didn't care if my room ended up looking like a nursery before long, his comfort was all that mattered to me.

As I was heading toward the toy section, my cart already half-full, I found a dragon pillowcase on an endcap. It was too perfect, and given that it was clearly out of place, I decided it was meant to be and tossed it into the cart with my other purchases.

I knew I was going to be in trouble in the toy section because I wanted to buy everything I saw. I managed to remind myself that, aside from a handful of stuffed animals Caleb tended to alternate between, his favorite toys seemed to be the blocks and little wooden cars he had. The blocks were easy to find, and, since I couldn't decide which of the three sets he'd like more, I bought all three. The cars were harder to find. One of the sets had a few wooden cars, and I found two more a bit farther down the aisle, but finally resigned myself to needing to buy more online. Satisfied with the toy finds, I set off to get a bin to keep them all in. I had a feeling the number of toys at my house would grow rapidly.

By the time I got my groceries and a few other impulse buys—a stuffed animal, three new coloring books and crayons, a few DVDs, and a picture book about a dragon— my cart was overflowing, and I was thankful I had a truck. I still didn't know when he'd get to the point when he was ready to accept me as both his boyfriend and his Daddy, but I hoped it would be soon and I wanted to be ready for that eventuality.

I realized it was later than I'd anticipated by the time I got home and unloaded the truck. There was no way I'd be able to get everything put away properly *and* make dinner that night. Deciding it was more important to have the house ready for Caleb when he arrived than it was to have dinner at home, I set to work putting everything in its place.

I started a load of laundry so Caleb's new pillowcase would be clean. I hand-washed the bottles, sippy cups, and various dishware I'd purchased because I didn't have enough other dirty dishes to justify running the dishwasher.

Despite living in my house for years, it had always been too big for just me and most of the kitchen cabinets still had very little in them. I put Caleb's new bottles, cups, plates, and silverware in the cupboard next to the dishwasher. The crayons and coloring books went into the drawer next to the silverware. Figuring out where to put the toys and the box I'd bought for them was more difficult.

Everywhere I set the storage box felt out of place and like it was the focal point of the room. While it didn't bother me, I knew it would make Caleb uncomfortable, especially if anyone came over. He was so private about his likes, he wouldn't like anyone seeing his toy box, or worse yet, opening it because they didn't realize what it was. After moving the thing all over the living room at least twice, I finally spotted the throw blanket I usually kept on the ottoman and decided to drape it over the box. When I was satisfied that it was concealed I pushed it to the far side of the couch, against the armrest, and put it out of my mind. I'd already been moving things around the living room for so long that the washing machine had finished.

After tossing the laundry into the dryer, I focused my attention on my room and the bathroom. I stashed the bubble bath and bath toys in a storage bin under the bathroom sink, and that just left a small pile of items on my bed that needed to find homes in my room.

I spent a half an hour cursing at the rail while I put it together and stuffed it between my mattress and box spring before running down the steps to grab the pillowcase out of the dryer. Caleb had texted me twenty minutes earlier to tell me he was leaving work, meaning I only had a few minutes before he arrived. I ran back upstairs to stuff the pillow into the case and place the new stuffed animal in the center of the bed.

My room still looked far more grown up than Caleb's, but I hoped the little things on the bed would help him feel welcome. I gathered up the trash scattered throughout the house and had just gotten it into the trash can outside when Caleb's car pulled into the driveway.

"Hey." He smiled at me as I came around the side of the house to greet him.

I pulled him into me, not caring that I was giving old Mrs. Taylor something to talk about at her next Garden Club meeting. It was hard to care about what all the old birds thought when my boy fit so perfectly in my arms. It felt like it had been longer than eight hours since I'd last seen him.

"What's the plan for tonight?" he asked when he pulled back from our kiss. He didn't go far, allowing his head to rest on my shoulder and his face to press gently against my neck.

Running my hand through his hair, I brought up dinner. "Well, I'd hoped to make dinner here, but I ran out of time.

I thought maybe we could go out for dinner then come back for a little surprise."

Caleb's head came off my shoulder, and he looked up at me with curious eyes. "What kind of surprise?"

"We'll talk about it at dinner. For now, are you ready to go?"

"Yeah, I'm good," he assured me.

CHAPTER 24

Caleb

When Travis left his appointment that morning, he'd given me a tender kiss that promised so much more. It had made me think. I had been halfway through the day when I'd finally figured out that part of my hangup was that I hadn't been completely honest with Travis about my family and why I was so hesitant to go for what I needed.

The surprise Travis had promised had been pushed to the back of my mind as I tried to figure out how I was going to tell him about something I didn't ever talk about. When the waiter came around to take our order, I wasn't entirely certain what I'd chosen.

"I need to tell you something. Nothing bad, just… something," I said in a rush as soon as the waiter left the table.

Travis's brows furrowed and he leaned forward. "You've been quiet all evening, and I'd love to know what has you so lost in your head."

I closed my eyes and tried to figure out exactly where to

go from there. "People want to point to a bad childhood to try to find a reason for why someone is drawn to age play. But, like I told you before, age play seems to be something I've been interested in since a pretty young age. I really did have a great childhood."

Travis sat quietly, listening to everything I was saying. I knew I was explaining things out of order, and I hadn't given him a lot of context about where this conversation was going, but I needed to get it all out. The only person who even knew *most* of it was Dexter and that was because he'd lived a lot of it with me.

"My mom got sick when I was about fifteen. At the time, I was just coming to terms with my sexuality. Even though I'd never heard her say anything negative about gay people, I didn't know how she'd take it if I told her how I was feeling. She had enough on her plate dealing with her cancer diagnosis, going through chemo, and still trying to be there for me, so I never told her. I didn't want to burden her, and I didn't want her to be disappointed in me." My voice cracked as I finished the sentence, and Travis reached over to take my hand, offering me silent support.

I took a moment to compose myself. I didn't often think about the time when she'd been sick. I allowed myself to think of the time afterward even less. It always dredged up pain I wasn't sure I was ready to deal with even over a decade later.

"She died when I was going into my junior year of high school. After she died, my dad… changed. He'd never been the most attentive dad, but he'd never been angry like he was after her death. I always thought it was his grief over her death, so I stayed away as much as possible. It seemed like his anger was always directed at me. I spent a lot of time at Dexter's house. He was the first person I told I was gay."

Travis rubbed my hand slowly, silently supporting me and encouraging me to continue.

"When I went home, my dad tended to ignore me if he wasn't yelling at me, so I spent a lot of time in my room and on my computer. That was when I discovered the age-play community. For the first time in my life, I realized I wasn't alone. There were other people out there who shared my interests. That was when I discovered what a Daddy was, and I knew as soon as I saw the first pictures of a Daddy and his boy, it was what I needed to be happy."

Talking about discovering age play and Daddy kink was the easy part of this conversation, oddly enough. I let my eyes drift shut as I figured out where to go next. "So my senior year didn't get any better at home. My dad was even worse, honestly. I applied for college without his help or input. Dexter's parents actually took me in and helped me figure out where to apply, write my essays, and apply for scholarships. Dex and I were applying to the same colleges so it was easy enough for them to help both of us."

I played with my fingernail and waited for more words to come. Thankfully, Travis didn't rush me. Even as our drinks arrived, his attention stayed on me.

"I was surprised when my dad volunteered to drive me

to college because I hadn't spent any time with him in over a year. We'd just unloaded the last box into the dorm and he turned to me and told me not to come home again.

"I'd been dumbstruck, and I didn't understand. So he spelled it out for me. He told me that he couldn't support my immoral life. He couldn't accept having a deviant for a son."

I sighed thinking about the last conversation I'd had with my father. "He told me I'd never find someone who would want someone as broken as I was. Then he got in his car and left and I haven't seen or heard from him since."

Travis got up and came over to sit next to me. He pulled me into his side. "And Dexter was there to pick up the pieces."

It hadn't been a question, but I nodded. "He's been there every step of the way… like it or not."

"You don't need me to tell you that your dad was wrong. Maybe it was grief or maybe it was his true colors showing through, but either way he was wrong. You are perfect, just the way you are. Gay, little, dodi. There's not a single thing I'd change about you."

"Even my diapers?" *Shit, hadn't meant to ask that.*

Travis nodded without thought. "Diapers, dragons, or dinosaurs. Everything about you makes me happy."

I couldn't help but thank my lucky stars I'd found him. I didn't know how it had happened, but I'd found a man who accepted all the things about me that I'd struggled accepting for years.

I turned my head into his shoulder. "Thank you."

Travis paused for a moment while he gathered his thoughts. "Thank you for telling me that story. I understand so much better where you're coming from now. I couldn't imagine trying to come to terms with your sexuality and your kink and having your dad react the way that he did. I'm honestly shocked you're as open to exploring what you want as you are."

I felt myself smile. I'd long since accepted that I was a little, but I'd never allowed myself to believe that there was a man who would love me that way. My dad's words still echoed through my brain enough that I struggled with letting others see all of me out of a fear of rejection. I knew that for me being a little and wanting a Daddy were not bad things, but I also didn't know if I could handle it if someone made me feel wrong because of my desires.

Travis made me want more, and he made me feel like I deserved it. Looking at the strong, driven man sitting beside me, there was nothing that seemed odd or wrong about him or what he wanted, and he wanted me, just the way I was. He wanted me little and big and everything in between.

As his hold on me relaxed, so did the uncertainty that had wrapped around me for a decade. For the first time, I *felt* completely accepted by a lover. There was no hiding. No need to hide. Travis had just taken everything I'd just dumped on him, processed it, and told me exactly what Dexter had been trying to tell me since the afternoon I'd returned to our dorm room heartbroken and with tears

231

running down my face—my dad was wrong. But for the first time, I was at peace with it. I might never have closure with my father, and that old wound might reopen again in the future, but I would have a man by my side who would be there to close it up and make me whole again.

Travis moved back to his side of the table, and by the time our meals arrived a few minutes later, I was beginning to smile again. Looking at the steak and potato with some form of sauce on them, my mouth began to water. "I'll be honest, I don't even remember what I ordered. My nerves were all over the place."

"I can't imagine why." The smile in his eyes told me Travis was teasing and it made me feel better.

The first bite of perfectly cooked steak caused me to moan and my eyes to roll back slightly as flavors exploded in my mouth. Travis's eyes darkened. "You're enjoying that food a little too much, Caleb."

As I brought a second bite to my lips, a wicked thought crossed my mind. I opened my mouth slightly, allowing my tongue to dart out and wet my lips before I opened wider and slipped the bite into my mouth, closing my lips around the fork and pulling it back out as slowly as I could manage.

I'd always played it safe, stopping when I knew I was driving Travis nuts, not wanting to chase him away, but after our conversation, I knew he wasn't going anywhere. Now I wanted to see what I'd have to do to earn the spanking I knew would help settle the last of my nerves.

I sighed as I chewed the bite slowly and watched as

Travis scooted around on his chair trying to find some relief. He growled low in his throat and leaned over. "You need to behave, boy."

"What am I doing?" I looked at my plate, trying not to let him see the cheeky grin that was spreading across my face.

I played up eating and enjoying my dinner so much that by the time we ordered ice cream, even I was having a hard time sitting still. I totally forgot to be teasing when the chocolate ice cream drizzled with strawberry sauce and covered in slivered almonds came to the table.

I grabbed my spoon and slipped the first scoop into my mouth, moaning as the bite hit my tongue.

Travis groaned in frustration. "You are not listening very well tonight."

My breath hitched. "I'm sorry... Sir," I managed to get out. Definitely not what I wanted to call him, but it was more than what I'd managed previously. Thinking of him as Sir and not simply as Travis seemed to help settle some of my nerves. The way his eyes darkened and his voice deepened, I'd apparently said the right thing.

Travis nodded. "When we get home, I'm going to remind you how to listen." He leaned in close so he didn't have to raise his voice. "First, I'm going to lay you out. Then I'm going to pull down your pants and undies and turn your bottom a beautiful shade of red."

I had to bite the inside of my cheek to keep from moaning. "I understand, Sir." The word came out more easily that time and Travis seemed to be gaining confidence as he continued.

"Red looks so beautiful on you." He seemed to be talking to himself, so I didn't say anything and let him continue. "Yes… Red is a beautiful shade for your bottom. I love how heated your skin gets when it's been spanked."

I squirmed. If he kept talking about heated skin and spankings, I was going to cum sitting in the middle of a restaurant. I gnawed on my lip for a moment before finally nodding. "I've been naughty tonight, Sir. I think I need to be reminded to behave in the future."

Travis let out a groan that shot straight to my dick just as the waiter returned with our check.

CHAPTER 25

Travis

Caleb had been adorable throughout dinner. I'd enjoyed watching him push limits. At first, I hadn't realized what he was doing. Caleb was rarely stubborn or defiant, and I couldn't figure out what was going on. I'd thought maybe he was overwhelmed by what he'd told me or maybe he wasn't feeling well before I realized he was trying to earn a spanking. It was the first time he'd initiated any type of role-play and I loved watching him gain confidence throughout dinner.

By the time I'd threatened to spank him, he was clearly having fun tormenting me from across the table. He'd practically made out with his spoon and the ice cream as he'd eaten his dessert. If anyone could turn eating ice cream into foreplay, apparently my boy could. After he'd opened up about what had happened with his dad, I knew we'd had a major breakthrough in our relationship. There was no longer a question in my mind—Caleb was finally my boy.

As soon as the word "Sir" had passed his lips, the ideas

I'd had floating around my head for the last week came to the forefront—putting him over my lap and spanking him until he was right on the edge before laying him across the bed and fucking him.

His breathy response to my fantasy had me throwing enough bills on the table to cover the meal and a nice tip. It was so vivid in my mind I could almost hear his little moans and gasps as I spanked him. A picture formed of Caleb laid out on the bed, his red ass filled with a plug, and his skin glistening with oil as I massaged him. I knew exactly how I wanted the night to end.

Caleb laughed as I pushed back from the table and grabbed his hand, rushing us out to the truck before either of us could overthink our plans for the night. He giggled as we made our way to the door. "People are staring at us."

"Let them stare. They'd be rushing too if they had the same plans we did."

As we drove home, Caleb wiggled in his seat and nibbled at his lower lip as he thought about what we were about to do. "You were naughty at dinner, weren't you, boy?"

Caleb jumped slightly at the sound of my voice and his head snapped over to me. "Yes, Sir. I didn't listen very well. I'm sorry."

My dick got even harder in my jeans at his sweet words. "And what happens to naughty boys?"

"They get spanked," he told me as I pulled the truck into my neighborhood.

I nodded, forcing myself to focus on the road and not

the sexy boy next to me. "Do you get to cum during your spanking?"

Out of the corner of my eye I saw him shake his head.

"I need words, Caleb."

He squeaked, but finally found his voice. "No, I-I don't get to cum when you spank me."

"Good boy. Remember that."

"I will," he assured me, his tongue tracing his lip nervously as we pulled into my driveway. I wanted to lean over and take him right in my truck, but I had better plans for him, and his ass.

As we exited the truck, I pulled Caleb closer and squeezed his ass through his snug pants as I kissed him deeply. I loved how he leaned into me as we kissed. As I pulled back I gave his ass a light swat. "Where's your bag, baby?"

"My trunk," he answered automatically as he pulled his keys out of his pocket. He pushed the button on the remote to pop the trunk, and I swiped the bag out as we passed the car. We went inside through the garage, and I had to resist the urge to strip him down in the mud room, but if I did that, we wouldn't ever make it to the bedroom.

"Please go sit on the chair in my room. I'll be there in just a moment." Allowing Caleb to sit and wait would help build the anticipation and I hoped it would put him in the right headspace for his spanking. I needed just a few minutes to get everything I was thinking about ready.

Caleb walked toward my room while I followed behind him. When he took a seat on the chair, I continued on to the bathroom, finding the massage oil and the plug tucked safely away in a small tote in the back of the closet. I took the box back to the bedroom and set it on the nightstand.

Caleb was sitting patiently on the chair, his eyes cast downward and it didn't appear as though he'd noticed anything different in my room. Crouching in front of him, I put my thumb under his chin and pulled it gently up so he was looking me in the eyes.

"Time for your spanking."

CHAPTER 26

Caleb

Being laid out naked across Travis's lap was becoming a familiar feeling. What wasn't familiar was being in Travis's room and not mine. Also being across his lap while he sat in a chair instead of on a bed felt strange.

I was over Travis's lap, my hard cock wedged between his legs, as he massaged my ass. In the past, the biting pain of the smacks on my tender skin would change rapidly to a beautiful pleasure that erased every worry from my mind to the point that nothing mattered but my orgasm. This time, I was bent into what amounted to an upside down "V" and couldn't quite get comfortable.

When he seemed to decide I was in the right position, Travis squeezed my ass one last time. "Count your spankings, Cal."

"What?" I craned my head around to look up at him when the first crack landed across my ass.

"Count," he repeated to me.

"One."

He hummed in pleasure. "Good boy." A second spank landed in the same place.

My back arched up. The spanks seemed to sting more in this position, but I remembered to count. "Two."

The next three were softer, but they came in rapid succession and all on my left cheek. "Three. Four. Five." Numbers six and seven landed sharply on my right side, right where my cheek met my thigh. I yelped at the sting but still counted as expected.

By the time I'd counted to thirteen, the pain had been replaced with a desire to cum, and I felt my hips buck into the space between Travis's legs with each spank. I was starting to understand why I was in such an uncomfortable position. I knew it was one of the only things keeping me from cumming or slipping into that realm where nothing mattered.

The knowledge that I was draped over his lap and was being "punished" for misbehaving had added a whole new level of pleasure to the spanking. I should have been upset with myself for being naughty enough to end up over Travis's knee, but logic had left with the second smack. Instead of feeling guilt or shame, I felt loved and cared for. He cared about me enough that he wanted to help me remember to behave.

Counting had become automatic as I thought about how crazy hot it was to be spanked. I hadn't even realized the spanking, and my counting, had stopped until I suddenly felt only cold air running across my skin instead of the heat of new spanks. I forced myself to focus on what was going on in the room. I hadn't found that floating space where nothing mattered, and I was still firmly in reality. I definitely hadn't forgotten my erection trapped between Travis's legs.

"You did very well. I'm proud of you, Cal." His soothing voice washed over me, helping me forget the stinging feeling in my ass cheeks. "Can you sit up for me?"

I nodded and slowly maneuvered myself up with his help. Once I was finally upright again, large, protective arms wrapped around me and held me tight.

"How are you feeling?" A glass of cool water was brought to my lips. I didn't know where it had come from, but I was thankful to have it.

After a long drink, I smiled and nodded. "I'm good. Promise. My butt will feel it tomorrow, but I'm good.".

"Let's get you to the bed. I'll be able to make you feel even better there."

I snuggled into his arms and nodded. "Yes, please. But you're going to have to give me a push."

Laughter filled the room, but Travis gave my back a little push to get me standing. He didn't let his hands leave my sides as he gently guided me to the foot of the bed. "Lie on your stomach for me.".

I did as he asked, but I didn't know what to expect, so when cool lotion touched my warm ass, I felt myself flinch and tense up. "Sorry," he soothed. "This will make it feel better in the morning. You're usually pretty far out of it when I do this after a spanking," he mused mainly to himself.

Between the comforting words, the gentle massage my ass was getting, and the feel of the soft blanket under me, my dick was confused about how to react. It decided it wanted friction, and I thrust against the bed, moaning slightly as my cock dragged along the soft material.

A light smack to my upper thigh had me stopping in mid-thrust. "You don't get to cum yet. You need to wait."

I groaned and tried to relax. A finger ran down the crack of my ass, stopping at my hole, and I couldn't help pushing back against the finger slightly. "I'm going to plug that beautiful hole so you're ready for me tonight. I already know I'm not going to want to wait to prep you when we're done."

The words sent chills through my body and my ass arched off the bed. *Was it okay to beg to be plugged?* Because I needed to be plugged like I needed my next breath.

I heard lube pour from a bottle, and then I felt a thick finger press against my hole. I was so desperate to be filled, my body seemed to pull Travis's finger in immediately. There was no need to adjust, no need to wait. "More. Please. More." I was willing to do anything to get a second finger inside me as I used my hands to push my body, specifically my ass, toward his hand.

"Patience, my needy boy. I'll give you what you need." He pulled out of me, eliciting a groan when I felt the emptiness. Thankfully, the empty feeling lasted only a second before he sank back into me with two thick fingers.

"Oh…oh yes." I groaned at the fullness.

Fingers scissored and rotated inside me until I felt like I was more than ready for a third. Before I could say anything, his fingers left only to be replaced with the tip of a metal plug. The slicked metal slipped into me with ease, and I could feel how much thicker it was than his fingers had been. It caused a stretch as Travis pressed it in so it was properly seated. A gentle tug told him it was where he wanted it and sent sparks of electricity running up and down my spine. My body shook, and I felt a tingle in my lower back, a telltale sign that I was barreling toward orgasm.

I gasped. "Gonna cum." Thankfully, he stopped playing with the plug and waited for me to come back from the brink.

His next touch was to my back. "Good boy. I know that wasn't easy. You did great, though." His words sent a sense of pride coursing through me. "Roll over, Cal. I want you on your back. I don't think you're going to be able to hold off if I keep you on your stomach." He chuckled to himself, but I knew he was right. I was one thrust into the mattress away from cumming.

I'd already forced myself to push my boundaries to earn a spanking. I didn't want to end up with an actual punishment on the same night. I scrambled onto my back, and my cock swung proudly before finally settling along my stomach. As I settled back down on the bed, the plug pushed against my prostate, and I felt my cock straining again. I whimpered at the sensation.

Travis moved to the side of the bed. "You've definitely earned a reward tonight. You were so good during your

243

spanking, and you haven't cum yet, even though I know it's been hard."

I nodded my head rapidly. Rewards were good, right? If it weren't for the fact that my body was already singing from the spanking and the plug, I probably would have been more curious about what the reward was. As it stood, all I could think was a reward would likely lead to an orgasm. I desperately needed to cum.

He ran a hand lightly up my leg. "Tonight is all about us. I want to be able to touch you and feel you."

My body relaxed, I didn't care what he did with me, as long as I could feel his hands on me I'd be happy. "That sounds perfect."

"That's what I thought you'd say. You just lie there and enjoy."

CHAPTER 27

Travis

I poured some of the lavender oil I'd found into my palm and rubbed my hands together to warm it before finally touching his shoulders. Caleb let out a little sigh at the contact. I slowly worked the oil in, moving across his shoulders and down his arms, watching as his muscles rippled with each touch and squeeze.

I could see he was beginning to drift off as I worked on his arms and didn't want him to totally fall asleep on me. I added more oil to my hands and moved slowly down his chest.

Caleb gasped and his cock jumped as my finger ran from his sternum to below his navel before I flattened my hand and worked my way back up his body. I'd always appreciated the care he took to keep his body hair-free, but right then, I was even more thankful. I had miles of smooth, hairless skin to explore from Caleb's chest to his thighs. From the amount of precum leaking from Caleb's dick, I knew he was also enjoying the slow exploration.

When I needed more oil, I drizzled some out of the bottle, directly onto Caleb's abs. His muscles tensed and his cock jerked. "Fuck," I heard him gasp as he bucked his hips upward.

"Language." I watched a pink blush spread across his chest and up his neck. I may not be his Daddy yet, but I was going to show him that I wanted to be. If that meant reminding him to watch his language, I would do that.

He groaned. "Sorry."

He let out breathy moans and if there'd been an ounce of tension left in him, it was now gone. It was clear he was enjoying both the massage itself and the sensation of the oil on his skin. Watching Caleb fall apart as he gasped and bucked into the air while his cock dripped precum was stunning. Each time the plug moved in his ass, he'd moan, and I'd watch his cock spasm. One stroke would likely have taken him right over the edge. My dick was so hard in my jeans it was aching, and I'd barely started with him.

Goosebumps covered Caleb's arms and legs as my hands lightly trailed across his stomach, but he remained still. I moved down, almost touching his cock before sliding my hands over his hips and thighs.

Standing beside him as he was sprawled across the foot of the bed allowed me to easily skim my fingers from his knee to his groin and back down the other leg. As I worked, his moans became soft pleas for more. Each time I got close to his erection or allowed the oil to drizzle over his tight balls, his cock would jump. When I finally allowed my palm to run up the length of his cock, Caleb gasped loudly, and his hips bucked off the bed.

I looked down at him, his chest, abs, and dick glistening from the massage oil. I couldn't help but take a moment to appreciate how lucky I'd gotten when I'd hobbled into his office. I'd stopped moving my hands as I took his body in and apparently, the lack of contact was too much for my sweet boy to take.

"Please," he whispered.

"Please what, baby?"

"I—" he started but then stopped. "So horny." The ability to make a full sentence had escaped him and I felt a surge of pleasure in knowing I was the reason.

His admission made me want to wrap my hand around his cock and stroke him until he exploded. I knew it would only take a few strokes, but then I wouldn't be able to feel his body contract around me as he came.

"Let's take a shower, Cal."

Caleb reached out and took my hand, allowing me to help him up. The plug must have moved inside him because he gasped and bit his lip. When he finally opened his eyes again, he gave me a deliciously wicked grin. "I, yes. Like that."

When I had the water started in the shower, I reached for my shirt. "Can I?" Caleb's timid question took me by surprise, and as I turned to see him standing naked and aroused, I nodded. "Of course, baby."

He took two steps toward me until his hands grazed my

chest, and he skimmed his fingers lightly across my shirt until his fingers found the buttons. One by one, Caleb popped the buttons loose, exposing more of the gray hair on my chest with each button he undid. Once the last button was undone, he ran his hands up my stomach and chest, baring my nipples and running his fingers over them as he slid the shirt from my shoulders and down my arms.

Slowly, almost reverently, Caleb moved to the button of my jeans. He used both hands to unbuckle my belt and then worked on my button and zipper. By the time he knelt down to work the jeans down my legs, I was having a difficult time controlling myself, and he was out of breath from the plug nudging his prostate with every movement. I wouldn't last if Caleb paid the same amount of attention to my underwear as he had my jeans, so I guided him up using his elbows and leaned in for a kiss while I worked my briefs down my legs and kicked them to the side.

Thankfully, I was standing next to the sink and was able to rummage through the top drawer of the vanity until I found a strip of condoms and the bottle of lube while we were still locked in a kiss. Once they were in my hands, I walked us toward the shower. I pulled back from Caleb, gasping for breath, and swatted the side of his ass causing him to jump slightly.

"Travis!" he giggled as he rubbed the spot I'd swatted. I knew it hadn't hurt, and I'd been careful to not hit the tender flesh that had already been spanked.

"Get in the shower, or I'll spank the other side."

Caleb raised an eyebrow and appeared to be deciding if he was going to make me make good on my promise or if he was going to get in. Finally, he stepped in, wiggling his naked butt ever so slightly in my direction, the base of the plug peeking out from between his cheeks. I let out a low growl and roughly grabbed the base of my dick to stave off an orgasm.

As I joined him in the shower, I set the supplies on the shelf and grabbed the body wash and the new scrub I'd picked up at the store. Caleb was already under the far showerhead. His hair was wet and water was sluicing down the firm planes of his abs. I took a moment to watch him and gave myself a little pinch to make sure it was real.

He pushed the water from his face and opened his eyes a crack. When they settled on me, he smiled. "It's not fair. You look just as good wet as you do dry."

"Oh, my sweet boy, you have no idea how stunning you are right now." I stepped toward him as I clicked the lid of the soap open. "You are absolutely gorgeous all wet and wearing my marks.

Caleb ducked his head, but the smile on his face was obvious. I lathered the sponge and brought it to his chest, taking my time to wash the remnants of oil from his skin. I washed his chest and back thoroughly before dropping down to wash his legs. I cleaned his dick gently, aware of how his knees trembled and his abs quivered with each movement. When he bucked into my fist, I knew I had to stop.

I stood up again and moved him so he was facing the tiled wall. "Spread your legs for me." The command had barely left my lips when Caleb moved to comply, bracing himself on the wall with his legs spread slightly. I ran the sponge between his cheeks and nudged the base of the plug one more time.

He whimpered as I watched his legs shake.

"I gotcha, Cal," I assured him. I didn't leave my spot, but I reached over and grabbed the condom and lube from the shelf.

When he realized what I was doing, he pushed his ass back to bump against me causing us both to moan. "Let me get suited up," I teased as he impatiently wiggled his hips at me.

"Need to get tested," he complained as I worked the condom on. There was nothing about the statement I didn't agree with. We could go in the morning if that was what he wanted. For the time being, we had to deal with the condoms, but I was already sheathed and ready.

Gripping the base of the plug, I gave it a gentle pull and began easing it out of his body. The desperate moan he let out as the widest part slid from him went straight to my dick. Caleb was just as on edge as I was, and I knew this wasn't going to last long.

"Travis, please. I need you in me," Caleb begged as I set the plug aside and grabbed the lube.

The squelch could barely be heard over the running showerheads on either side of us, but I knew Caleb heard it when he moaned and wiggled again, his stretched hole pulsating as he waited for me to enter him. Placing a hand on his back, I steadied myself and used my free hand to guide my dick toward his entrance. As soon as the tip grazed him, Caleb's head fell forward and rested against the tiles, and his back arched to provide me with the best angle possible.

The plug had been in long enough that I slid in with almost no resistance and bottomed out in one long push. We both gasped as my balls hit his ass.

"Fast, please," Caleb begged me.

"Is someone being bossy?" I teased as I eased back and almost completely out of him.

His head bobbed up and down. "Yes. So bossy. You feel so good."

I pushed back in with more force, causing Caleb to arch off the wall and his shoulders to press against my chest. "Please, harder."

I wrapped my right arm around his chest and my left hand held onto his hip as I began to rock my hips in and out. Caleb's left hand clung to mine as his right braced him against the wall. He pushed back against me as much as he could with each thrust I made into him.

"You're perfect," I whispered into his ear before I sucked lightly at the tender skin where his neck met his collarbone. "And beautiful." I licked up his neck and nipped at his earlobe causing another shiver to run through his body.

"So close," Caleb gasped as I took a step closer, pushing him against the wall.

I could feel how close he was when his muscles began contracting around me, attempting to pull my orgasm from me. I finally reached around Caleb's waist and gripped his erection with my hand. In a matter of seconds, he was begging me to let him cum as he ground his ass against me. "Please. I need to cum. Please."

I grunted and almost agreed when Caleb continued. "Travis, please. I need to cum." I couldn't deny him or myself any longer.

"Cum, baby," I told him as I thrust into him over and over again.

Caleb screamed out, making me thankful we weren't in his shower where, at the very least, Dexter would hear him. His dick jumped in my hand and coated my fist and the wall before the water washed it away just as quickly. Feeling his release all over my hand pulled my orgasm from me, and I stilled as I filled the condom.

I sagged against Caleb's shoulder as he rested his head on his forearm and leaned into the wall as we caught our breaths.

"That was amazing."

There was nothing else to say, and I simply nodded my head. When I finally felt like I could move again, I gripped the base of the condom and pulled out, causing Caleb to inhale sharply. I kissed his shoulder. "Sorry, baby."

Caleb slipped under the spray again and rinsed off while

I tossed the tied-off condom into the trashcan and slipped under the opposite showerhead. "We need to get out of here and get you ready for bed. You're falling asleep."

Caleb looked at me with a lazy grin. "You're tired too."

I chuckled. "You're right, I am. I need to clean up a bit before bed. I think there are a few cartoon DVDs in the bedroom you can watch while I clean up." I reached over and turned off his showerhead then mine.

Caleb's eyes lit up. "You bought me cartoons?" His smile was genuine, and I was happy the impulse buy would bring him joy. "I think there's a dinosaur one and one about cars for sure. Maybe another one too."

"Dinosaurs!"

"Okay, PJs then cartoons. Once I'm done cleaning up, you can have your bottle, and we can go to bed." It wouldn't take long to strip the old blanket off the bed, take it to the laundry room, and clean up the massage oil, but if I didn't give Caleb something to watch, I was sure he'd fall asleep on the chair as soon as he sat down.

I could see the wheels turning in his head. Caleb wanted to help with cleanup, but he knew I'd tell him to watch his show instead. Finally, he nodded. "That sounds like the perfect end for tonight."

CHAPTER 28

Caleb

I was sitting in the same chair Travis had sat in earlier while I watched TV with my dodi and bear. I felt bad about not helping to clean up, but the one time I even thought about asking if I could help, he'd given me a look that said to not even think about going there. Instead, I kept my mouth closed and watched the dinosaur cartoon.

The only thing that would have made the night even more perfect would have been if I had diapers instead of training pants. I knew he wasn't turned off by them, and while he'd not brought them up, I had a feeling he'd had to have seen them in my room. They were hidden from view, but with any amount of looking, they could be easily found.

For years, the idea of finding a man that would be accepting of my little side was completely unfathomable. My dad's parting words to me had left me believing no one would love me. While I knew that wasn't true, I definitely hadn't seen how someone could love me and want me if they knew I liked to wear diapers. Since I'd been so convinced no one would accept little Caleb, I'd not even let myself think about the possibility of finding a Daddy.

But, sitting in Travis's room, I was realizing that the only thing holding me back from having exactly what I'd always wanted was my own hangups. Travis had bought me cartoons to watch because he knew I'd like them. He bought them for me even knowing that I liked diapers. With a start, I realized Travis had done all of this because he already saw me as his boy. He'd been calling me baby and his sweet boy for weeks but I'd never put it all together before then.

Looking back, there had never been a moment where Travis had even hinted that he wouldn't like me just as much in diapers as he did in underwear. The first time I'd let him see me in my training pants he hadn't batted an eye. He'd been more surprised by the rainbow hibiscus covering my upper arm than my choice of underwear.

It was too late in the evening to do anything about it, but I knew I was ready to let Travis seem me as little Caleb, diapers and all. Before I got emotional about it, I forced my attention back to the show. Within a few moments, thoughts of what it would be like to be little in front of Travis were replaced with the cartoon's characters. I was so drawn into the show, I'd even managed to ignore the sounds of Travis moving around the room.

"Cal, baby. Time for bed."

Travis's voice from beside me and his gentle hand on my shoulder brought me back to the room.

"What about the show?"

"You can finish it tomorrow. You've had a big day, and your eyes are drooping."

I couldn't deny that I was tired. Now that he'd brought it to my attention, I could admit I was exhausted. As I took his proffered hand, my eyes fell onto the bed and they misted over instantly.

My dodi slipped from my mouth and landed on the floor. "Travis…" I didn't know where to go with the sentence. A dragon-printed pillow was on my side of the bed and on top of it, a brand-new owl was placed carefully. I could tell from across the room that it's fur was soft. I turned so I could slip into his arms and allowed his scent and strength to wrap around me.

Without lust and thoughts of the future clouding my vision, I noticed the little things that had changed since the last time I'd been in here. The pillow and the stuffy weren't the only changes. There was a bottle on the nightstand that wasn't from my place, the small stack of cartoon DVDs on the top of the dresser hadn't been there before nor had the picture book.

Travis's room had always been immaculate and the picture of masculinity. This room, though, was filled with things just for me. He'd changed his room for me and I didn't have the words to describe how special that made me feel.

His hands rubbed up and down my back for a few minutes before he finally kissed my head. "Let's get into bed, Cal. When you're ready, you can tell me what has you so emotional."

I nodded and climbed onto the bed, crawling up to the top and waiting for him to join me. I grabbed my bear and the new owl that was just as soft as I'd expected it to be. He stooped down and grabbed my dodi off the floor, examining it for anything that might have gotten it dirty before he walked toward me and handed it over. To my surprise, he bent slightly and pulled a wooden safety-rail into place. It was almost exactly like the one on my bed, but this one was bright blue instead of brown. He'd really thought of everything.

Leaning over, I got the sweetest kiss from him before he swiped the bottle off the nightstand. As he climbed onto his side of the bed, he pulled me close so I was draped halfway over his lap. "Do you want to talk about what has you all teary-eyed?"

"You changed your room for me."

I felt him nod. "Of course I did. I want you to feel like this is your house too."

"But your room was beautiful and looked like it could be in a magazine before. Now it—"

"Is perfect. Before it was a place to sleep. Now I see the place where I get to share something special with my boy. The most important person in my life."

I had to blink back the tears stinging my eyes. I didn't know how much I could cry in one night, but he seemed to be determined to find out. "Thank you." I may not have been able to call him Daddy yet, but I tried to let my words convey my thoughts. It wasn't just the overwhelming sense of belonging, but the love and trust that came wrapped up with having a Daddy that I was experiencing. I knew then that Travis would be fine seeing me as little Caleb, and more importantly, I was ready for that step.

The way his arms stopped moving and his breath caught for just a moment told me he understood what I was trying to convey.

"No need to thank me, sweet boy. I want you here, always." I knew they weren't just words to him. It was too soon to say "I love you" but we'd both come about as close to saying it as we could.

He must have known I wasn't able to say much more because I felt the nipple of the bottle graze my lips, and I opened instinctively. A lot had changed that night, but this was the same as it was every night, solidifying in my mind that what we'd been building over the last weeks was real and wouldn't change.

I must have been both physically and emotionally drained because when I woke up the next morning, I didn't remember finishing my bottle. I was curled into Travis's side, his arms wrapped protectively around me even in his sleep, my dodi was between my lips, and both the owl and my bear were resting between my arm and his bare chest. My half-full bottle was sitting on his nightstand confirming that I'd fallen asleep quickly the night before.

Instead of overthinking everything that had changed, my mind drifted back to the cartoon I'd been watching. I wanted to know how it was going to end. I realized how right everything was in my life when I was thinking more about what was going to happen in a cartoon than worrying about if Travis would accept me when he saw me in my diapers for the first time. The answer was quite simple, I didn't worry about it because I *knew* he would. I couldn't help the smile that spread across my face or the little chuckle that escaped my throat.

A sleep-roughened voice interrupted my musings. "What's so funny?"

I giggled. "I was wondering what was going to happen in my cartoon."

"Why is that so funny?"

I felt the need to hide my face even though he couldn't see me. "Um, because I was more excited about that than I was worried about the rest of the weekend?"

Laughter bubbled from his chest. "My worrier. I think I should just say I'm glad and not overthink this one too much."

My head bobbed up and down. "Definitely."

"Well, how about I turn on the TV while I get ready for the day? Maybe we can go out for breakfast then pick up some stuff at your place so you can stay here this weekend?"

The hope in his voice made me smile. Travis didn't want me to leave any more than I wanted to leave. "I like that idea." And it gave me an excuse to gather my diapers from my house too.

Five minutes later, I was seated in the middle of the bed with a bowl of dry Cheerios, a sippy cup of juice, and a new blue dinosaur. It had been hanging out on the dresser, and I'd missed it the night before. Travis had remembered it and gave it to me that morning. I made a mental note to grab Branson when we went home so they could meet each other.

Thinking about bringing one of my stuffies to Travis's house made me smile. Thinking of spending more time here and less time at my house wasn't as scary as I thought it would be either. The only thing I was worried about was not getting to see Dexter as often. We hadn't been seeing as much of each other lately, but I'd always known he was just a wall away.

CHAPTER 29

Travis

Caleb had been all smiles from the moment he'd woken up. It was like a weight had been lifted off his shoulders. I wasn't sure what had changed since last night, but I could tell something was different with him.

I was going to continue to do everything I could to show him how I felt, even if that meant painting my room primary colors. If I could continue to get those adoring smiles and this carefree boyfriend, I'd do just about anything. I knew I loved him, but it was too soon to tell him, and I recognized that. I'd probably scare him off, even if he was feeling the same things I was.

Through breakfast, he'd smiled more freely than I'd ever seen and had had no hesitations about allowing me to order his meal for him. Caleb had even grinned when I'd asked the waitress for chocolate milk instead of coffee. I knew the lack of coffee would probably catch up with him later, but we had nothing planned, and he'd be able to take a nap when he got tired.

We did need to get to his place to get more of his things so he could spend the weekend. We'd never spent much time at my house, and I hadn't expected him to want to stay all weekend when I'd packed his bag the morning before. I'd brought up the idea of him staying casually, and I would have been happy to go back to his place, but he'd quickly agreed to stay another night.

My phone buzzed in my pocket, and I pulled it out to see a text from Dean. I couldn't help but sigh when I opened the message.

Dean: *Logan's latest GF broke up with him last night. We're going out tonight to try to cheer him up.*

Me: *They couldn't have been dating* that *long. I didn't realize there was a woman left within a 20 mile radius who hadn't dated him.*

Dean: *LOL! I was surprised too. You know how Logan is. He wants to go out.*

Me: *I'll talk with Caleb about it and see if he wants to go.*

"What's up?"

"Logan broke up with another girlfriend. The guys are going to go out tonight. Do you feel like going out with them?"

To my surprise, Caleb nodded eagerly. "I'd like that. Let's go."

I picked up my phone and typed a text to Dean asking him to let us know when and where and telling him we'd be there before I turned my attention to the breakfast that had just been delivered. The waitress chuckled as she set Caleb's drink down. "Sorry, I put in the order for chocolate milk and they put it in a kid's cup. Do you want me to change it out?"

"This is fine. It all goes down the same." The bashful smile that spread across his face was confirmation that he liked the mixup. Once the waitress left, I reached over and pulled his plate toward me so I could cut up his pancakes.

He picked up his cup and took a sip to try to hide his slight blush, but as I slid the plate back he muttered a barely audible, "Thank you."

"Anytime. Now eat up so we can go get your stuff."

Caleb had finished everything on his plate, and the waitress appeared as he was sucking the last drops of chocolate milk from the bottom of his cup with a loud slurp. She set the check on the table. "Well, since you've already got the cup, why don't I refill it for the road?"

Caleb blushed, but nodded. "Thank you."

By the time she returned with the refilled cup, I'd already left enough cash to cover the bill and tip, and we were ready to leave. Caleb didn't seem to know what to do with the cup as we stood up, so I took it from him as we left and didn't hand it back until we were in my truck.

"Did you enjoy your breakfast?" I questioned as I backed out of the parking space.

A grin split Caleb's face. "It was good. The chocolate milk is really yummy."

"I thought you'd like that. The cup was a happy mixup too." I reached over and squeezed his knee as he took another sip of his drink.

Caleb was squirming in his seat when we reached his house, the chocolate milk and his juice from that morning having gone to his bladder. I barely had the truck turned off when Caleb was running toward his house. The door was hanging open when I made it to the porch, still shaking my head in amusement. "I left Branson on the couch. Make sure we grab him. Charlie's lonely at your house."

Dexter must have heard us arrive because he followed me into the house. I couldn't help the amused chuckle that escaped at both the way he went running up the steps and his statement. But it left me wondering about who Charlie was. Before I could ask, Dexter was giggling, almost uncontrollably, beside me.

"Dex, quiet." I shushed him and called up the steps. "Baby, who's Charlie?"

"A guy from a movie we saw in high school. He had a mohawk and Cal had a huge crush on him."

"Dex! Quiet."

The toilet flushed and the sink ran for a minute, then Caleb came bounding down the steps. "The dinosaur you got me yester—" he cut himself off when he saw Dexter standing beside me. Caleb smiled seeing his best friend and I decided to give them a few minutes alone.

I gave him a kiss on his forehead. "I'll be upstairs packing things up for tonight. Holler if you need me."

I got a simple nod from him before I headed upstairs. On my way up the steps, I saw Caleb smack Dexter's arm. I didn't know why, but I figured Dexter probably deserved it.

I shook my head and began to focus on what Caleb would need. I didn't want to overstep, so I left the diapers under the bed alone and packed a few of his shirts, pants, and underwear for him to wear at my house.

I killed as much time as I could before I finally got curious about why Caleb and Dexter were so quiet downstairs. I found them curled on the couch. Caleb was tucked securely under Dexter's arm while they spoke quietly. I'd known they were close, so the affection didn't surprise or bother me. If anything, I was thankful Caleb had had someone to hold him close and give him what he'd needed before I came along. Despite being curled close, there was nothing about their body language that spoke of more than friendly intimacy.

"You know, your lease expires in two months." The way Dexter glanced up at me, I knew he was aware of my presence.

I cleared my throat before Caleb had a chance to answer. I didn't know if it was because I didn't want to hear him say it was too soon, or if I didn't want him to have to answer his nosy friend.

Caleb's head shot up and he smiled when he saw me standing there.

"I've got your stuff packed up. Do you have Branson?"

Caleb held up the green dinosaur and smiled at me. "He's ready to go to your house to hang out with Charlie." He turned to Dexter. "What about you?"

"What about me? I'm not going with you."

Caleb shook his head. "Sorry, that came out wrong. What will you do if I move out? We haven't lived more than two houses away from each other since we met."

Dexter's face softened, and he pulled Caleb closer to him. For as bouncy and mischievous as Dexter was, he was also a kind and attentive friend. "Cal, I knew one day we'd end up living away from one another. But that doesn't mean we won't still see each other or talk to each other. You've found your wings, baby bird."

Caleb seemed to choke up as he pointed to the wall behind him. "But you've always been right there."

Dexter squeezed Caleb's shoulders and kissed the top of his head. "But you have Travis now, Cal. I'll *always* come running if you need me, but I don't think you're going to need me like that very often."

I was about to tear up listening to Dexter's words. I didn't know if his talk would convince Caleb to move in with me in two months, but it really didn't matter to me if it took two months or two years, I'd be ready for him. Of course, I hoped it would be closer to two months.

"I'll think about it." It was far more than I'd expected, and I felt myself fill with hope that I tried to tamp down before it got out of control. I didn't want to end up pressuring Caleb into moving too fast.

Caleb pulled back from Dexter's embrace and gave him a quick peck on the cheek. "Thanks, Dex. Love you."

"I love you too, Cal. I always will. Now go with your man. He's looking impatient over there."

Caleb got up from the couch and headed toward me. "We're going out with his friends tonight."

"Well, have fun."

"Will you be okay?" Caleb questioned earnestly.

"Cal, I'll be just fine. I'm probably going to head out tonight too. I was actually just making sure you weren't going to be here alone. I need to get going." With another light kiss on the cheek, Dexter bounced out of the house. I started to follow before Caleb spoke up.

"Oh, wait! I almost forgot something." He handed me Branson and bounded up the steps like there was a fire under him.

"I'm going to drop this stuff off in the truck. I'll be right back." I was pretty sure Caleb called down a consent but it was muffled. I couldn't figure out where he was or what he was doing, but I headed out the door.

I hadn't even made it to the truck when my phone buzzed.

Dexter: *Don't let him convince himself he needs to stay here. He needs to be with you. I'll be fine.*

A funny winking face followed by an eggplant followed the first text.

Me: *TMI, Dexter. Caleb's his own man and can make his own decisions.*

Dexter: *If you wait for Caleb to decide to move in with you, you'll be waiting until you move into the old folks' home together.*

I laughed and pocketed my phone.

CHAPTER 30

Caleb

As soon as Travis had gone upstairs, Dexter leveled me with a serious look.

"You haven't shown him all of little Caleb yet, have you?"

"What do you mean?" I was perfectly content playing dumb, not that it would get me out of talking about it with Dexter, but I could at least try.

"You know damn well what I mean. You're still scared to show Travis your really little side, aren't you?"

"I'm not scared, exactly. It's just *big*." I didn't know how to explain it. He knew I liked diapers and I knew he liked that I did. It had just gotten out of control in my head.

Dexter pulled me into a hug. "I get that, Cal. You won't even let me see you in them, so I know this is huge in your mind, but you need to let him in. The way that man looks at you, I swear, you could wear nothing but diapers for the rest of your life and he wouldn't go anywhere."

I groaned at my friend, but couldn't help agreeing with

his assessment. I didn't know that it was in the way he looked at me, but I knew it was in the little things he did. Okay, big things… the big and little things he did. Like changing his room for me.

"I know, I know. Honestly, Dex, I know it's time. I just need to do it."

Dexter's mouth hung open. "Seriously? I didn't think you'd actually agree with me! Part of me thought that you'd go the rest of your life without ever showing anyone little Caleb!"

I smacked his arm again. "I'm not that bad! He changed his room."

"Huh?"

Not enough words. "Last night, I was there. He had cartoons for me and a new pillow and new stuffed animals. He even had a bed rail on his bed for me. I sat there and thought about it and I knew it was time to show him."

Before I could finish, Dexter threw his arms around me. "Oh, Cal, that's so great. He's going to be the perfect Daddy for you!"

I groaned, but I knew he was right. "I was going to take some… stuff… over to his house today."

"Do you need help picking things out to take?" The pure excitement in his voice should have annoyed me, but I knew Dexter was happy for me.

"I'm good. I think this is something I need to do for myself."

Dexter beamed with pride. "My Cal is growing up. Or is that down?"

I smacked him with Branson but couldn't help laughing myself.

Once he recovered from his own giggling fit, he decided it would be a good time to harass me about my lease. I'd been glad Travis appeared when he did, if he hadn't we were probably going to start discussing the long-term future and it was the one thing I wasn't quite ready to think about.

With Dexter gone, I needed to get upstairs and gather the stuff I needed for Travis's house. As I sat on my floor, putting bags of diapers and onesies into a box, I couldn't help but wonder how long it would be before Travis really was Daddy. Knowing that I was putting the diapers into the box told me well enough that I was ready to take that step. After it being such an unobtainable fantasy for so long I'd never thought of what it would be like to actually call someone Daddy.

How would I even know when the time was right?

In my gut, I knew whenever I chose to say it would be the right time for Travis. Truthfully, I'd rapidly reached the point of feeling like it was overdue as well.

I pushed the bags of diapers into the box, then folded the onesies carefully on top of them. I closed the box, tucking each end into the other like a puzzle before taking it down the steps.

I'd always found it humorous how the thing that made me feel the littlest weighed so much. The struggle to get the full box down the steps and to the door left me annoyed and glad that this was the only box of diapers I had at my house.

Travis was shaking his head at his phone with an amused smile on his face when I finally wrangled the box to his truck.

"What on earth do you have in there?"

I felt myself turn red. "Um… stuff?"

I watched Travis glance down at the box as he took it. Because I hadn't taped it shut, the top had opened enough that a package of diapers and my airplane onesie were visible. His eyes got wide and he looked at me trying to figure out if I was serious.

"I kinda thought they'd be better at your house." I chewed my lip nervously. This was so far out of my comfort zone I didn't even know how to talk about it with anyone but Dexter.

Travis set the box into the back of the truck and pulled me into a tight embrace. "I'm so glad you think so." He kissed my forehead. "Let's head back. I may have some surprises for you when we get there."

Surprises were enough to get me to hurry into the truck and buckle my seatbelt. Looking over, Branson was in the center seat waiting for me. I grabbed him and was ready for the trip back to Travis's.

CHAPTER 31

Travis

After we got back to my house, I climbed out of the truck as Caleb skipped up the driveway toward the front door with Branson in his hand. The only neighbor near enough to see my house with ease was Mrs. Taylor. She wasn't out, but I didn't think Caleb would have cared if she had been. His focus was completely on getting to see his surprise.

Once I opened the door, I let Caleb scurry in. "I'm going to unload the truck. Why don't you head to the living room? There may be a surprise in there for you, but you'll have to look around for it."

Caleb's natural curiosity took over, and he headed toward the living room while I went back to the truck to get his bag and the box. The box was deceivingly heavy, but I was able to get it to my room to unpack it and find a place for the items. If he wanted them here, I was determined to make sure he felt like his things belonged in the bedroom.

As I opened the flaps, I was curious about what I'd find.

I'd never seen the items in the box before. Aside from a glance at a package under his bed, I had made it a point not to snoop around in his things. Caleb had more onesies than I'd expected. There were easily over a dozen at the top of the box.

The brightly colored airplane fabric unfolded to be a long-sleeve onesie. The one below it, a gray short-sleeved onesie, had a giant dragon on the front. I started laying them on my bed as I unfolded them, enjoying the little pieces I was learning about Caleb in the process.

Most of the onesies were fairly plain and could be worn with a pair of jeans and no one would ever know he was wearing a onesie. Some of the others ended up being one piece shorts suits I knew would show off whatever diaper he was wearing. Before unpacking the diapers, I took the time to hang his clothes in my closet next to my work shirts. I got lost in enjoying the bright colors and soft textures of his stuff next to my pressed dress shirts and jeans.

I finally had to pull myself away and address the diapers I hadn't unpacked. I found them to be just as unique as Caleb's onesies. The first bag was bright and printed with rainbows and unicorns. The next pack were basic white diapers. The next two were more muted patterns, but still colorful. I wasn't sure where to keep them, though. Another trip to the store for some buckets or maybe a new shelf system for my closet was in order. Until then, I didn't want him to feel like we were hiding them or that I didn't want them in the room. I finally decided to put the diapers on the floor by the bathroom door before I broke the box down to take it to the garage.

I made it all the way to the steps before I realized the living room was shockingly quiet. I'd expected to hear blocks being moved around at the very least. I headed down the steps and stuck my head around the corner to peer into the living room. Caleb was sitting on his knees in front of the toy box. His hands were braced on the edge, and he wasn't moving.

I set the box down, completely forgetting about taking it to the trash. "You okay, Cal?"

His head whipped around to face me. "Y-you bought me toys?"

I nodded. "I hope you like them. We can go back to the store and pick out more together. I didn't know exactly what you'd want." It was then I noticed the tears streaking down his face as he looked into the box.

I walked over and knelt beside him, placing a hand on his lower back. "Are you okay, sweet boy?"

He nodded and swiped at the tears. "You bought me toys."

It wasn't a question that time, but I answered anyway. "Yes. I want you to feel comfortable spending time here."

A dam seemed to open as he threw his arms around me and pushed his face into my neck. I had to fight to keep my balance, but eventually I was able to ease us both down so I was sitting on the floor rubbing his back. "Do you like them?"

Caleb nodded rapidly. "They're perfect. Thank you."

There was something he wasn't telling me, but I couldn't even begin to unpack what it was. I leaned forward and pressed a kiss to Caleb's forehead. "Now, how about you play for just a few more minutes, and I'll be back for you."

He nodded as he looked back at the toys in the box. "Thank you, really."

"I meant it, Cal. I want you to feel like this is your home as much as your own is. I want you here."

He grinned before turning his attention back to the toys.

I ran my hand through his hair as I stood up, thankful my ankle was no longer a constant source of pain. Caleb was just as good at his job as I was at mine, and I was thankful because I had a feeling he was going to keep me on my toes for the foreseeable future. Hopefully, the rest of my life.

"I'll be right back, baby." I needed to get the box to the trash or it would drive me crazy for the rest of the afternoon. I didn't want anything to distract me from spending time with Caleb as he explored the toys at my house for the first time. I had no other plans until we had to get ready to meet the guys that evening.

By the time I returned, Caleb had spread his blocks across the floor so they created a track for his cars to follow. He was lying on his stomach as he zoomed a car around the track. I took a seat on the couch and watched him play.

He'd let himself drift into his little space fairly easily that afternoon. I wasn't sure what it was, but something had seemed to tip him into that headspace easily. He'd played fairly quietly for almost half an hour before his glances toward the steps began.

At first, they were quick glances that I'd been able to brush off. They almost looked like he was looking for me. But they slowly became longer and more pointed. I could see questions starting to form in his eyes. Admittedly, it took me too long to piece together what Caleb was thinking about.

Once I realized he was glancing at the steps, up to the room where I'd taken his box, I knew what I needed to do. It was the opportunity I'd been waiting for. I needed to put on my Daddy hat and take the uncertainty away from him. "Cal, baby." My voice caused him to snap his head toward me. "Let's go upstairs for a few minutes. We'll come right back down so you can play. Don't worry about cleaning up."

He hesitantly climbed to his feet and took my hand, apprehension evident on his face.

Kissing the tip of his nose, I tried to take away some of his fear. "It's okay, sweet boy."

We walked quietly up the steps and into my room. He sat nervously on the bed. I don't know what he thought was going to happen, but I swiped his dodi from off the nightstand where I'd put it earlier in the morning.

Once he had his dodi in his mouth and his teddy bear in his arms, I headed to the closet. When I returned, Caleb was staring at the bags of diapers lined up by the door. As he saw me coming out of the closet holding one of his short-style onesies, Caleb's eyes widened.

276

"I'm pretty sure this is what you've been thinking about for the last half hour, and probably for the last month and a half."

The dodi started moving in and out of his mouth rapidly as he watched me set the outfit on the bed. I watched him carefully for any signs that I was misreading his desires, but he just continued staring at me as I looked over the packages of diapers, deciding which one to put on him. I finally reached for one of the brightest.

Caleb's eyes closed, but I didn't stop. "You have your safewords, Cal."

He nodded rapidly, but his eyes remained shut.

"These are quite cute," I told him with a smile.

His eyes cracked open enough that he could see which one I was holding. "They only come out once a year for Pride," he mumbled around the pacifier in his mouth.

"They're adorable." I set it on the bed and took a minute to find the container of baby powder I had in the bathroom, but I was back by his side a few moments later. He'd not moved, though he was looking at the diaper like it might bite him.

He was nervous enough that I started to worry I was pushing him too far. "What color are you, baby?"

Caleb blinked up at me in confusion for a moment before seeming to process what I'd asked. "Green."

I wasn't going to give him time to second guess what we were doing. I reached for his T-shirt and guided it over his head. "Lie back for me, Cal."

He flopped back onto the bed. Caleb lying across the bed in the same place where I'd massaged oil into his skin the previous night was every bit as erotic and gorgeous as he'd been then, just in a different way. With his dodi and bear, a thick diaper and a cute one piece outfit on the bed beside him, he was the picture of innocence, but his well-trimmed beard and firm muscles were a beautiful contrast to the innocence.

I worked his pants and training pants down his legs and pulled them completely off his legs. I tossed the undies into the hamper. My boy was clearly nervous because he would normally be hard as a rock at the mere thought of me undressing him, but he was soft and that didn't appear to be changing as he lay naked on the bed.

I picked up the baby powder and dusted it across his front. Even as I was coating his dick and rubbing it into his balls, Caleb remained soft. I wiped the excess powder off on my pants, not worrying about the white stains that would come out in the wash and grabbed the diaper from beside him.

"Still green?"

He nodded slowly. "Yes, green."

That was all I needed to hear and unfolded the brightly patterned diaper. "Lift your hips up." Caleb reacted quickly, his body remembering the steps even if his nerves were not as certain. I centered the diaper under him and tapped the side of his leg. "Back down." He collapsed quickly, his eyes peeking hesitantly at what I was doing once the front was pulled up and smoothed over his stomach. I pulled each of the four tapes into place while he watched carefully.

Caleb hadn't moved while I'd diapered him, but by the time I was grabbing the outfit, he was watching me closely. I hoped that I was showing him I was okay with his diapers. The only nerves I had about the entire situation were strictly related to how he would react.

I took his hand and helped him to sit up so I could guide the shirt over his head. He pushed each of his arms through the holes as I held them open and lay back again so I could finish getting him ready. He lifted as needed, and waited patiently for me to secure each of the five snaps.

Once I was done and he was again covered, his muscles were no longer so tense, he wasn't sucking as furiously on his dodi, and the death grip he'd had on his bear had loosened. I hoped the day would come when Caleb didn't feel nervous about letting me see this side of him.

"You're so beautiful." The words slipped out without any input from my brain and caused him to blush and shake his head.

"It's the truth. You look so sweet lying there in your cute outfit with the alphabet on it and your thick diaper."

Now that he was in his diaper and dressed again, the fear he'd had earlier was being replaced by arousal. I didn't know if it was from the feeling of the diaper rubbing against him, or the fact that my own erection had to have been visible even through my jeans. Whatever the cause, I could see Caleb getting hard. Even the thick padding wasn't enough to hide it.

I reached down and patted the front of his diaper, feeling his hard length under the padding. "When you're diapered, there's no playing with yourself. Do you understand?"

Caleb groaned. The sound was something between frustration and excitement. "That's not an answer, Cal. Do you get to play with yourself when you're diapered."

He groaned again but shook his head. "No."

"Next time you cum, it's going to be under my terms."

"Fuuuck."

I smacked his thigh. "No bad words."

He flushed but nodded in understanding. I knew we needed to get out of the bedroom before we were both too turned on to leave without one of us cumming in our pants. While it would be fun to watch him lose that control, I was supposed to be the Dom, I couldn't be walking around with cum-stained pants all afternoon and still be taken seriously.

"While I could watch you lie here all afternoon, I'm pretty sure I told you we could go back downstairs so you could keep playing with your toys." Reminding him his toys were waiting for him in the living room had Caleb nodding eagerly and a small smile breaking from behind his dodi.

"Well, let's go, then." I waited until he was holding my hand and we were on our way to the steps before I continued talking. "When you're wet, you can let me know, and we'll get you changed and ready for a nap."

Caleb's eyes widened in surprise and his voice cracked slightly. "Wet?"

"Yes, sweet boy. There's no need to hide it. When you're

wet, I'll get you changed and then you can nap for a bit before we have to leave." Truthfully, I would probably nap too.

CHAPTER 32

Caleb

The mortified feeling I'd had when we first went back to the living room had subsided greatly as I played with my toys. Finally being back in diapers was a balm to my soul I hadn't realized I needed. I'd been so worried for so long about what Travis would think when I finally let him see me in them that it seemed almost anti-climactic now that it had happened.

The diaper under my pants crinkled loudly as I moved around grabbing toys from the bucket or moving them around the table. Adult thoughts had slipped from my mind almost as soon as I'd sat back down. A few minutes after I was playing again, my dragon sippy cup appeared in front of me filled with apple juice, and a plate of fruit and veggies was placed on the other side of me.

The few times I looked up from where I was playing, Travis was sitting on the couch watching me play with a content smile on his face. I thought it would have been boring to watch me play with toys, but he didn't seem to

282

mind. Had I not sunk so fully into little space as quickly as I had, I probably would have noticed that my sippy cup was refilled as soon as I'd finished it. I'd managed to forget about the thick diaper crinkling under me, and I definitely wasn't thinking about how much I was drinking or how long I'd been sitting there.

I'd moved the blocks up to the coffee table and it was almost completely covered when I noticed my bladder was full and, just as quickly, it began to empty. It wasn't until I was already wet that I remembered Travis had never seen me with a wet diaper. It had taken years for me to get to the point that I could wet a diaper without much thought, and I'd never expected that habit to come back so quickly when someone else was around.

As I got nervous about what Travis would say, a little voice in the back of my head told me he had expected it and, in a way, encouraged it as we were coming downstairs. There wasn't much I could do about it anyway because I was already wet and my toys were still calling my name.

Of course, with the warm, wet material pressing against my dick and balls, every movement reminded me of the diaper hugging me. Before long, I was wiggling needlessly as my cock began to thicken.

Travis's voice cut through my thoughts after a few minutes. "Cal, do you need to go potty?"

That was easy to answer. "Nope."

"Then stop wiggling."

"Sorry." I focused back on my blocks again, pushing the wooden cars across the table.

I got lost in my toys, but I must have continued to wiggle because Travis's exasperated voice behind me caused me to jump slightly. "Cal, you're wiggling like you have ants in your diaper."

The cycle seemed never ending. Travis would remind me to stop, I'd focus back on my toys, and the next thing I knew, Travis would be reminding me to sit still again.

I lost track of the number of times he'd reminded me to stop moving around but when I was no longer able to sit still, even after being told to stop, Travis finally sighed. "Come over here, little one." He was exasperated with me, but I was too aroused at that point to care about not listening.

I headed over to the couch and climbed up so my legs were draped over his lap and my head was resting on his shoulder. At least in that position, the swollen material was pushed against my groin providing constant stimulation, and I didn't feel the need to wiggle quite as much.

"I think my boy needs to go potty."

I shook my head. "Nope."

His hand snaked between us and came to rest on the front of my diaper, likely expecting it to still be dry. His hand pressing against my already hard dick had me grinding into his touch. A rich laugh filled the room. "Well, I read those wiggles wrong."

I nodded and pressed my cheek into his shoulder.

"You aren't supposed to be playing with yourself. Did you forget that?"

"Sorry. I didn't even realize I was!" It wasn't a lie, I'd been oblivious to the movements I was making until he'd bring them to my attention.

He shook his head, but I was pretty sure I saw a twinkle in his eye that said he was more amused than upset. "If you can't control your wiggles when you're in your diapers, we may need to look at getting you a cage."

A moan escaped my lips and my hips bucked upward of their own accord.

"And it seems you like that idea." I should have been worried about how much desire I heard in his voice, but right then, all I could think about was how hard my cock was and how much I wanted to cum.

Forcing my brain to find words, I was proud of myself when they finally came. "Can't cage an already hard cock."

"Cheeky boy. You better get upstairs before I decide to put a cockring on you and leave you hard and needy for a while."

"No, no, no, no. Need *your* cock in me!" I scrambled off his lap, leaving my toys on the table, and hurried up the steps to our room. I was already lying across the bed by the time he got upstairs. It had been torture getting up the steps and onto the bed with my bulky diaper, and the urge to jerk myself off was getting harder and harder to resist.

I must have looked as desperate as I felt because Travis started laughing as he entered the room. "You are something else. Let me get the wipes and a new diaper, and I'll be right back."

The whimper that escaped my throat at the thought of having to wait any longer was totally unintentional and far from attractive.

"Patience. It will be worth it."

He grabbed the bottle of lube, a condom, and a pack of wipes I hadn't seen before and was between my legs in seconds. As he unsnapped the crotch of my outfit, I became embarrassed to be lying in front of him in just a wet diaper and a onesie shoved up on my chest. Travis must have picked up on my discomfort because his hands began trailing up and down my thighs.

"I bet you don't have any clue how gorgeous you look right now. Your shirt pulled up and your stomach exposed." His fingers grazed the waistband of my diaper "You lying there, so beautifully, waiting to be changed." He pulled the top tab and the sound seemed deafening in the room.

"I love when you let me take care of you." He bent down and kissed my lips to emphasise his point. "It doesn't matter if it's holding your bottle, cutting your food, or changing your diaper. Each time you trust me with another part of you, I feel that much closer to you."

I tried to blink back my tears, but the sweet words had them brimming in my eyes and spilling over. He really did enjoy it. And he liked me just as much in the thick diaper as he had in my training pants. I knew then I'd found my Daddy. Travis was the man I'd been so certain didn't exist. I wanted to cry, and I wanted to laugh.

I swallowed as much emotion as I could. Despite wanting to scream it from the top of the roof, it wasn't the right time to say it. Not while we were about to have sex. "You take good care of me." That wasn't what I'd wanted to say but thankfully, he seemed to understand because I got another kiss as the second tape loosened around my waist and my dick was finally able to move. I thrust upward, barely making contact with his stomach, but it caused me to groan.

I took a second to clear my head and find what I felt like I needed to say to him. "You're the only person I could ever think about sharing this side of myself with."

Travis pushed my onesie up higher and bit down on one of my nipples causing me to arch off the bed. He pulled the outfit over my head and tossed it to the side, taking in my body. "Damn good thing, because I'm not good at sharing."

I giggled at his possessiveness. Some people might not understand how important and loved his attention made me feel, but it never failed to turn me on, and it was driving my desire to have him inside me even more. "Not going anywhere," I assured him as he freed the last two tapes of my diaper.

He stepped back for just a moment as he reached for a wipe to clean my skin off. I shivered as it touched my overly heated skin, but even the cold didn't affect my raging hard-on, though it did make it jump and gave me goosebumps.

Watching Travis make sure my skin was clean and dry before he wadded up the diaper to throw it away just reinforced how seriously he took his role as caretaker—as Daddy. He was perfect. He could have so easily tossed the diaper to the side and slid into me and I wouldn't have cared or even realized what I was missing. But watching him refrain from turning into a caveman, putting his wants and needs aside, to make sure I was taken care of struck a chord with me. When he returned to the side of the bed he was already naked, and I couldn't help but smile at him. I hoped it wasn't as watery as it felt, but the odds were my emotions were clear on my face.

"You really are my sweet boy." The almost reverent quality in his voice was addicting, and I knew I'd do just about anything to hear it for the rest of my life. I had to force the thoughts out of my head before I got overly emotional again.

Thankfully, a slick finger pressing against my hole quickly chased any emotional thoughts out of my head. In a matter of seconds, there was a finger in me, swirling and twisting and I was a writhing mess on the bed.

He worked quietly, rubbing my thigh or stomach with his free hand as he methodically stretched me until three fingers were moving inside me with ease. When they slipped out of me, I heard myself groan, instantly missing the fullness.

Travis pulled the condom open using his teeth and the cleaner of his two hands. It took him a moment to roll the condom on. I heard the snick of the lube bottle opening and shutting before Travis's dick was at my entrance. His head slid in with ease, my body ready and eager for him. Moving slowly, he gradually worked his way into my ass. Tender kisses peppered my jaw and chest while his cock remained firmly seated inside me. It was clear he planned to take his time with me.

This—the feelings, the attention, the contentedness to just *feel* each other's bodies—was making love. Time could have been standing still or going at light speed, and I wouldn't have known the difference.

By the time Travis began moving again, I'd almost forgotten his cock was buried in my ass. That changed quickly as he slid against my prostate, setting nerves alight and causing me to gasp into his mouth. "Feel good?"

Did he really need to ask that question? I nodded and rocked my hips so they met his incoming thrusts. "So good." I had no idea how long we stayed in that position, need and desire building gradually as he worked his lips from my nipples up to my mouth and back down. I was going to have hickies all over my chest and neck, but I couldn't bring myself to care. There were plenty of collared shirts I could wear while the marks lingered on my skin.

Eventually, I began to grind my hips upward with each thrust of his hips. The motion allowed my cock to drag between our bodies, bringing me closer and closer to orgasm. I was almost incoherent with my pleas by the time Travis put his hands under my ass and pulled me to the edge of the bed.

The new angle allowed Travis to hit my prostate with every movement causing my babbling pleas to turn into screams and begging for him to touch my cock. It would only take a few strokes and I'd explode, but Travis wasn't ready for it.

Beads of sweat were gathering on his chest and forehead as he picked up his pace. The torturously slow love making had been abandoned for fast, furious bucks of his hips. "Do you want to cum?"

"Yes, dammit!"

A sharp smack to my left hip had me gasping for breath. "Language," he reminded me with a growl.

"Want... need... cum... please!" I screamed when I couldn't take it any longer.

A large hand wrapped around my cock as he slammed into me again and again. "Cum for me, beautiful."

He didn't even have a chance to finish the sentence and I was exploding all over his hand and my chest. Travis pushed into me two more times before I felt his cock pulsate then his body shook as he stilled.

My body was still humming with pleasure as he slid out of me and leaned down to kiss me. "You're so beautiful, Cal. I don't know how I got so lucky, but you're everything I've ever wanted. Thank you for sharing your desires with me."

"Thank you for understanding." My face scrunched up as I felt the cum cooling between us.

"I'll get you cleaned up." He kissed my cheek and got up to get a washcloth.

In minutes, I was cleaned up with a new diaper taped securely around me.

CHAPTER 33

Travis

Caleb's eyes were getting heavy by the time he was diapered, but he didn't seem quite ready to sleep. "Can we read the book you bought?"

"Sure, sweet boy." Before grabbing the book from the nightstand, I pulled the rail up on his side of the bed. It didn't matter that he'd only slept in my bed twice, it was already his side.

With the book in hand, I climbed into the bed and propped the pillow up behind me. As soon as I held out my arm, Caleb snuggled in close and let out a contented sigh. He had his bear in one arm and the owl in the other. I wasn't sure where he'd found his dodi, but it was in his hand.

"Shoot, I forgot a bottle."

Caleb shook his head. "It's okay. Just need you."

I kissed his forehead and opened the book about dragons. I'd only read a few pages when Caleb scooted himself so he was draped across my lap, his head on my chest while he watched the pages. By the time I read, "The End," he'd gone quiet and hadn't moved for a few minutes. I'd thought he'd fallen asleep about four pages back, and was resigning myself to being stuck half seated in bed while he napped.

I was surprised when his head came up off my chest and he gave me a small kiss on the cheek. But when he spoke, I was struck almost speechless. "Thank you, Daddy."

My vision blurred as tears sprang to my eyes, and I fought to keep them back. That one word held so much love and trust it was hard to explain how hearing it from my sweet boy made me feel. With great difficulty, I managed to get words out around the lump in my throat. "Oh, Cal. You're welcome." I didn't say more because I knew my words would be broken and halting.

With one word, everything in my life changed. I hoped I'd always be able to make my boy feel as special as he'd made me feel, and I was more determined than ever to not do anything to mess that up.

As I loosened my grip on Caleb and pulled back so I could see him more clearly, I noticed the surprise in his eyes. He gave me a shy smile and a whispered almost reverent, "Daddy," escaped his lips.

I didn't want him to think for even a second that I didn't cherish the word and what he'd finally found the courage to say to me. "Yeah, Cal, Daddy's got you." He leaned his head back against my shoulder and breathed deeply. As he relaxed into me, I let us both stay like that for a few minutes while my hand ran through his hair and down his back. He didn't seem to be in a rush to pull away, and I wasn't in a hurry either.

When he finally pulled back, he smiled then laughed lightly. "Dexter's going to be so proud of me."

I fought a laugh of my own. "Yes, he will."

Caleb fell asleep quickly after that. I hadn't had the heart to move him, but at least we'd slid down slightly in the bed so I was no longer sitting upright and was a lot more comfortable as I drifted in and out while he napped mostly on my chest. I didn't really care if we made it out or not. I had my boy in my arms and nothing else mattered to me.

Unfortunately, what felt like all too soon, Caleb began to stir awake. His head tilted upward and his eyes cracked opened slightly. He smiled lazily then seemed to tense.

I wrapped my arms tightly around him. "Whoa, baby, tell Daddy what's going through that head of yours."

He buried his head in my chest. "That wasn't a dream, was it?"

I had a feeling I knew what he was talking about, but I wasn't going to give him an easy out. Caleb needed to hear himself say it enough that he'd understand I cherished the word. "Not enough words, Cal. Want to try that again?"

He huffed but moved his head so he could speak clearly. "I really called you Daddy, didn't I?"

I nodded. "You did. And it sounds even better when you say it and you aren't half asleep."

I didn't even have to see my boy's face to know he was

blushing, I could feel the blush against my chest. He took a few slow breaths before saying the next thing on his mind. "You don't care?"

It was hard to stifle the laugh that wanted to escape, but I knew it would do far more harm than good. "No, sweet boy. Quite the opposite. I love hearing you call me Daddy. It's such a special word, especially from you, and I'll cherish each time you say it."

Caleb tilted his chin upwards so he could look me in the eyes. When he spoke, his voice was more confident than it had been. "I like saying it." He paused briefly before adding a quiet, "Daddy."

I couldn't help but kiss him. I was happy staying where we were for the rest of the night. I had my boy in my bed. There was nothing more I needed in my life. Of course, Caleb lifted his head and looked at the clock. "We need to get ready to go. It's getting late."

I grumbled and reluctantly let him out of my arms, but not before planting a few more kisses on him that promised more.

CHAPTER 34

Caleb

Meeting up with Travis's friends that evening felt much less daunting than it had when we'd gone to Steve's. Maybe it was because I'd already met them or maybe it was because it wasn't Travis's parents' bar and I didn't have to worry about seeing Steve and Delilah. Odds were, it was a combination of both, plus I was walking in knowing I was holding my Daddy's hand.

Dean was the first one to greet us when we arrived. He'd been standing at a high-top table watching the group of men who surrounded a blond mop of hair that was unmistakably Logan.

Dean didn't turn to us, but he clearly knew we were there. "He's going to be feeling this one tomorrow."

"Who was he dating? I didn't even know he was dating someone."

From the looks of it, Logan wouldn't even remember dating the woman the next morning. It was hardly nine and he was well on his way to wasted.

Dean shook his head. "No clue. He was bitching about someone named Aubrey or Andi or Amy? Ugh, it started with an A. How long do you think it's going to take for someone to have to carry him out of here?"

"Knowing Logan as well as I do, a long time. Though I feel bad for Trent. You know he's going to be the one to have to take care of his drunk, hungover ass tomorrow. Speaking of drinking, I'm going to get a drink for Caleb and myself. Do you want anything?"

"Nah, I'm good. I'll keep your boy company while you go to the bar."

Travis quirked an eyebrow in my direction, a silent question to make sure I was okay staying with Dean.

"Sounds good to me. This place is packed, and I'd rather have a chance to keep our table."

Travis squeezed my hand reassuringly and leaned over to give me a quick peck on my temple. "I'll be right back, baby."

I felt myself flush. As soon as Travis was out of ear shot, Dean leaned forward slightly. "He's been one of my best friends since I was about seventeen. He's a good guy. I've been waiting for him to find a guy like you for a long time. Someone who makes him happy. You do that."

I furrowed my brow while trying to decipher what Dean meant.

He smiled comfortingly. "At work, Travis is a bit of a control freak. He can also be a bit intense and it's run a number of guys off in the past. I'm glad to see you're not intimidated by his need to... care for his partner."

I laughed. "He's not *that* bad, though. He just likes to know I've got what I need."

Dean threw his head back and laughed. "That doesn't surprise me. I think you've got him wrapped around your little finger."

Was there a right way to respond to that statement? "I like that about him."

He nodded in understanding and was quiet for a brief second. "I figured you did. Those assholes"—Dean pointed over his shoulder to the group of men in the middle of the room—"are some of the most accepting men I've ever met. Don't be ashamed of what you and Trav are building. As someone who's known Travis for fifteen years, I've never seen him this happy or relaxed. What you two do behind closed doors is your business, but seriously, keep it up."

"Thanks."

Dean leaned in closer to me, yet still kept an eye on Travis. "Listen, I just want to tell you not to worry about what you call him around me. In my past life, I was a Daddy Dom too. I understand and I won't judge."

My eyes widened. I should have been mortified that Dean told me he knew Travis was my Daddy, yet I could only think about one thing. "In your past life?" How did someone just give up being a Daddy? Wasn't it in their DNA or something?

Dean laughed, but it was forced and almost bitter. "I guess that's the wrong way to put it. If I ever had the opportunity again, I'd love to be a Daddy, but I don't see that happening."

I wanted to ask more questions about what he'd said, but I got the feeling he didn't want to talk about it. I forced myself to change the subject. "So, if you know Travis is a Daddy, you probably know a lot more about my life than I care to imagine right now."

Laughter sparkled in Dean's eyes. "Probably. But don't worry about who you are. You and Travis are perfect together and that is all that matters."

"And you don't mind?"

He shook his head. "Not in the least. Just keep doing what you're doing. It's good for Travis. He thrives on being able to care for someone."

"Oh… okay." I had no clue where to go from there, but thankfully, I didn't have to figure out anything else to say because Travis reappeared with two beers and handed one to me.

Travis looked at me closely then looked over at his friend. "Dean, what did you do to my boy?"

Dean's hands went up in mock surrender. "Nothing. I just told him that we were glad you'd found someone that makes you happy."

Knowing Dean was likely just as kinky as we were, I didn't feel so bad teasing slightly. "Oh no, that's not what you said. You told me he's a controlling micromanager and you're glad he finally has someone to focus that energy on."

"Dean, you're not supposed to scare him away."

Dean winked. "Oh, believe me, I don't think I came anywhere near scaring him away."

I shook my head. "Nope, I'm here to stay."

The arm that snaked around my waist and pulled me close told me better than any words could that Travis felt the same way. The gentle kiss he placed on my lips had me melting into him slightly and sighing. "I'm glad to hear that because I don't plan on going anywhere either."

Dean interrupted our little moment when he cleared his throat. "We should probably go help Merrick. Logan's having a bit too much fun."

Looking over at the blond hair bopping around the center of the circle, I had to laugh. "I think he needs a spanking."

Travis laughed. "If you were that drunk, yes, you'd be getting a spanking once you sobered up. But, Logan's more likely to be the spanker than the spankee. Come on, let's go try to get some water in him."

Trent looked relieved as we joined them. "He's going to have one hell of a hangover tomorrow." I didn't think that needed to be said. If the hangover headache didn't make Logan want to die, I was pretty sure the headache he got from whipping his head around as he... danced? Flailed about? I honestly didn't know what to call what he was doing... would probably make him wish he'd died.

"Logan." Travis's voice was stern and deep and I hoped I never had *that* tone aimed at me.

Logan stopped and looked at Travis with wide eyes.

Merrick spoke next. "Come with us. You need to take a break for a few minutes."

The way Trent put his hand at the small of Logan's back and whispered something that looked like a warning into Logan's ear, I began wondering what crazy Dom party I'd managed to find myself in. How was it possible all these dominant men had just accidentally become friends in college?

Larson looked a bit like a deer in headlights, probably similar to how I looked at that point. There were so many dominating personalities in the group that I was struggling. Being in the middle of a Dom sandwich was probably some sub's idea of a good time, but not mine. The look of confusion on Larson's face told me he was feeling similarly. *Maybe they weren't* all *Doms after all.* I could have reached out and grabbed my Daddy's hand if I needed it, but the big quiet firefighter didn't have that option in this group. I dropped back a little and smiled up at the big man.

"They're all crazy, right?"

He let out an uncomfortable laugh. "Sometimes I think so."

"Are they always so…" How did I ask if they were always so Dom without saying it. Larson looked a bit more freaked out than even I felt so I didn't want to spook him. "Take charge?" I finally finished.

Larson nodded. "Usually. It can be a bit overwhelming sometimes. But their hearts are all in the right place."

"Logan's going to feel like sh-crap tomorrow." It was probably okay to curse around Larson, especially when Daddy couldn't hear, but I didn't want to press my luck.

Larson smirked. "Good catch. Doms don't like it when their subs have potty mouths."

My eyes widened. Was he a Dom who didn't like his sub to curse? In that moment, I couldn't see Larson as a Dom, though. He looked lost in the crowd of his friends. Was he a sub? Was I misreading his words?

I managed to nod and caught myself before I rubbed my backside. It didn't hurt, but I could still feel the spanking from the night before when I moved certain ways. The tight training pants I was wearing wasn't helping matters any.

"Sometimes it's fun to misbehave though. It feels good to be reminded you belong to someone." There was a wistful tone in his voice, and I knew Larson had just given me a very private part of himself.

It wouldn't do me any good to deny it or lie. He got it and he'd see right through any excuse. "It does."

The smile that spread across Larson's face was genuine and just like that, I knew I'd gained a new friend. We got each other, and I had a feeling it had been a long time since Larson had felt understood in this group of men who seemed to take control in every situation. Doms were awesome, but I already knew how exhausting it could be to hang out with a number of them for an hour or two. I didn't know how Larson had made it fifteen or more years being the only submissive in the group. No wonder he was quiet.

I enjoyed talking with Larson while the others tended to Logan for most of the night. Travis would send questioning looks my way from time to time, trying to figure out if I was okay. Each time I smiled and nodded and went back to talking with Larson.

"I've never seen him like that before," Larson admitted after a while.

"Like what?"

He shrugged. "*That.* He doesn't want to let you out of his sight. He's looking over here every few minutes like he can't figure out what's going on, and it's driving him insane."

"He doesn't have enough time to be crazy right now. He's got his hands full with Logan." One of the things I admired about Travis was that he cared about his friends as deeply as he did about me. It would have been easy for him to step back and let Merrick, Trent, and Dean take care of Logan, but he was standing side-by-side with them as they all tried to help him through his breakup with tough love and solidarity. He'd probably have me over his knee if I was behaving like that, but the care and attentiveness was there just the same.

"No wonder Logan's gone through women like candy. Four Doms are having a hard time keeping him from making a fool out of himself. Could you imagine being on a date with him? He'd be almost impossible to handle."

I giggled thinking about Logan on a date. It was hard to think about the man being on a date with anyone. He was so… intense.

"You two have been huddled over here for over an hour." Travis's voice beside me made me jump and squeak.

He wrapped an arm around me and gave me a quick kiss

on the temple. "Sorry, didn't mean to scare you. Are you two okay?"

We both nodded but Larson spoke. "Looked like you guys had it under control for the most part. Too many cooks and all that."

I nodded in agreement and looked over to where Logan and Dean were standing. "Is Logan okay?"

"Trent's trying to take him home right now. He's going to feel like hell tomorrow, but he's okay."

"Serves him right," Larson mumbled causing me to laugh.

Travis looked between the two of us suspiciously but apparently chose to ignore it. "Sorry I haven't been able to spend the evening with you. This was not how I expected to spend our night."

"It's okay. I made a new friend." I smiled at Larson who let a small smile spread across his lips as he nodded his head.

"You've got a keeper, Travis."

"Don't I know it." He squeezed my ass causing me to jump slightly.

"Daddy!" The word was out before I had a chance to think about it, and I felt my cheeks turn red. Larson gave me a reassuring smile I was pretty sure was masking sadness.

"And don't forget it," Travis growled in my ear.

Was he getting jealous of me talking with Larson? I almost laughed because he apparently had no clue his friend was no threat to his place in my life. That made me wonder if it was really possible the men had no clue Larson was submissive?

How could so many Doms have never picked up on it?

Larson laughed. "He's all yours. We were just chatting."

CHAPTER 35

Travis

Dealing with Logan's drunk ass was not the way I'd expected to spend my evening when I'd initially accepted the invite. However, watching Larson and Caleb chatting for an hour also hadn't been what I'd expected. At first I'd thought it was one of them just trying to be friendly, but as time went on, I'd realized Larson was talking more than listening. I'd never seen him do so much talking in all the years I'd known him. To say my curiosity was piqued would have been an understatement. I wanted to know what they were talking about, but Logan was being absolutely impossible.

I'd seen Logan drunk before, but that night he was ridiculous. Even Trent, the man with endless patience for his best friend and co-worker, seemed about ready to snap. Merrick leaned over to me at one point and growled into my ear about wanting to take him over his knee and spank the disobedience out of him. It caused me to bark out a laugh, but I also remembered Caleb saying the same thing.

When we finally convinced Logan to go home with Trent for the night, I felt like I'd won a major war. That was, of course, until I saw Larson and Caleb still talking at the table. Larson was always so quiet and reserved, but around Caleb, he seemed relaxed. Logically, I knew Caleb was completely devoted to me, and Larson didn't have a deceitful bone in his body, but that didn't change the fact that I couldn't figure out how they'd managed to find so much to talk about.

Caleb brought out the possessive and jealous caveman in me, and I felt the need to stake my claim on him. I knew I was being paranoid even as I approached the table. Caleb's startled squeak when I'd spoken to them didn't help to squash my paranoia. Then I remembered he'd had his back toward me and had no way of knowing I was coming up behind him.

Larson, for his part, was more relaxed than I'd seen him in, possibly ever, which made me realize how absurd I was being.

I heard Caleb mutter something to Larson about "possessive Doms," which caused them both to laugh. I felt like I'd entered the twilight zone. My normally shy and reserved boy was joking openly about my possessiveness with my equally shy and reserved friend. How was it possible they'd both come so far out of their shells in such a short amount of time?

Larson didn't like to be the center of attention and he didn't speak much unless we asked him direct questions and... *ohhh*, it was suddenly making sense.

My sweet boy was drawn to the quiet giant across from us for a totally different reason than I'd expected. They both understood each other on a level I'd never be able to fully comprehend. My caveman went back inside the cave and tucked himself into bed as I looked at Larson in a new light. I'd let him talk to me, or one of the other guys, when he was ready, but I was happy my sweet boy had picked up on what we'd missed for many years.

As the other guys, minus Trent and Logan, rejoined us, Larson's walls came up and he slipped back into his shell. Even Caleb's gentle prodding didn't seem to be able to bring the smiling, talkative guy back. When it was clear Larson wasn't going to open up again, I squeezed Caleb's hand. "Ready to go home?"

He nodded around a yawn. "Yes, give me just a minute." He scooted himself closer to Larson and whispered a question. I watched as they both pulled out their phones and tapped quickly at the screens. A few seconds later, Caleb bumped shoulders with Larson, then waved goodbye to the rest of the group and we were out the door.

"You had an interesting night."

"And you got jealous of your friend," Caleb retorted. "Did you really think you had anything to worry about? You call me a worrier!"

I nodded in defeat. "You're right. It was unfounded jealousy."

"Is it bad that I kind of like that you were jealous?"

I reached over and squeezed his leg. "It's probably a

good thing you like it, because with you in my life, I see it happening a lot. Though, it won't happen with Larson again, and you never have to worry about me being jealous of Dexter either."

Caleb seemed satisfied with that answer. "Okay. I like Larson a lot. As a friend," he quickly qualified.

"Clearly as a friend. And I'm glad you two hit it off so well. It seems as though he's needed someone to connect with for a while now."

Caleb wasn't going to offer anymore information on Larson and I respected that. "Well, I think I can safely speak for the rest of the guys when I say that any friend of ours is a friend of yours."

Caleb yawned as he changed the subject. "Can we go to sleep when we get back home? I know it's not late, but I'm really tired."

I loved how easily he called my house *home*, and I hoped he really felt like it was his home. It had been fun earlier in the afternoon to watch him set Charlie and Branson on the chair together. He'd explained to me that dinosaurs liked to be in larger groups so they needed to stay together. Whether that was true or not, it didn't really matter to me, to my sweet boy, dinosaurs lived together so my reading chair was now home to two dinosaurs, and I couldn't think of a better use for the chair. I had a feeling that soon, my room wasn't going to look anything like the space I'd designed years earlier. The control freak in me, the one that wanted everything exactly where it was meant to be, didn't even have an opinion on the matter.

CHAPTER 36

Caleb

I quickly fell into a routine with Travis. We spent almost every night at his place, but that also meant that I got to be little whenever I wanted. Having a Daddy meant I didn't have to decide when to get diapered or when I had enough time to play with toys. Daddy seemed to enjoy getting me changed as soon as we got home in the evenings, and I got to play or hang out in the kitchen while he made dinner.

I wasn't little every night, but it seemed like more often than not I was diapered after work. I could usually decide what I wanted to do after that. Some nights I helped make dinner, other nights I colored at the table, and sometimes, I spread my toys out in the living room.

As an added bonus, Travis was heading home from work a lot earlier than he had in the beginning of our relationship. While he'd always made time with me a priority, I'd known he was moving meetings around and working on projects after I'd fallen asleep at the beginning of our relationship. Now, he was out of the office by five and usually home around the same time I got there. If he wasn't at the house when I got there it was okay because I had a key and could come and go as I pleased. Though, I tended to stay over more often than not.

As I spent more time at Travis's house, more and more of my stuff migrated to his place as well. At first it was my toothbrush and toothpaste and some clothes, but after a few weeks, most of my clothes and a number of my toys were there too. I'd realized the night before that I needed a pair of shoes in my closet at my place.

After work I decided to head to my place to grab what I needed. As I was pulling into the parking lot, I remembered I had my cars still in my toy bucket in the living room, and I wanted to take them with me so I had more cars. We'd talked about ordering a few more online, but I'd insisted it was pointless since I had them at my house. I just kept forgetting to grab them.

I hurried up the steps, determined not to forget the things I needed to collect before heading back to Daddy's house for the evening.

I'd managed to grab my shoes and was heading down the steps when Dexter's voice filled the living room, causing me to jump and almost fall down the stairs. "You need to cancel your lease, Cal."

When I'd recovered from the shock, I blinked at my best friend. "What do you mean?"

He shook his head at me like I wasn't catching on to something obvious. It was a gesture I hadn't seen from him in weeks, if not months. It had been a long time since he'd been exasperated with me. "Cal, you haven't slept here in weeks! You haven't even noticed that I cleared out your fridge last month."

"You did what?" I wanted to be mad but then realized how petty that was. I hadn't opened my fridge in so long that, had Dexter not cleared it out, it would have been a science experiment. I sighed and thought about what he'd said.

So far, Dexter and I hadn't gone much over twenty-four hours without seeing each other. We saw each other every day at work, and on the weekends, Daddy made sure to set time aside so Dexter and I could go out for a few hours.

Since I'd been spending more time away from my house, Dexter had been going out more frequently as well. If anything, I felt guilty that he was just now starting to live his own life. Until I'd met Travis, Dexter had always seemed content hanging out at home with me. When I'd brought it up the weekend before, he'd patted my arm and told me I hadn't held him back from anything, and he'd always been exactly where he wanted to be. That hadn't changed my feelings.

"You know what? Thank you, that's one less thing I have to worry about." There was no point in being frustrated with him.

"I knew you'd see it my way." His grin was contagious. "So, you'll call the leasing office this afternoon and cancel your lease."

"Dex, I haven't even talked to Travis about moving in yet."

He gave me the *look* again. "What sheets are on the bed at his house?"

"The dragon ones."

Dexter looked at me for a few seconds. "Would those sheets have been on that bed six weeks ago?"

"Well, no... but I wasn't spending the night there very often then!"

"So why are there dragon sheets on the bed? Or that safety rail?"

I thought for a moment about the best way to answer. I was pretty sure I was walking into a trap no matter how I responded. "Because I like them?"

Dexter ruffled my hair. "Maybe because he wants you to feel at home?"

"Of course I feel at home there, Dex. If I didn't, I wouldn't be there...Oh, oh I see what you did. You're a sneaky ass."

Dexter laughed. "Call the leasing office."

I sighed and looked up at the ceiling before picking up my phone. The night I'd changed Travis's contact info in my phone to read "Daddy" had felt huge to me. Even bigger than calling him Daddy for the first time had. It seemed to give me permission to call him Daddy all I wanted.

Me: *So, my lease is up in three weeks.*

Daddy: *I believe Dexter has mentioned this a time or ten.*

312

Me: *I don't know what to do… I don't know if I should renew my lease or not.*

Daddy: *I don't want you to make a rushed decision, but I certainly like my house more with you in it than I ever have before.*

Daddy: *Did I say something wrong?*

Me: *No. You said everything right. I feel like I shouldn't ask this over text, but would you mind if I didn't renew my lease?*

I couldn't believe how fast the response arrived on my phone.

Daddy: *If you want me to, I'll be there in a few minutes to help you pack your stuff.*

I stared at my phone and smiled at how funny he was.

Me: *Well, we don't have to move everything today. We have three weeks. But I think I'll call the leasing office and give them my notice.*

A text message with a string of emojis from hearts to houses to celebration banners appeared on my phone a moment later and I knew I'd made the right choice.

I looked over at Dexter. I wasn't sure if I was excited or nervous, but either way, I knew I was making the right decision. "He said I could move in."

"Well, duh."

I laughed and pushed at Dexter's shoulder before making the call to the leasing office to give my notice. Dexter spent a few minutes helping me gather some toys from the living room to take home, because Travis's house really was my home whether I'd accepted it before then or not.

As I was getting ready to leave, Dexter gave me a hug and danced out my front door. He pulled it shut as he left, but before it could close all the way I heard a muffled. "Umph." Then Daddy's deep laugh filled the porch.

I flung the front door open just before it latched and smiled when I saw Travis on the front porch. His gorgeous salt-and-pepper hair and well-maintained silver beard almost sparkled in the early evening sun. When Dexter finally moved out of the way, I saw his well fit jeans and the red dress shirt tailored to fit him perfectly. I couldn't help but grin widely. He was perfect and I'd gotten lucky enough to have him as my Daddy and boyfriend.

I didn't bother hiding my shock and excitement at seeing him standing there. "Daddy! Shouldn't you still be at work?"

He shook his head, but Dexter's gasp from beside us drew our attention.

"You called him Daddy!" he hissed excitedly, bouncing from foot to foot.

I stared at my friend in disbelief. "Umm, yeah?" I couldn't understand why he was so stunned. Surely I'd said it around Dexter in the weeks since Travis had become Daddy.

Dexter giggled. "I mean, you've been occasionally referring to him as Daddy, but I've never actually heard you call him Daddy. It's so much more real hearing you say it, finally! Even more real than seeing all the texts on your phone from Daddy."

I glared at Dexter. I needed to change the password on my phone.

A throat clearing from beside me had me turning my head, remembering that Daddy was standing on my porch. I flung my arms around him. "What are you doing here?"

He pressed a kiss to my forehead and hugged me tightly. "Well, I was basically done for the day and nearby when you texted. I figured we could get a jump on things and take some stuff home tonight."

I giggled. "Home. I like that."

"Let's gather some stuff to put in the truck."

An hour later, Travis was taking out the last of what would fit in the truck, and Dexter and I were sitting on my couch trying to figure out what stuff could be donated instead of moved. As Travis disappeared off the porch Dexter turned to me and gave me a gentle smile.

"I'm so happy for you. I always told you the right guy was out there for you. Now look, you've found him, and he loves you so much it's almost sickening!"

I blinked. I knew I loved Travis, and I loved Daddy. Hell, the two were so intrinsically intertwined it was hard to separate them at times. Travis instinctively knew what Caleb needed and Daddy knew exactly what little Caleb needed and he switched between the two roles effortlessly. Once I'd let him see me in diapers, any hesitation he had about taking control of a situation or stepping in when I was tired or stressed out had completely evaporated. I'd learned quickly that it didn't matter which headspace I was in, he cared for me just as much.

"Do you really think he loves me? It's not too soon to say that?"

Dexter sounded like an exasperated parent again. "Cal, I know—" his words were cut off when Travis began talking.

CHAPTER 37

Travis

The guys hadn't noticed that I'd walked back in, but I'd arrived in time to hear Dexter tell Caleb that I loved him. I could sense the unease in Caleb without even seeing his face. I'd not said those three words to him because I hadn't wanted to scare him if his feelings weren't quite there yet. I *thought* I'd done enough to show him I loved him, but that little bit of hesitation told me I needed to clearly spell it out for him.

"Oh, my sweet worrier, come here." He jumped slightly and turned to see me standing near the door. Opening my arms, he left Dexter's embrace and came quickly to me.

Once I had him wrapped tightly in my arms, I began talking. "I know it probably feels too soon to you. I've not said it before because I didn't want to scare you off, but I've been in love with you since we went to the dinosaur museum and we bought Branson as we were leaving. I knew you were the one for me when you set aside your fears about what was appropriate for an adult and you allowed me to buy you the dinosaur you wanted. Every time I see Branson in our house, he makes me think of you and I smile."

His lips found mine and he kissed me gently. "I didn't *have* to see you in diapers to know I loved you. And I didn't *have* to hear you call me Daddy either. Those things are special and important to me, but they aren't why I love you. Yes, you look sexy as hell in your diapers, and I enjoy getting to take care of you when you're little, but I love you because you're my Caleb and my sweet boy. Caleb Masterson, I love you and I'm looking forward to getting to be with you every single day."

I felt wet spots on my shirt as Caleb's eyes teared up, and his breathing became ragged. He squeezed me tightly. "Really?"

I nodded. "Really, baby. I love every part of you and I have since our first date."

Caleb blinked up at me. "I think I fell in love with you the night you tucked me into bed after sitting on my dodi. Instead of freaking out, you chose to make sure I got ready for bed and had what I needed before you tucked me in."

I rubbed his back, remembering the night fondly. It hadn't been how I expected our first night to end, but looking back on it, it was perfect for us.

"And that's my cue to kick you two out of here. Take Cal home, Travis."

Caleb shook his head and grumbled something about Dexter being a pest, but I nodded in agreement. "That

317

sounds like the best idea I've heard all day. Let's head home, baby."

I'd taken a few minutes to really look at my room as we unpacked the things we brought home with us that evening. My life had changed so much in just a few short months, but I could hardly remember what my room looked like without random stuffed animals littered across the surfaces or what used to be on top of the dresser that had been replaced by the stack of cartoon DVDs. I'd come across the bright red and purple dragon sheets online one afternoon and hadn't thought twice about ordering them for our bed. The grayscale room I'd lived in for years seemed almost sterile compared to what it looked like now.

There were little touches of Caleb all over my house. A cupboard of children's cups and plates and bibs were in the kitchen. There were now three dodis in the house, one in our room with a red dragon holder with purple wings, his original one stayed in the drawer of the coffee table in the living room, and another was in the kitchen with an elephant attached to it. Each dodi had a different animal on the button. I'd been surprised when he'd taken to the dinosaur one over his old dragon one, but he'd told me it reminded him of Charlie and Branson and he liked it. No matter where we went in the house, there was one handy for him. He never seemed to hesitate to grab one if he wanted it, no matter what headspace he was in. I'd even put one in the glove box of my truck, just in case he ever decided he needed one while we were out of the house.

We'd discussed it over dinner and there wasn't much left in his place that he was truly attached to. He was ready to donate most of his furniture so that left a TV, a gaming system, and a few personal possessions. We'd easily be able to take care of everything in a few truckloads, and I'd already sent a text to the guys to see if they could help us out that weekend.

Caleb was pretty sure there was nothing left at his place that he'd be embarrassed to have someone see, which meant we could start moving him the next morning. By Sunday night, Caleb would be moved out of his apartment and into our home. In the end, that was all that mattered to me. I really didn't care how it happened, as long as I knew my boy would be with me every night.

EPILOGUE:
THREE MONTHS LATER

Caleb

"Seriously, how are things with you and your Daddy?" Dexter questioned as we got our drinks from the bar and found a booth along the back wall.

Larson laughed from beside me. "Well, I know Travis is happy. He was all smiles last night at Steve's."

I pushed his arm and laughed. Travis had been surprised the first time Larson had invited me out to dinner, but he seemed to be thankful Larson was finally opening up to someone.

Once he was away from the over-the-top Doms, Larson was not only talkative, but funny as well. I knew he was submissive, but I had a feeling there was more to him than just that. I just didn't know how to ask the question. Instead, I hung on every word trying to figure out what else he might be into.

By that point, I'd ruled out age play, though he never seemed to have a problem when I slipped up and referred to

Travis as Daddy around him. He'd made an offhand comment about having a fear of being trapped so that seemed to eliminate shibari and bondage in general. After a highly invasive round of questioning from Asher one night, I knew without a doubt he wasn't into more traditional BDSM either. There was a chance he simply liked to submit in the bedroom, but I felt like it was bigger than that. Larson wasn't going to give it up easily, though.

I smiled at the question because it was a very Dexter thing to ask. "Things are good. I need to head home after this drink though."

Larson got a far off look on his face. Sometimes he seemed almost wistful when we started talking about me getting home. He seemed so desperate to have someone to welcome him home, that sometimes I invited him over, but he'd never accepted the offer.

Looking over at Larson, I could see the crease in his brow as he thought hard about something. "What are you doing tonight?"

"I have to write some reports for work, but I think I'm going to do it from home instead of at the fire station for a change. I usually wait until I'm on duty, but there's no reason not to get them done at home where I can wear my underwear while sitting on the couch and writing up reviews.

Dexter snorted a laugh and shook his head. "Damn, Larson. That's quite a mental image."

"Why are you thinking about me in my underwear?"

For a moment I thought Larson might have stumped Dexter, but when Dexter's eyes lit up, I knew I was in for something. "I'm trying to decide if they're pretty, pink lace panties."

Larson barked out a laugh loud enough that people at other tables turned to look in our direction. "Definitely *not* lace. I hate to break it to you, but I'm a plain boxer briefs guy."

Dexter shook his head. "You two are so boring."

"Hey, my underwear are totally *not* boring! They have race cars on them today."

Larson and Dexter both laughed at my statement and I blushed. "You guys totally didn't need to know that."

Dexter patted my arm from across the table. "I've seen your race car undies before."

Larson was shaking his head at us. "You two share way too much."

My face was still red, and I decided to cut out while I was only a little behind and before I ended up telling them that I needed to go home and get diapered for the night. Though that was exactly what would be happening once I walked through the door. There'd only been a handful of nights I'd not been diapered since I'd moved into Travis's house, and I was happier than I'd ever been.

"Okay, I'm heading home."

"You're no fun," Dexter pouted.

Larson was still laughing as he slid out of the booth. "Honestly, I need to be getting home too. If I stay for

322

another drink, I'm not going to be okay to drive, and I do have work to do tonight."

Dexter sighed and shook his head but stood up. "I guess I'll go find someone else to hang out with. You guys have a good night." He pulled me into a hug and kissed the side of my head. "Have fun with Daddy tonight," he whispered.

I blushed but nodded. "I will. See you Monday at work." It had been hard to get used to not seeing Dexter every night, but we had both adjusted fine—just like he'd told me we would.

"See you guys," I called over my shoulder as we headed out of the bar and to our cars.

Daddy was standing in the doorway when I pulled into the driveway and the last remaining stress of the work week melted away in seconds. I locked the car and headed toward the door.

I burrowed my face into his neck and wrapped my arms around him. "Daddy."

He pressed a light kiss to my forehead. "Did you have a good time with Larson and Dexter tonight, sweet boy?"

I nodded but yawned.

"It's time to get my boy ready for bed." Daddy took my hand and guided me toward the bedroom where he proceeded to undress me. There was nothing sexual or teasing about the actions.

That night, Daddy was clearly in caretaker mode. He wasn't going to let something like an inconvenient erection stop him from making sure I was ready for bed and had a little time to unwind before he tucked me in.

As I stepped out of my pants, Daddy guided me directly to the bed where a diaper was already waiting. "Lie back and let Daddy take care of you."

Lying naked while waiting to be diapered was no longer awkward. Even the process of getting diapered was natural to me at that point. A few months earlier, I'd have been a mess of nerves and questions about how Travis really felt. Now I could lie back, grab my dodi, and enjoy every light touch and the way Daddy made sure each tape was secured in just the right place and the leak guards were adjusted just right before he'd announce me good to go.

That night, he'd chosen a diaper adorned with puppies and had slipped a red T-shirt over my head. "Come on, the house is warm enough that you don't need pants. We can go downstairs and watch a show before bed."

I nodded, the dragon holding my dodi bobbing up and down with my head, and let Daddy lead me to the living room. I normally played with my toys while we watched TV, but that night, the only place I wanted to be was snuggled up on the couch and wrapped in Daddy's arms, so I waited for him to get comfortable before I sat down.

I sprawled out across his legs and body. The TV clicked on, and I placed my ear against his chest, the top of my head resting under his chin, listening to the steady thump of his heartbeat. Daddy's left arm wrapped around my back and rested at the back of my diaper and I curled my legs around his.

As the show began to play in the background, the world went fuzzy as I thought about how much my life had changed that year. I'd gone from a self-proclaimed bachelor, convinced no one would ever accept my needs and wants, to happily curled in my Daddy's lap with my dodi in my mouth and a thick diaper wrapped around me while we watched TV. The last thing I remembered was Daddy's lips touching my forehead and him whispering, "My sweet boy." I snuggled closer and drifted off to sleep thinking about how lucky I was that we'd taken a chance on each other. I now had a loving Daddy by my side and no reason to hide my wants or desires.

ALSO BY CARLY MARIE

At Home, Finding Home Book 1

Be My Home: An At Home Valentine's Day Novella Book 1.5

Coming Home, Finding Home Book 2

CHAPTER 1

Derek

"Hey, Derek, we're going to the bar. You coming?" Harrison called to me, as I headed to the dressing room at the back of the arena.

We were the founding members of the country music band, Hometown. Harrison was the bass guitarist and had grown up with me in Oklahoma. I was lead vocals for the band and played acoustic guitar as well.

I nodded. "Give me twenty." An evening at the bar would be just what my frazzled nerves needed, but first, I needed a shower. My hair was soaked with sweat and my black t-shirt clung to my body. Another two-hour set was in the books and we were almost halfway through our first headlining tour.

Harrison and I had spent a few years playing small bars for a little pocket change while we were in college. We had never intended to become famous or to end up with a number one album. But that is exactly what happened. We were approached by a talent scout after playing at a honky-tonk in Tulsa. In the blink of an eye, our little side gig turned into our livelihoods.

Within a few months of that chance encounter, we were in a studio in Nashville recording our first album. Our current headlining tour followed a six-month tour opening for one of the hottest country artists in the nation.

Since playing that bar in Tulsa, I had gone from Derek Edward Scott, a twenty-two year old ranch hand on my family's ranch, college student, and struggling artist and songwriter, to twenty-four year old Derek Edwards. Derek Edwards was a country music sensation, playing sold-out arenas, various music awards shows, and oh yeah, a Grammy award-winning artist.

How the fuck did that *happen?*

Our first single had shot straight to the top of the charts and our lives had been an insane roller coaster ride ever since.

There was a part of me that missed just being a college student and working on my parents' ranch in the summers. As quickly as that thought entered my mind, it was joined by memories of the uncomfortable Christmas I spent with my family three weeks earlier. I'd been dragged to church to listen to the pastor drone on about Jesus, Mary, and Joseph. I'd heard the same sermon so often I could practically recite it by heart.

What I hadn't expected was the extra fifteen minutes of the pastor lecturing the entire congregation about how the "gay agenda" was threatening Christianity and the sanctity of this holy time. I'd sat in the pew with my mouth hanging open, wondering how the gays were killing Christmas.

Okay, so, maybe being a chart-topping country artist who only had time to go home for a couple of days every four or five months wasn't so bad after all.

I showered as quickly as I could and headed to find Harrison and whoever else was going to join us at the bar. We had just finished playing in Nashville which proved to be every bit as insane as we expected. We knew we couldn't go to a bar anywhere in the city because we'd be mobbed by fans. Instead, Harrison was on his phone searching for bars off the beaten path to hopefully give us a bit of anonymity and allow us some much needed time to relax.

"Where're we going?" I questioned, as I pulled on a black and white plaid button-up over a white undershirt. I rolled the sleeves halfway up my forearms and grabbed an old college ball cap before being satisfied with my appearance.

Harrison grinned. "Franklin. It's about thirty minutes from here, kinda the middle of nowhere."

Gina, one of our backup singers,turned vital member of the band, clapped happily. "Night out!" She was a petite little thing, topping the scale at maybe one hundred and ten pounds soaking wet and was no more than five-foot-three. Her hair was purple, at least that week, by the next week it would likely be a different color.

The first few weeks of the tour, Gina had flirted with me

almost constantly, but after pulling her aside one night and telling her I wasn't interested in her, or any woman, she backed off and became a friend and fierce ally.

I'd been out in college and our management team had been quick to separate Derek Scott and Derek Edwards. The thought was if they could bury the existence of Derek Scott, an out gay man, then there wouldn't be much dirt on me. I hadn't been all that comfortable with the idea at first. I'd just gotten comfortable enough with my sexuality to come out to friends. The last thing I wanted to do was go back into the closet. A number of worst case scenarios had been thrown my way before I finally agreed to the name change.

It had been over a year and there didn't seem to be many, if any, people who had figured out we were the same person. The media finding out had quickly become my biggest fear. Country music wasn't ready for a gay musician, yet.

I had reluctantly agreed to go back into the closet with the understanding I would be able to tell the band. When we signed the contract, I didn't want my personal life to be public knowledge anyway. I'd always been a private person and I prefered to keep it that way. In private though, I didn't want to hide my sexuality. I needed the band to know I was gay because it was a part of who I was. Unfortunately, the fear management had ingrained in me made it hard to be open, even with the band. It had taken me months to come out to everyone on the tour with us. We were a tight knit group and so far nothing about my sexuality had been leaked online or to the media.

I was happy to keep it that way.

Gina, Harrison, and I were joined by Clayton, Vance, and Neil, all backup musicians hired by the label, but we had quickly become friends. We climbed into a black SUV and Harrison leaned forward to input the address into the driver's phone. "Please, keep us under the radar. We just need a night out," he said to the man.

The driver nodded and began to follow the directions on his phone while we laughed and chatted in the back. The farther from Nashville we got, the more I was able to relax. It had been too long since I was Derek Scott and I missed going out with friends. The last eighteen months had been a whirlwind and it was nice to be able to take a step back.

"We've just snuck out," I said with a laugh. "Sneaking out of Nashville is a lot harder than it was to sneak out of our houses growing up."

Harrison laughed too. "Remember that night in high school when we snuck out of your house to go to the movies with our girlfriends and your dad was sitting on the front porch as we rounded the house?"

We dove into a row of bushes on the side of the driveway, both forgetting they were my mom's roses. By the time we got ourselves untangled from the bushes, we were scratched and our clothes were torn from the thorns. Thankfully, we were able to keep our pained screams muffled and got away before my dad found us.

Gina shot me a mischievous grin. "Girlfriend?"

"You didn't grow up in an Evangelical household. I faked it until I was in college. I didn't come out to my immediate family until just before the tour started. I'm still not out to our fans. At this rate, we'll be retired before I find a guy to be with."

I was on track for the longest dry spell ever.

Harrison bumped me with his shoulder. "There's no reason that has to be the case. You've made enough money on this tour to never need to go back to Oklahoma again. Be happy for once."

I rolled my eyes at him as the SUV pulled into the parking lot of a small bar in the middle of a tiny town. "Good job, Harrison, you found a bar off the beaten path!" Clayton said, his voice laced with sarcasm. There were two SUVs with Sheriff Department markings in the lot and maybe ten other cars and trucks. We piled out of the back and headed into the bar.

There was a slight lull in conversations as the six of us walked in the front door of Steve's Tavern. The most generic bar name in the most generic looking place ever. *Thank you Harrison!* I had to refrain from turning and hugging him in the middle of the bar.

Most of the bar's occupants allowed their eyes to sweep over the five men in our group when we first entered. It was clear this was a local bar and outsiders were uncommon. And none of us were small guys, Neil was the shortest and slightest built of all of us, but even he was almost six feet tall and solid muscle. Once they took us in, they all seemed to notice Gina standing behind us and more than one set of male eyes appraised her. I pulled my ball cap down farther to avoid recognition.

"I'm here to have fun," Gina whispered, "and so help me, if any of you pull the big brother card and gets in the way, I'm going to have your balls."

We all laughed and headed directly to the bar. Gina already had a man approaching her, offering to buy her a drink, so I grabbed a beer with the other guys and we headed to a table in the corner.

An hour later, I excused myself to use the restroom in the back of the bar. On my way out, I was distracted by a text from my brother and I ran face first into a solid wall of muscle, knocking my ball cap to the ground. My six-foot frame was nothing compared to the tall, dark, and handsome man standing in front of me wearing a dark green uniform shirt that read "Sheriff Westfield." His sleeves were rolled up over his elbows and his exposed arms were thick with sinewy muscles that moved hypnotically. He put his hands on my shoulders to steady me as I took a few steps back. I felt electricity zing through the spots where our bodies touched. "Sorry," I muttered, as I bent to pick my ball cap up off the ground and slid my phone into my pocket. My brother could wait.

I had a hard time looking the gorgeous man in his piercing green eyes.

"No problem," the guy, Sheriff Westfield I presumed, said in a deep voice with a slight tip of his own hat.

He walked into the bathroom and I had to pull myself together, quick. *"Not now, Derek,"* I scolded myself. *"This is not the time, or the place. Jesus fucking Christ, you are on tour."*

My growing arousal was going to be a problem, so I started thinking of mathematical equations, the next tour stop, anything to make me stop thinking about the Adonis who had just walked into the bathroom. I finally pulled my phone out of my pocket again, thinking maybe returning my brother's text would distract me enough my cock would stand down, and I could go back to my friends without a hard-on in my jeans.

"Can't seem to get away from you," a deep voice said from in front of me, causing me to jump slightly.

So much for distraction.

THANK YOU

Dear Reader,

Thank you for reading *Undisclosed Desires*. Caleb and Travis spoke so loudly to me that I had to put Jasper's story from the Finding Home series on hold to focus on this book! Travis, Caleb, and their friends will be seen again as the Undisclosed series continues.

Undisclosed Desires wouldn't have been possible without my editor, Susie, who pushed me to write the best book possible, or those who kept me motivated when I was ready to give up. A special thanks to the amazing Tracey Soxie Weston of Soxational Cover Art for the beautiful cover!

Next up, I will be finishing the Finding Home series. Jasper, Declan, Ty, Derek, and Colt will all be back in *Close to Home* and *Already Home*. The two books will follow Jasper as he learns to navigate life with his adoring men.

Thank you again for your support! If you enjoyed reading Travis and Caleb's story, please consider leaving a review on Amazon or Goodreads. A short review is invaluable to independent authors like myself and helps others find our books.

With Love,

Carly

ABOUT THE AUTHOR

Carly Marie has had stories, characters, and plots bouncing around her head as long as she can remember. She began writing in high school and found it so cathartic that she's made time for it ever since. With the discovery of m/m romance, Carly knew she'd found her home. She was surprised to learn not everyone has sexy characters in their head, begging for their stories to be written. With that knowledge, a little push from her husband, and a lot of encouragement from newfound friends, she jumped into the world of publishing.

Carly lives in Ohio with her husband, four girls, two cats, and 14 chickens. The numerous plot bunnies running through her head on a daily basis ensures that she will continue to write and share stories.

Connect with Carly!

Mailing List: Carly's Connection

Facebook: www.facebook.com/groups/CarlyMarie

Instagram: instagram.com/carlymariewrites

Goodreads: goodreads.com/CarlyMarieWrites

Website: www.authorcarlymarie.com